THE BRIDE
BARGAIN

© 2008 by Kelly Eileen Hake

ISBN 978-1-62029-719-3

All scripture quotations are taken from the King James Version of the Bible.

This book is a work of fiction. Names, characters, places, and incidents are either products of the author's imagination or used fictitiously. Any similarity to actual people, organizations, and/or events is purely coincidental.

Cover design by Lookout Design, Inc.

Published by Barbour Publishing, Inc., P.O. Box 719, Uhrichsville, Ohio 44683, www.barbourbooks.com

Our mission is to publish and distribute inspirational products offering exceptional value and biblical encouragement to the masses.

Member of the
Evangelical Christian
Publishers Association

Printed in the United States of America.

THE BRIDE
BARGAIN

KELLY EILEEN HAKE

BARBOUR
PUBLISHING

DEDICATION/ACKNOWLEDGMENT

Seven years ago I dedicated my first novella to "the two unstoppable forces in my life: God and my mother!"

Since then, my blessings have grown, and so has the list of incredible people who've supported my writing. I want to personally thank Rebecca Germany and Aaron McCarver, my wonderful editors; and Julia Rich, Kathleen Y'Barbo, and Elsa Carruthers, whose encouragement and prayers meant more than they know.

This wouldn't have been possible without all of you!

CHAPTER 1

Nebraska Territory, Oregon Trail,
two weeks journey past Fort Laramie, 1855

That does it!" Clara Field gritted her teeth and tugged harder on her leather glove, which was currently clamped between the jaws of a cantankerous ox. She didn't know whether to laugh or cry.

"I'll get him in a headlock for you, Miss Field, and cut off his air so he'll open his mouth." Burt Sprouse sauntered over. "That should take care of things quick enough."

"Oh, choking him wouldn't be the right answer." Clara struggled to hide her disgust at the very suggestion. "I have to marvel at how similar animals and humans can be. Neither group likes to be forced into anything, and try as I might, I can't seem to convince him we're trudging toward freedom."

"Well, I reckon I could knee him in the chest to make him let go." Sprouse shuffled closer. "Hickory's got an eye on you."

"Thank you, Mr. Sprouse. I'll handle this." Clara

waited until the burly ex-lumberjack wandered away before pleading with the ox. "Your antics are going to get us kicked off the wagon train, Simon!"

At the sound of his name, the ox perked his ears and his mouth went slack, allowing Clara to yank away her glove. How an ox had a taste for leather escaped her, but bovine cannibalism counted as the least of her worries at the moment. She held up the mangled thing and sighed.

Thank You, Lord, that I brought an extra pair just in case I lost one. Her lips quirked at the tooth marks on the leather. *Though I never thought things would come to this.*

Yanking on the length of rope she'd tied around Simon's neck, Clara urged him toward the makeshift corral the trail boss had set up for the night. The obstinate animal refused to budge, his eyes fixed on her glove with a greedy gleam.

"There's lots of good forage and fresh water," she tempted. "And plenty of rest." Oooh, how good that sounded. A verse from Psalms floated into memory: *"He leadeth me beside the still waters. He restoreth my soul."*

For it being a river, the Platte came as close to still water as any running water could ever hope. Wide, shallow, and dark with mud, it was their constant guide and water source. Clara tried not to compare it to babbling brooks, flowing streams, or any other clear, flowing water with a friendly rush of sound.

As for the earlier part of that scripture. . .well, they'd only just stopped for the night. Until she got this last ox to the corral, gathered enough fuel for the campfire, and cooked dinner for herself, Aunt Doreen, and the blessedly helpful Burt, she wouldn't be lying beside anything.

But we're one day closer to Oregon. Eleven miles farther toward a new start. Not even Simon's snacking can take that away.

Tension eased from her shoulders as Simon ambled toward the enclosure. She and Aunt Doreen had already lost two oxen on the trail, and when they settled in Oregon, the remaining stock would be used for food or trade. The sadness creeping over her at the thought explained, at least in part, why Clara wasn't an accomplished driver. Even after weeks on the trail, she couldn't bear to use a whip harshly.

With Simon safely tucked away with the rest of the train's livestock, Clara began hunting for buffalo chips. The tall, dry grass rustled around her skirts as she searched. Typically, the prairie held a large and ready supply of the quick-burning fuel. But the recalcitrant ox had cost her valuable time. The areas closest to the circled wagons were picked over by the other women on the train whose husbands saw to the animals. She needed to go farther, though never too far, to scrape together a fair-sized load.

By the time she got back to camp and started their fire, Aunt Doreen already had vegetables—the same supply of potatoes, carrots, and onions that they'd been using since the stop at Fort Laramie—chopped and in the pot for cooking, and the batter ready for johnnycake. Once the fire burned hot enough to heat the Dutch oven and cook the stew, Clara gratefully sank down beside the makeshift kitchen.

A healthy breeze carried away the smoke from the fire, bringing welcome coolness as the sun faded. The moon came into view, its modest glow bathing the plains in whitish blue light.

"Grub ready yet, Miz Field?" Burt Sprouse's head tilted forward as he sniffed the air like a hopeful bear. In exchange for their cooking, alongside a bit of washing and mending, the ex-lumberjack provided them with fresh meat whenever possible, took on the night watches assigned to their wagon, and lent a hand when he could.

"Not quite, Mr. Sprouse." Apologies wouldn't make the rabbit cook any faster. "I had difficulty finding enough buffalo chips tonight."

"Looked like the oxen gave you some trouble tonight." Burt's voice held no censure as he squatted down. "I'll take on your watch tonight, like we agreed, but Hickory's getting antsy about having you and your aunt in your own wagon. You were last in the row and last to set up camp tonight."

"Sure were." The trail boss, Hickory McGee, stomped over to glower at them. Disgust filled his tone. "Same as every day on this trail. I warned you gals I didn't want to take on two women with no menfolk to shoulder the night watches, wagons, and livestock. You know the law of the trail—pull your weight or be left behind."

"We know." Clara forced the words through

gritted teeth. Men who believed women to be inferior in every way put up her back as little else could. *If you spent more time helping and less time harping, things would get done faster. As it is, you accomplish nothing with threats, yet Aunt Doreen and I hold things together in spite of them. A true gentleman—the kind of man a mother would be proud to raise and a woman would be glad to claim as husband—would be respectful and helpful.*

She kept the thoughts to herself. Speaking her mind was a luxury she couldn't afford if it angered the trail boss. A quick prayer for patience, and she swallowed her ire.

"I haven't completely mastered the art of un-hitching the oxen," Clara admitted before staring him down. "But Mr. Sprouse makes sure our watches aren't shirked, and you know it." She cast a grateful look at Burt.

"You ain't the ones doin' it," Hickory groused. "No call for a man with his own wagon and responsibilities to shoulder yours."

"I don't mind taking the extra watch in exchange for their cooking," Burt put in.

"Don't recall askin' you, Sprouse." Hickory turned his glare from Clara to the lumberjack. "But anyone causin' problems can be left behind."

"Worse comes to worse"—Mr. Sprouse shrugged—"I can sear some meat. Got an iron stomach, I do."

"Glad to hear it." The guide returned his attention to Clara. "You're lagging behind as it is. Not being able to control your animals is one more hassle to endanger the train. One rampaging ox can set off a stampede."

"We managed to sort it out." Aunt Doreen tugged a bucket of water toward them. "We always do."

"It didn't put anyone else out." Clara shoved aside her remorse over Mr. Sprouse's late dinner. "We'll be ready to pull out at dawn, same as everyone else."

"Better be." The disagreeable guide punctuated that statement by launching spittle toward their cookfire. It hissed as he stalked away.

When we get to Oregon, it will be worth it, she vowed to herself for the thousandth time since they left Independence and started out on the trail. *The Lord will see us to a new life and a happy home.*

"The johnnycake should be about ready." Clara pushed the ashes off the top of the Dutch oven with her ladle handle, wrapped her hand in a dishcloth, and lifted the lid. The sweet smell of warm cornbread wafted toward them. "Let me slice a piece for you to have now while the stew finishes."

"Mmmph." A moment later, Mr. Sprouse plunked himself down and set to munching the hot bread. His obvious enjoyment didn't soothe Clara as it usually did—not when he'd made it clear that their agreement wasn't as strong as Hickory's warnings.

"Here, Aunt Doreen." Clara made sure her aunt got a large portion. After weeks on the trail, not only did their simple dresses boast enough dust to plant a garden, but also the calico also hung from her aunt's thin frame. After a grueling day of travel, any moment they could use for a good night's rest was another small loss her aunt didn't deserve to bear. *Unacceptable.*

Aunt Doreen passed Mr. Sprouse another piece before he asked. Their success on the trail depended on keeping the man well fed. So long as they did that and kept pressing onward, the trail boss couldn't leave them behind.

Clara filled a tin with the steaming stew. Onions came from their supply, greens they'd gathered along the way, and the rabbit came courtesy of Mr. Sprouse's shotgun. If it weren't for their little arrangement with him, she and her aunt would be surviving on jerky.

"Best deal I ever made." His grunt made both of them smile. Burt made no bones about the fact he liked to eat but couldn't cook. Another's misfortune was rarely cause for prayers of gratitude, but. . .

"I was just thinking the same thing." Clara knew Aunt Doreen's reply came from the heart, to say the least.

Until now, Mr. Sprouse was just one more example of how the Lord watched over them and would see them through this arduous journey, which had become more wearing than Clara anticipated. A continuous stream of mishaps drained their supplies and energy. And they'd yet to make it past the prairie to the hardships of the mountains.

"When we reach the mountains, things will go more slowly." She meant the words as a comfort to her own aching bones and her aunt's worries, but Burt Sprouse didn't see it that way.

"Yep. Snow can make us lose days, get off the trail, have so many delays food runs out and animals freeze. Everything's harder once you hit the Rockies."

"Our oxen are too ornery to freeze." Clara couldn't help smiling even as she muttered the words.

"Even so, we'll all probably lighten our loads." Burt shrugged. "I hear the mountains are littered with furniture and heirlooms abandoned by travelers so they can get free of a snow bank or make it up a steep pass."

Her aunt's gasp made Clara wrack her brain for something positive to say.

"After that rough river crossing, we already lost several items." She quelled the sense of loss that overcame her at the memory of her childhood trunk, filled with her doll and doll's clothes. The last thing her father gave her, lost in the Platte forever. "So we probably won't need to leave anything else behind." She forced a smile.

"For all those reasons, you have to be careful not to get on the trail boss's bad side." Burt waved his spoon in the air. "We won't make it without him, and he's dead serious about leaving behind anyone who causes problems."

He does care. Surely Burt said that nonsense about having an iron stomach just to placate Hickory. She eyed him fondly as he made his way back to his own wagon. Who would have thought a burly ex-lumberjack looking to make his fortune gold mining would be their saving grace?

"You go on ahead and get to bed," Clara encouraged her aunt after they'd eaten their fill. "I'll clean up and join you in a few moments."

Aunt Doreen's lack of protest and grateful nod spoke of her weariness more eloquently than if she'd carped over the long day. Yet the older woman never uttered so much as a word of complaint. Not that she ever had, even throughout the long years of living under Uncle Uriah's thumb.

No matter how many verses her uncle warped out of context, how often he misinterpreted her own words or actions, Clara held firm to the conviction that Uriah's chauvinism was personal prejudice, not truth. Oft-repeated lectures against the frail values and fragile mindsets of the so-called weaker sex only underscored the quiet strength of the woman who'd raised her.

The few months when she'd had Doreen's sole attention soothed her soul, pulling her from the endless cycle of guilt and anger over Ma's and Pa's deaths. Clara owed everything to the self-sacrificing love of Doreen. Then she'd married Uriah Zeph, and their world tilted once more. For the worse.

Hopes ahead; regrets behind. Grandma's saying had become their motto over the years and seemed more appropriate with each passing day. Tonight, as Clara fell into her quilt, she added one more phrase....

And God alongside.

Outskirts of Baltimore

Filth everywhere. Dr. Saul Reed shook his head as he made his way from the room he rented to the area of the Baltimore outskirts that housed businesses. Brackish water and mud splotched the street. The odor of stale urine in the alleyways fought for dominance over the smell of stewed cabbages and onions.

To think, this was the better area of town, where most of the residents had roofs over their heads and cabbage to eat. There were others less fortunate, left to burrow under garbage or be chased away from bridges until pneumonia or fever took them away. The illness he could treat, the neglect of hygiene and sanitation he could fight, but all he could do was pray for the indifference neighbors showed for one another.

That's why he'd chosen this place. A cozy practice in a whitewashed building in the heart of Baltimore would bring affluent clients, respectable standing, and a nice living. Here, though, he could put his knowledge to the best use. These were the areas where people otherwise denied medical attention needed his help.

If only You will open their ears, Lord, he prayed as he entered the post office. His youth became an impediment in the eyes of some, who saw more value in years than in his Edinburgh education. They didn't take into account the school's reputation as he had when making his choice. The university's renown for technological advancement didn't transmit beyond the medical community.

"Letter come for ya, Doc." The post office worker thrust the note at him.

"Any packages?" Saul peered into the cubbyholes

14

behind the desk to no avail. "Those forceps I ordered should be coming in any day now."

"Any day ain't today." The man chewed his tobacco before sending a thick stream of sludge onto the floor beside an obviously oft-missed spittoon. "While yer here an' all, though. . ."

"What's ailing you?" Saul prayed the man wouldn't do as he had the last time he'd asked for help and pull down his britches to display a carbuncle on his hip.

"M' mouth." The tobacco tucked into his cheek, he opened wide.

Holding his breath to avoid the foul blast of air, Saul tilted his head and surveyed browned teeth, yellowed gums, and a sore the size of his thumb on the man's tongue. Saul pulled back to a safe distance and inhaled.

"You've got an open sore on your tongue."

"Heck, Doc, even I knowed that much." The man rolled his eyes. "What can I do about the thing?"

"I'll make you a rinse of witch hazel to clean it out. Be sure to drink a lot of water and use the rinse after you eat anything." Saul set his jaw. "Most of all, you must stop using the tobacco."

"Wha'?" His jaw gaped, treating the doctor to another view of that open sore and losing the tobacco altogether. It landed with a soft thud on the dusty floor.

"Good. The tobacco is what's causing the problem."

"Naw." The man stooped down, scooped up the

wad, dusted it off as best he could, and plopped it right back in his mouth.

"Yes." Saul closed his eyes. "Though taking things from the ground and putting them in your mouth doesn't help, either."

"Dirt don't hurt." Crossing his arms over his chest, he rolled the chaw in his mouth, sending another stream toward the ground. This time it landed perilously close to Saul's boot. "Even a quack'd know that."

"People track in more than dirt." Saul's voice became more stern. "The more you chew, the worse it'll get. Keep on, and you'll see more sores until they spread down your throat and you can't speak."

The man's laughter followed Saul outside—another example of the ignorance that ruled this area. *How can I make a difference if they won't let me? What do I have to do, Lord, to make them see how to take care of themselves? Give me the chance to make a difference.*

As he rounded a corner, a shaky voice sounded. "Young and untouched. I'll give ya a good time, sir."

"No." He made to move on, but her gaunt face stopped him in his tracks. The girl couldn't be more than eleven. Shadows smudged her eyes, and bony wrists protruded from beneath too-short sleeves.

"I swear it's true." She drew closer, obviously misinterpreting his pause for interest. In the brighter light, livid bruises bloomed along her throat. Whether they'd been pressed there by a violent customer or an enraged pimp was impossible to say.

"Stay there." He held out a hand to stay her progress. Between her youth, her assertion of innocence, and those bruises, he couldn't walk away. "What is your name?"

"Whatever ya like." She raised a nervous hand to the marks on her throat. "Whatever ya want."

Enraged pimp then. Saul peered down the alleyway to see if the brute lingered behind. No one there.

"What can you do—no, not that." He stopped her hastily as she prepared to speak. "Can you sew? Cook? Clean?"

"What?" Astonishment replaced the desperation in her gaze.

"I know a lady who runs a boardinghouse and is in need of some help." Saul kept his voice muted. "If you're an honest sort and not afraid of solid work, you might do."

"I sews real fine—it's what he used to have me do." The glow of pride left her abruptly. "He'd find me." The whisper almost floated past him unheard, but when her hand fluttered toward her neck again, Saul understood her fear.

"Where is he now?"

"Pub." She jerked her head toward a side street.

"Come with me now, and he'll never know." Saul shifted his doctor's bag so it came into a more prominent view, hoping the symbol of trusted authority would put her at ease.

"You're one of them what purges babes when one of us gets unlucky?" Suspicion blazed to life in her pinched face. "Like him that came last night?

He took the baby, right, but m' sister hasn't stopped bleeding since."

"Absolutely not." Saul closed his eyes at the image she evoked. "Where's your sister?" Obviously the woman needed immediate help—if it wasn't too late.

"Inside." She backed away a step. "Be on yore way, sir. M' sister don't need any more help from no doctors. She didn't want the first one to come, but he didn't give 'er no choice."

"The quack who did that to her was no doctor." Rage boiled in Saul's chest. "If she keeps bleeding, your sister will die."

"And I'll be alone wif"—her gaze darted in the direction of the pub she'd indicated earlier as her voice went hoarse—"*him*." Though Saul wouldn't have thought it possible, her face became even more pale. "He said he'd take care of us, but he turned Nancy out within a week. After last night he said I'd have to take her place."

"No, you won't. Take me to Nancy."

CHAPTER 2

P anting, she spun and darted back down the alley, shoved open a warped door, and waved him inside. "Nancy's there."

When Saul's eyes adjusted to the dim light, he sank to his knees and examined the poor girl's face. Completely waxen, her skin was cool to his touch. Cold. No breath stirred her chest, no heartbeat pumped life in her veins, and the reason was clear. A dark pool of blood stained the base of the pallet. Saul pulled the worn sheet over the woman's face.

"Nancy!" With a choked scream, the little girl threw herself over her sister. "Wake up, Nancy. Please, Nancy. This gent's going to help us. Just wake up." She dissolved into tears as Saul gently pulled her away, only to spring from his arms, grab her sister's shoulders, and violently shake them.

"Nancy! You come back here," she ordered. "Nancy. . ."

"She can't hear you." Saul pulled her back and

kept his grip firm this time. His words carried over the sobs wracking her thin frame. "You need to say good-bye. We have to go now. You aren't safe here."

Her eyes widened in fear, and her sobs jerked to a stop with the realization. "He'll be back." She tenderly reached out and folded the blanket away from her sister's face. "Good-bye, Nancy."

A few stray tears spilled onto her sister's dress as the little girl unclasped a brass locket from around Nancy's neck and clutched it in her shaking hand. "May the angels welcome you, and may Mama make yore favorite bread pudding when you see her in heaven." Finished, she pressed a kiss to her sister's forehead, raised the blanket once more, and rose to her feet. Shoulders slumped but chin raised, she allowed him to whisk her away.

Hoping to make her feel safe, Saul spoke past the lump in his throat. "I'm Dr. Reed, and we're going to Mrs. Henderson. With a bath and new clothes, no one will recognize you." Seeing the fragile glint of hope in her expression, he added, "She'll keep you indoors for a few weeks to be on the safe side."

"All right then. I'm Midge." She meekly kept pace as he led the way back to Mrs. Henderson's. The farther they walked, the lighter her steps became until she murmured, "I hope she likes me."

"She will." Saul's words must have done the trick, because a small, cold hand slipped into his as they reached the stoop. "And you'll be treated well."

I'll make sure of it.

Clara cupped her hands to her mouth and gave an unladylike bellow. "Si-iimon!" *Where is that stubborn ox?* In a burst of inspiration, she whipped her chewed-up glove from the pocket of her apron. "Here, Simon!"

She moved up a slight rise in the landscape and surveyed the area. Seeing no sign of Simon, she turned back. Perhaps her ox had traveled south? She lifted her skirts as she hurried down the rolling hill and back toward where the wagon train already began to break camp.

A swift journey to the south gave her no more hope than the north. Clara took several deep breaths before rushing eastward. Without Simon, their wagon was one ox short.

"Lord," she gasped slightly as she spoke, still gripping the ruined glove and searching frantically for the ox, "without Simon, we won't make it in the mountains. Please help me find him before Hickory discovers he's lost!"

Several minutes passed before she had to give up the search and head back toward their wagon. Sure enough, Hickory waited there. A swift glance showed Aunt Doreen was trying not to cry.

"I'm sure we'll find him in a moment." Clara tried not to wheeze and forced a smile. "If you could just ask a few of the men to help, we'd be ready in no time."

"No. We're leaving. Your oxen are your business."

"How did he get out of the enclosure?" It

went against the grain to point out someone else's carelessness, but Simon should have been safely corralled with the rest of the team.

"If you were hitched up on time like everybody else, the stupid beast wouldn't have been left back there long enough for it to be a problem. The way things stand right now, you're out."

"You can't do this!" Clara's jaw tightened. "You have no reason!"

"You're slowing down the whole train, and we don't have time to spare." Hickory McGee's glower could singe the fur off a polar bear.

"This is the first time one of our oxen wandered off," she objected then softened her tone in an attempt to placate the man. "Same thing happened to the Jamesons two days past."

"They have a newborn to look after. You don't have any excuse. We're leavin' soon as I git back to the front, whether you and your aunt are ready or not." He jerked a thumb toward the start of the train. "Keep pace or git left behind."

"You know we can't." Though it almost stuck in her throat, she pled with the man. "Without that ox, we can't make it through the mountains."

"Lighten your load." He shrugged. "Others have had to do the same."

"So have we!" Her temper rose as she recalled everything they'd left at home and more lost in a rough river crossing when their spare ox floundered and drowned. "We've the bare minimum as it is, and you know it!"

"I saw you lookin' at a picture album the other

day. And from here I can spy a rockin' chair in there."
He folded his arms and planted his feet. "You don't
need those...or that awful flute thing I know you've
still got tucked away."

"Yes, we do." Aunt Doreen came alongside
Clara. "My grandfather carved that rocking chair
for my mother when I was born. My father shipped
it to America when they left England, and I won't
leave it behind."

"You don't have to leave it." Hot pinpricks of
tears stung Clara's eyes. After all Aunt Doreen had
done for her, had sacrificed to raise her. . . "The
chair stays."

Clara wouldn't defend her decision to bring
along the large album full of tintypes. They were
the guardians of what few memories she had left of
her parents, before the accident. When she shut her
eyes, it was the photos she saw now, not the sway of
Ma's fancy skirts or the scent of Pa's spicy cologne.

"Necessities. That's all you take. Told you at the
start, anything that don't help you holds you back.
What you've got is a bunch of sentimental claptrap
that won't help you, missy." Hickory's brows knit
together. "You can't keep the chair and the pictures
and whatever else ain't vital. The sooner you reckon
with it, the more chance you have of makin' it. The
trail brings enough tears without women fussin' over
foolish things."

"Life is more than food and livestock, Mr.
Hickory." Clara drew in a deep breath. "We only
need a little time."

"What you need is a man to take you in hand

and make decisions. I've said it from the start, and you ain't proved me wrong." The trail boss narrowed his eyes as he looked from them, to their wagon, to the five oxen already yoked to it, to Simon's empty space. "A wagon train can't afford dead weight. You're out. Next town you'll be left behind."

Clara's throat tightened as she struggled not to yell at the man. "You can't kick us out."

"Yes, I can." His assertion came with cold confidence.

"What if I take 'em on?" Burt Sprouse lumbered over from behind their wagon, where he'd been lurking during the argument.

Clara battled between anger over his assumption of responsibility, exasperation that he'd been eavesdropping rather than finding Simon, and hope that this could be a solution. Mr. Sprouse already exchanged duties with them, so a slight modification of the arrangement wouldn't be too onerous.

"You sure you want to?" Hickory glowered at Clara. "Troublesome female you got there. Once you make the decision, you can't take it back, neither."

"I could use a wife." Sprouse shrugged before adding, "And Miss Field is easy on the eyes."

"Wife?" She spluttered at the word.

"See what I mean? Not much in the brainbox." Hickory tapped the side of his skull as he spoke to the other man before turning to Clara. "Sprouse here, against good judgment, is offering to take you two on."

"I heard that. Surely we can work out a partnership between our wagons," she began.

"Already tried that." Sprouse threw a beefy arm around her, tucking her against his sweat-stained underarm. "Only way is for you two to join my wagon."

Clara tried to shift away from the damp fabric and stale odor pressed against her cheek. She couldn't suppress a shudder.

"See? Women are fragile." He clamped her closer. "Even in the heat of the prairie, she's shivering. Go on ahead and get your clothes. Then you and your aunt can settle into my wagon."

"Leave this stuff behind." Hickory thumped the side of their wagon, casually dismissing every last thing they owned.

"I'll get the food." Sprouse finally released her as he turned toward their wagon, eyeing it as though trying to decide which crates held their cooking supplies.

Clara couldn't squeeze any words out until she saw Aunt Doreen's horrified, hopeless expression. "There's no...we have no preacher." She straightened her shoulders. "We can't make the change until we find one." *And by then I'll have thought of something.*

"Buttonwood may be tiny, but we'll make it there today. They've got a preacher." Hickory scratched his stomach. "You might be able to sell some of your things in town. Join up with Sprouse before he changes his mind or stay behind. You waste time trying to find that ox and press on, I wash my hands of you."

"She'll marry me." A huge grin split Sprouse's face. "It's the only way."

No. Clara backed away, reaching blindly until

25

she caught Aunt Doreen's hand in her own. She couldn't seem to draw enough air into her lungs. *It hasn't come to this. After seven years, we're not in the same situation where we began. Lord, give me the strength not to fall into the same dreadful trap.*

"Give us a moment, gentlemen." Aunt Doreen drew her away, the rustle of their skirts the only sound until they'd gone far enough to speak in private. "Clara, there will be another way."

"How can you say that?" Tears pricked the back of her eyes. "I failed you, Aunt Doreen. When my parents died, you married Uriah to be able to provide for me so we could stay together."

"Selfish and cruel as Uriah turned out to be"— Aunt Doreen tightened her clasp—"you know the cost of marriage to the wrong man. I want better for you, Clara."

"How can I do less for you than you've done for me?" Heat pressed against her chest, almost cutting off the words.

"You wouldn't disregard all I've done to give you better opportunities. Together, we'll do what I should have done so many years ago and trust God to provide."

"This is my fault. I brought us here, to the middle of the prairie." Clara bowed her head. "We're supposed to start fresh, not live under the sway of a man because he can make his way in the world and we can't. But it's the same in the middle of the Nebraska Territory as it was back home."

"Not quite. It's not God forcing you to marry Sprouse."

"No." Clara's head came up. "It's Hickory and Sprouse." Her jaw jutted forward. "You're right. They're manipulating the situation to make us do what they want. It's not a sign of my failure or a marker of God's will—it's another example of self-serving stubbornness."

"Are you ready to give up on yourself, stop looking for God's path, and marry Sprouse to stay on the wagon train?" Aunt Doreen drew a deep breath. "Because that's not the niece I raised."

"Marriage isn't an easy answer. We'll press forward on our own terms." Clara lifted her chin. "The only stubborn male we'll be looking to keep today is Simon."

CHAPTER 3

Town of Buttonwood,
between Fort Laramie and Independence Rock

Josiah Reed! What are you doing here?" Kevin Burn plunged a red-hot horseshoe into a water barrel. As it sizzled, he gestured for Josiah to come inside.

"Need a new crowbar, Kevin," Josiah answered, stepping into the heat of the smithy. The forge sat in the middle of the structure, its stone chimney reaching through the ceiling. Orange flames that would be cheery come winter blazed as though to compete with the stifling August weather. "I sold the last one, so just tell me when I can pick it up."

"Take a seat." Kevin's eldest son, Matthew, came from the stables, where Josiah assumed he'd been shoeing a horse. He gestured toward the bench in the corner near the door, where visitors could get some fresh air and cool water from the bucket nearby. "A crowbar won't take me long."

"Sounds good." Josiah settled himself close to

the Burns so he wouldn't miss anything they said over the clang of iron on iron. "How've things been for you?"

"Good," Kevin grunted as he pounded a piece of metal on his anvil. "That last wagon train brought lots of business."

"I'd think that will be the last one until spring." Josiah removed his hat in a futile attempt to cool off. "Awful late for a caravan not to have made it to Independence Rock yet."

"Hickory McGee's ornery enough to make sure they get to Oregon before winter hits." Matthew's movements made him shift between the flickering light of the forge and the shadows beyond. "He knows what he's doing."

"That doesn't make it the right choice." Kevin plunged his work into the cooling bath, releasing a hiss of steam.

"Too often we think we know what we're doing when we don't." Josiah used his hat to fan the steam away as best he could, but the Burn men kept working as though the heat didn't register. "And sometimes a man makes a leap of faith and it works out just fine."

"What's on your mind?" Kevin made his way over to the bench. "You're not thinking of leaving Buttonwood?"

"No!" Josiah put his hat down. He'd known Kevin Burn for years even before the blacksmith moved out to the prairie. "You know I'd have come sooner if I could've."

If Gladys wouldn't have thrown a screeching, hollering fit. He squelched the unkind thoughts of his wife. She'd passed on years ago, and he prayed she'd found the peace she denied everyone else during her time on earth.

"All those years of talk, and now we're both settled out West." Kevin grinned. "Glad to hear you're not thinking of turning tail and scampering back East. That'd be a waste, with your store doing so well and that grand house you put up."

Josiah sobered at the mention of his place. Standing at two stories, built of brick and wood, that house took pride of place for hundreds of miles any direction. Oh, he'd started out in a one-room dirt soddy like everyone else, but once he'd set up the store, he'd made a house fit for his family.

Only hitch was, his family didn't come out West to join him.

"Yeah. She's a beaut." Matthew joined the conversation. "Isn't Saul coming out soon, now that he's back from Edinburgh?"

"He's a genuine doctor." Boasting about his son's achievement didn't do much to ease the hollowness of his home. "But he's decided to set up his practice in the outskirts of Baltimore."

"Sorry to hear that, Joe." Kevin clapped a hand on his shoulder.

"Say"—Matthew shifted his weight from one foot to the other as he spoke—"if you ever want to sell, I'd be interested."

"Naw." Even as he said it, Josiah suppressed a sigh. It was a house built for a family—the laughter of loved ones and the thumps of children at play. Unless Saul changed his mind, he'd be rattling around in the place until the Lord called him home. But it wasn't time to give up hope just yet.

"All right. Just keep it in mind." Matthew held out the new crowbar. "Here you go."

"Thanks. You want cash or store credit?"

"Credit."

"I'll be seeing you." Josiah waved good-bye and headed back to his store. In the time it took to put the crowbar behind the counter, he heard someone pull up outside. It sounded like a lot of commotion for a buckboard, so he craned his neck to look through the window.

A lone Conestoga wagon—a prairie schooner—stood outside.

The tinkle of the bell above the door announced customers. Josiah straightened his apron, surprised to see two strange women entering the shop. He didn't see any men with them.

"Afternoon, ladies." He stepped out from behind the counter for a closer look. Beauties, the pair of them, but bearing the telltale signs of the trail. The young gal was enough to turn any buck's head, but Josiah focused on her companion.

Beneath her dusty bonnet peeked swirls of soft mahogany threaded through with light touches of silver. Eyes that on anyone else would be dismissed as gray echoed the bright glint of her hair. *Now, there's a woman I wouldn't mind seeing every day.*

"Afternoon." The younger gal stepped forward, dark-blond hair escaping from beneath her sunbonnet to shine in the daylight. "We were hoping you could tell us whether you've seen

Hickory McGee's wagon train?"

"Two days past." Josiah heard a quickly stifled gasp. "You trying to find someone with that group?"

"We *were* 'someones' with that group." The girl muttered the words, but he heard them.

Surely the old coot hadn't kicked a family off the wagon train and left them to face the trail alone? Not even Hickory could sink so low. Josiah glanced out the window to see a lone wagon, oxen still yoked, standing outside. No men in sight.

"Two days." The silver beauty's murmur held none of the bitterness of the other. Instead, it was weighted with despair.

"Did your family start out late, hopin' to catch up?" Josiah craned his neck, looking for a father or brother—anyone—but the street remained empty.

"No." Tears shone in the older woman's eyes. "We got left behind, and if they're two days ahead, I don't see how we'll make it."

"Left behind?" Josiah had to force himself not to bellow. "Where are your men? You'd do better to wait for another train, but I can give 'em some tips on areas to skirt around so you'd have a better chance."

"Would you?" The girl pulled a pencil and a folded-up piece of paper from her worn purse. "We'd be much obliged."

Alarm bells sounded in Josiah's mind at her actions. "It'd be best if I spoke to the driver, ma'am."

She heaved a deep sigh but didn't slouch. "I'm driving."

"The two of you are alone?" He didn't bother

to hide his surprise. "Not even old Hickory would abandon two women."

"Oh yes, he would," the girl muttered again before raising her voice. "We hit a rough patch, but as time is of the essence, we really need to be on our way."

"It's late in the season to still be at this point." Josiah tried to make his words gentle. "Especially with a lone wagon. Truth of the matter, ladies, is that catching up with Hickory is a slim hope. If he left you behind once, he'll do it again." *The rat. Someone needs to teach that low-down snake a lesson or two, and I'd be happy to volunteer.* "Safest bet would be for you to stay here and join another train next summer." He watched as they reached for each other and linked arms as though trying to create a wall.

The younger woman spoke for them both. "We can't."

It didn't take an excess of brains to figure out the problem. Most folks headed West spent their money on the wagon and supplies. Time, then, wasn't the only commodity at stake. Josiah looked at the two, then beyond them through the shop windows at the house beyond.

He glanced at the gal again, affirming his impression that she'd spark an interest in any young man. If his son came to mind the store, the pair could be thrown together if he angled it right. . . . Could this be the answer to his prayers?

Josiah closed his eyes and waited for the Lord to give him that gut-wrenching sensation he always had when he'd made a poor decision.

Didn't come.

Yep. That settled it. For good or ill, he was going to invite these little ladies to stay.

Two days. Those words pounded in Clara's brain with the force of a sledgehammer, striking at her temples and sending a chill down her spine. *Two days. We're two days behind the wagon train after finding Simon and getting stuck in the mud after that rainstorm. Oh, Lord, what are we to do? So far we've clung to the hope that they're just a few miles away. That if we caught up with a full team, Hickory would accept us as part of the train. Now we know the truth.*

"Josiah Reed." The man's voice caught her attention. He gave a small bow. "Owner of Buttonwood General Store."

"Mrs. Doreen Edgerly and my niece, Miss Clara Field." Her aunt introduced them, her voice not betraying any of the worry Clara knew they shared. "Nice to meet you, Mr. Reed."

"My pleasure." The man's gaze lingered on Aunt Doreen appreciatively, making her flush a bit. "It's not often two such lovely ladies come to Buttonwood. And I do hope you'll be staying, though my motives aren't entirely selfless."

"Oh?" Clara's eyes narrowed.

"Yep." His posture slumped as he gestured around the well-kept store. "See, keeping up on everything around here is getting to be a big job.

Between this and the house"—he indicated the beautiful two-story brick and wood home she and Aunt Doreen had driven past moments ago—"I could use a hand."

"Where is your family?" Aunt Doreen craned her neck as though certain some grown children and a plump wife would appear momentarily. "Surely they pitch in."

"Gladys passed on years ago, and my children are grown. When I moved here, they opted to stay behind." He brightened with pride. "Hannah's married and in a delicate condition, and Saul's just come back from studying in Edinburgh. He's a doctor." The glow left his features and he slumped once more, heaving what Clara would have called a dramatic sigh. "So I'm alone and would be more than happy to put the two of you up in exchange for some cleaning and good cooking."

"Seems like everything's well in hand." Clara couldn't help but feel Mr. Reed was hamming it up. "And you don't know us."

"Oh, Clara." Aunt Doreen's disapproval came through loud and clear. "If the man says he'd like some help, why"—she faltered for a moment before swiping a gloved hand along a shelf, leaving behind a smudge Clara would have sworn wasn't there a moment ago and triumphantly displaying her dirty palm—"who are we to gainsay him?"

"Exactly so." Mr. Reed beamed at her aunt.

Clara tried to organize the mess of thoughts whirling in her head. If Aunt Doreen was willing to use a soiled glove to convince her to stay, that spoke volumes about her aunt's exhaustion. And desperation.

You failed. Uncle Uriah's voice echoed in her memory. *You couldn't take care of yourself, much less your aunt. Women are weak and need men to look out for them.* She shook away the lump in her throat at the thought he might have been right.

Simple truth of the matter was that they couldn't catch up to the wagon train. Not with the distance so great and their resources so small. *Is this Your answer, Lord? To wait for an early wagon train in spring and start again?*

"You're very generous," she demurred, "but it's a large decision based on such a short acquaintance."

"True." Josiah Reed stroked his salt-and-pepper beard. "I am trusting the two of you with my house, store, and everything I own. But I've learned to be a good judge of character, and there's plenty of crazier things a man will do for some good cooking."

"You don't know for certain that our cooking is any good," Clara pointed out, squelching an impulse to smile at the clever way he turned her doubts back at her. "You might not be able to tell our pot roast from coal. If it comes to that, then where will we all be?"

"Clara!" Her aunt's gasp held recrimination. "I'm an excellent cook, and I taught you everything I know. How could you suggest to this man that I would leave you rudderless in the kitchen?"

"Oh, Aunt Doreen," Clara hastened to mend the breach, "I wasn't saying we can't cook. The point was that Mr. Reed doesn't know one way or another, and he's willing to hire us."

"You wouldn't have made it this far if you couldn't cook." Mr. Reed's pronouncement hit home, making Clara think of Burt Sprouse—the man whose mouth worked only for eating, making unilateral decisions, and denouncing women who didn't go along with them. He didn't bother to speak a word in their defense.

Mr. Sprouse went along with Hickory when it counted, and he'd be sure to do so again. If that happened while they were in the mountains. . .Clara shuddered at the thought.

"What would the arrangements be?" She still didn't know enough to make a decision. Things had to be fair for Mr. Reed, as well.

"I built that house hoping my children would come fill it with grandbabies, so there's plenty of room." He rubbed the back of his neck. "If you take care of the cleaning, laundry, and cooking over there and pitch in over here from time to time, I'd be more than happy to put you up. Might even say you're an answer to prayer. Room and board till the next train comes along, and I'll find a place for your oxen to hole up come winter."

An answer to prayer. The phrase rang in Clara's thoughts long after Mr. Reed stopped speaking. The possibility that this situation was a blessing to everyone involved. . ."Will you excuse us for just a moment?" Clara ushered her aunt out the door for a brief consultation. "We don't know him, and to trust him with everything we own on such short acquaintance seems foolish." *Especially after Uncle*

Uriah. The thought hung between them, unspoken.

"I think we should agree." Aunt Doreen looked at her with wide eyes. "We'll stay together, and he has no legal claim. Besides, Mr. Reed seems a good man. It's a fair deal, he's not handing out charity, and we wouldn't have to use our savings!"

"It seems like a God-given answer to the problem," Clara acknowledged. "Catching up after we found Simon would have been difficult, but there's that creaking from the rear of the wagon. We're going slow and falling farther behind."

"Two days," Aunt Doreen repeated, her expression grim. "And that's *if* the axle holds. Taking the time to repair it means a longer lag, but breaking down in the middle of the plains. . ." Her voice drifted off, but there was no mistaking her meaning.

Clara clasped her aunt's chilled hands in hers. Wisps of hair flew away from her aunt's usually meticulous bun, dark circles beneath her eyes making her older than her thirty-nine years.

They'd given up the house to creditors, almost all their savings to outfit the wagon, and their life in Boston to make a new beginning. But Clara wouldn't allow her aunt's health to pay the price for their passage. Her aunt deserved rest from this grueling pace they'd set trying to catch up, and Mr. Reed's offer would provide that. Better still, they'd have a roof over their heads and access to any foodstuffs they might need.

Haven't I been praying for You to clear the way, to enable me to provide for us on the journey? The answer seems so clear, Lord. As simply as that, Clara made her decision. She gave her aunt a slight nod, gratified to see the smile blooming across the older woman's face as they went back inside.

"Mr. Reed, we'd like to accept your offer."

"Good." Of average height, in nondescript clothing, the shop owner hadn't made too much of an impression at first.

Now that Clara really looked, she could see that Mr. Reed's eyes sparkled and a distinguished smattering of gray adorned his temples and beard. He smiled broadly, a generous stretch with no clamped corners like Uncle Uriah, who constantly pinched away the joy in life. *Maybe this will work.*

"First things first." He pulled a pair of wire-framed spectacles from his pocket and settled them on his nose. "My larder isn't well stocked, so you'll need to have pretty much everything over at the house. Flour, sugar, molasses, beans, and the like are already set aside. You two just add on as needed, and I'll keep a list for my records."

"Truly?" Aunt Doreen's eyes widened at the thought.

"What are your favorite dishes?" Clara realized that Mr. Reed probably wouldn't have a garden or a fully-stocked cellar, so vegetables would be a problem.

"Can't say I'm picky." He grinned. "Though I do have a sweet tooth. What little we do have in the way of canned fruit is over there." He indicated a shelf to their left. "Got powdered milk but not the fresh stuff. Eggs are in the crates in the corner."

He wrote while he spoke, and Clara rushed to pile things on the counter.

Aunt Doreen added potatoes, baking powder, cheese, salt pork, a ham hock, a venison roast, and a side of bacon. She looked around the store twice before declaring she couldn't find vegetables.

"Fresh vegetables come in the spring from farmers hereabouts. Other than that, we make do with whatever gets preserved." Mr. Reed shrugged. "Not a lot we can do about it so far from the railroads. We're lucky if the stage comes through once a month."

"We've plenty in the wagon," Doreen pointed out.

"Anything you use from your own supplies, keep a list," Mr. Reed ordered, "and I'll replace it come spring."

"Thank you." Clara felt some tension in her shoulders relax at his sincerity. She sent up a prayer of thanks.

"If that'll do, leave that stuff behind. I'll haul it over." Mr. Reed headed toward the door. "For now, how 'bout I show you around?"

When he offered his arm to her aunt, Clara's conviction that they'd made the right choice grew. A few steps took them away from the store, leading them to their new home. As they skirted around their wagon, a great crack sounded.

"If you wanted an assurance you made a wise decision," Mr. Reed spoke, staring as the back of their wagon tilted ominously, the oxen pulling frantically against their yokes, "I'd say you just got one."

"Just one more." Saul passed Midge another peppermint. In the week since he'd brought her to Mrs. Henderson's, the little girl had become almost unrecognizable. A good scrubbing revealed Midge's hair to be a deep red rather than the dark brown he'd seen. And she'd already outgrown the hastily hemmed dress Mrs. Henderson unearthed from an old chest and bloomed under the kindness shown her. A few more weeks of good meals and the pale urchin he'd found in an alley would be healthy.

While Midge stood smaller than most girls of her thirteen years and showed the signs of being underfed for a prolonged period, her overall health was good. No signs of illness he would have expected from her poor living conditions—fever, weak pulse, coughing, and the like—seemed to threaten her. People didn't come any more resilient than Midge, who'd borne far more suffering than her years should hold and not let it destroy her.

"What color do you want for your new dress?" Saul led her over to the corner where bolts of fabric were stacked to the ceiling. "How about this?" He picked out a bolt of pink cotton. His sisters had always liked pink.

Midge, on the other hand, shrank away from the fabric as though it would bite her, pressing against his side and shaking her head. "The gents like a girl in pink." She was obviously repeating something she'd heard before. "He made Nancy wear it."

Saul stuffed the bolt back in place, jamming it against the wall as his other arm curled protectively around Midge. He stared at the fabric without seeing any of it. *What other simple things have been tainted for her?*

"Maybe the yellow?" She hesitantly pointed toward a yellow and white gingham, tucked high up in the corner.

He swung her onto a sturdy table nearby so she could pull it down. Saul didn't know much about fabric—and far less about little girls—but it seemed soft and cheery. A good choice.

He watched Midge run her hand along it then look down at him. "What do you think?" She chewed on her lower lip as though afraid she'd be denied.

He nodded. "It'll make you look like a ray of sunshine."

"I like it." Midge fingered the gingham as though it were made of golden thread. "This one, please."

"This one it is." Saul handed off the bolt to the store clerk and ordered more than Mrs. Henderson told him she'd need, just in case the hem would need to be let out or some such thing. "Now pick another."

"Really?" Midge's eyes widened until they seemed to take up her whole face. "Two more dresses? I'm to have *three*?"

"That dress was only meant to be temporary." Saul gestured to the old black wool she wore, a leftover from when Mrs. Henderson's first husband

42

had died and her daughter wore the traditional black. "It's too hot for summer."

"I don't mind, Dr. Reed. Honest, I don't." Concern replaced the excitement on her face. "The black is fine and"—she stooped to slide off the table as she lowered her voice—"fitting. Since Nancy passed on and all."

He could hear the tears threatening to overtake her, so he squatted down beside her. "Now, Midge, we talked about this. No one is to know where you came from, so he can't find you. Wouldn't Nancy want you to be safe and happy?"

"Yes, sir." She drew a shaky breath.

"In Nancy's honor, why don't you choose to have a dress in her favorite color?"

"Green." Midge didn't hesitate for a moment. "She loved green."

"Well then, green it is." He straightened as she eyed the fabric once more. "And every time you wear it, you can think of Nancy."

"She'd like that." Midge gave a tiny nod. "I know she would. 'Specially if it was a dark green."

Within moments they'd chosen a length of deep green reminiscent of a lush forest. When Saul paid for the material, he added in a few more peppermints. They were good for the stomach, and besides, Midge liked them.

As they made their way back to the house, they came upon a church. Saul stopped in front of it. "Would you like to say a prayer for your sister before we go back?"

"Naw." She shook her head vehemently. "Don't

want to keep Mrs. Henderson waiting." Midge wouldn't even look at the building. Odd for such a curious child.

"Midge, why don't you want to go inside?"

"Prayers aren't worth the time they take." She glowered at the cross on the door. "Nancy prayed every day, didn't she? And see what came of it. She died, and if it weren't for you and Mrs. Henderson, I'd be stuck alone with him, wouldn't I?"

Her ferocity took him aback, but he could see why she had that perspective. It would take time before she'd see otherwise. "But you're not alone with him. That means something, doesn't it?"

"Yes." She stared at him. "And grateful I am, too. But it don't have a thing to do with prayer, Dr. Reed. Rodney was right when he talked about church. I seen it same as him."

"You saw what?"

"Sundays was good days to Rodney." Her brows drew together in a ferocious scowl. "He said customers came fresh from church, all squeaky clean so's they could afford to muck about. There's some as would come straight from church to the alley. Nancy hated Sundays, and all her prayers couldn't change that."

"Listen to me, Midge." He sank down so their eyes were level. "That was the sin of men. The men who came to that alley were wrong, but it wasn't because of church. Nancy knew that, and it's why she kept praying."

"That's what she said." Midge shrugged. "But all I seen is the wrong side, and until I see the good part, praying is a waste of breath." She must have seen the sadness in his face, because she gave him an awkward pat on the shoulder. "Don't be put out by it, Doctor. I know there are good men, too. You're one of them."

"You said Nancy would see your mother in heaven," he pointed out. "If you don't believe in prayer, how can you believe in that?"

"Simple." She raised one brow. "Mama told us, and she were one of the good'uns, too. The way I figure it, if prayers work, it's only after you've gone to meet your Maker. Either way, it don't do much good while we're here."

Her words haunted him throughout the day and into the evening as he paced around his room. With all Midge had seen, her conclusions were logical. Problem was she based her understanding of the spiritual in the physical. How could he make her see how different the two were?

Lord, how do I reach her? If I'd pressed the issue, she would have gone inside and said a prayer. But she would have done it to please me, not because she believed in Your love. She needs to see Your hand in the world, despite the terrible things men do to each other. Here, it seems as though everything, even church, reminds her of the evil she's seen. It's a battle I'm unprepared for.

Between his pacing and the heat of the fire in the grate, he soon grew warm. Saul took off his jacket and laid it over the back of a chair, only to have it slither to the floor in a crumpled heap. He hung it up properly before the envelope caught his eye—the letter he'd gotten the day he found Midge.

He picked it up, breaking the seal as he settled in the chair.

> *My son,*
>
> *You know your sister is in the family way, and I want to be there for the birth of my first grandchild. I'm not getting any younger, and you're not getting married in a hurry, so it may well be my only chance. If it's a boy, they're going to name it Josiah. But if I'm going to be there when my namesake enters the world, someone's got to look after the store.*
>
> *That's where you come in. I want you to hop on the stage and come to Buttonwood for a few weeks. Take care of things as a favor to your old man now and set up your fancy city practice when you get back.*
>
> *Who knows? You might find the gal you want right here in town. At the very least, you can breathe some fresh air for a change.*
>
> *Love,*
Your father

Saul smiled. Dad had been trying to get him to settle down for years, never understanding the time it took to train properly. Now that he'd returned to America, his father was more determined than ever to needle him into marriage.

He ran his palm down his face. The building he had his eye on to become his office wouldn't be vacated for another month. And Hannah'd categorically refused to let him deliver his niece or nephew—no matter that he was a trained professional.

A peaceful little town on the Oregon Trail would certainly make for a change of pace. *Midge.* A small town of good people would go a long way toward helping heal her. Propriety dictated he couldn't travel alone with her, but Mrs. Henderson would probably bring her once he'd gotten everything ready.

It'd do Dad good to see Hannah, Saul could certainly watch over the store, and Midge could relax far away from her past. The slow, easy pace of life on the prairie could be just what they both needed. Buttonwood sounded like a godsend.

He rose to his feet, grabbed ink and parchment, and began to draft his reply.

CHAPTER 4

I never thought to see brick all the way out here." Clara surveyed the large house with curiosity.

"Everyone pretty much starts out in a soddy or a dugout." Mr. Reed led them around the back of the house.

A modest distance away stood an outhouse and one of the earthen homes that dotted the Oregon Trail. Dug straight into the dirt, with a slanted, mud-packed roof over the pit and blocked steps leading down to the entry, it seemed sad and dank.

"I built the big house after the store turned a respectable profit in hopes of talking my son into setting up his practice here." He turned toward a side door to the grander residence. "I special ordered these bricks from an old friend. Shipping 'em all here cost an arm and a leg."

Clara raised her brows and shot Aunt Doreen a glance at his casual mention of such an expenditure. Obviously, Mr. Reed's pockets were deep long before he came to Buttonwood and set up shop. It made a person wonder why he left a comfortable city life to rough it in a dirt hole. Of course, so many people back home wondered why she and Aunt Doreen chose to travel West, she had no room to speculate.

She moved closer as Mr. Reed opened the door to what looked to be a new kitchen, with a open-hearth fireplace in the far corner paired with a generous working table. Across the room, a large hutch guarded a door in the opposite wall. Clara could only assume it led to a pantry.

"Oh," Aunt Doreen breathed as she stepped into the room, trailing her fingers across the sturdy mantel over the hearth. She moved toward the worktable, tilting her head to peruse the shelf above it.

A jumble of items sat together—mixing bowls, sifter, pie tins, roasting pan, measuring cups, and more. If Clara were to guess, she'd say none of it had seen any use. Despite the assortment, the area boasted only one hook with a single skillet adorning the wall. Kettles and pots heaped together beneath the worktable. Slumped against one another in despair, the cookware gave the impression of once waiting in orderly stacks for a purpose that never arrived.

Until now. This muddle of a magnificent kitchen convinced Clara as nothing else could that Josiah Reed genuinely needed their help. She and Aunt Doreen would put his kitchen—and perhaps more—in order before they left.

"Don't say I didn't warn you," Reed reminded as he crossed the room and opened the door to a disgracefully bare pantry. "I would've stocked up before the end of fall, but during the warmer months I don't keep much here when the store's so near."

"May I?" Clara gestured to the closed cabinets of the pine hutch. Up close, she could see the thin veil of dust coating the entire piece.

At his nod, her fingers closed around one smooth knob and she tugged, finding a hodgepodge of dishes littering the shelves. A drawer beneath revealed a clatter of utensils. Forks clashed with knives, spoons bowed timidly away from the fray, and faded paper liner bore the brunt of the battle. Another compartment unearthed the silverware case. The deep depressions in its molded velvet stared up, rich and lonely.

Like Mr. Reed, his untouched kitchen, and his grand, empty house in the middle of the prairie. Clara closed the lid and slid the case away, only to realize the others were leaving. She hastily followed them past the door, to the dining room.

"Your room will be this way, if you like." Mr. Reed didn't linger over the oval table dominating the long, bare room. Instead, he moved into a narrow hallway of sorts. He bypassed the first door with a muttered, "Mud room," and came to a halt beside the other.

"How lovely!" Aunt Doreen exclaimed before Clara got a good look at the space. "Such beautiful windows!" She went over to trace the leaded panes melding waves of glass together.

"Yes." Clara couldn't tear her gaze from the

softened view of the prairie. Here there were no parched stretches of land where dirt dried into gray scales and grass grew as brittle as the ends of an old broom. The window blurred the landscape to a mixed mist of browns and green below and blue above—an oasis nursed by the waters of the Platte River.

"There's a door to the outside?" Her aunt pulled it open. "We can get to the kitchen and the washroom from right here!"

"I planned it that way in case of harsh winters." Mr. Reed's voice came from the doorway, where he hovered respectfully. "It's easier to heat just the downstairs and have quick access to the outdoors and such."

"Ingenious." Aunt Doreen looked at Mr. Reed with such admiration he practically beamed.

"There are plenty of empty rooms upstairs but"—he cleared his throat—"I thought you might want to stay close to each other."

"It's also good to be close to the kitchen," Clara agreed. Mr. Reed's decision would maintain propriety. It also dissipated any worries she or Aunt Doreen might harbor were they in separate rooms upstairs.

"After weeks in the wagon, staying in any house seems like a luxury." Her aunt moved toward the dresser on the opposite wall. "Staying here is. . ."

"A great favor to me," Mr. Reed filled in when Doreen couldn't find the words. "Having you two around will make the house less empty, and I won't have to fuss around the place."

"We'll see to everything," Clara promised. Her

resolve strengthened as Mr. Reed led them through the rest of the house. An air of abandonment hung over the still parlor. The wood of the stairwell banisters, while smooth, held no cheerful gleam. No flowers, photographs, or art enlivened the walls of the foyer as they climbed to the second floor.

Sheets twisted on the bed, towels slouched over the back of a chair, and thick curtains shut out any glimmer of sunlight in the master bedroom. A guest room bore no signs of occupancy. The worn quilt on the bed sagged toward the floor. One washstand and trunk huddled together on another wall as though joining forces against the sparseness all around.

While Mr. Reed wouldn't open the door to his office, the other two rooms boasted nothing but dust. No furniture claimed space, no hooks or pegs stood out from the walls, and no curtains hung over the windows. The barrenness of it all made Clara itch to weave rugs, stitch samplers, piece together quilts, lug in old bedsteads, sew cushions, and fill the space with signs of love and use.

A swift glance at Aunt Doreen told the same story. Her hands locked together as though clutching an imaginary lifeline. Silently, they made their way back outside.

"First thing we need to do is move your things out here." Mr. Reed's words stabbed at Clara.

"We can't put all that in your house," she declined with more vehemence than she intended. Putting their treasured belongings all over the place would be akin to settling here for good, which wasn't a possibility.

"You wouldn't want to haul everything upstairs." Mr. Reed's thin smile told her he knew there was more to her objection. "I planned to hitch up my buckboard and bring things over to the soddy. That way you can unpack what you'll need, and we'll be able to have Kevin Burn—he's our blacksmith but does a bit of everything—take a look at that axle."

"Perfect!" Aunt Doreen hurried after Mr. Reed, leaving Clara to follow. The two of them stayed at the wagon while he went to get his buckboard and mule from the stables, also managed by the Burns.

"Here we are." Mr. Reed pulled up in his buckboard, but another pulled up alongside it. Three strangers jumped out of the second one to line up alongside Mr. Reed. "This here's Kevin Burn and his sons, Matthew and Brett. Fellows, meet Mrs. Doreen Edgerly and Miss Clara Field."

"Nice to meet you," the father said. His sons quickly followed his lead. "Josiah told us you've hit a spot of trouble and plan to stay for a while, so we thought we'd lend a hand."

"Thank you." Clara couldn't help but compare all four of them to Hickory McGee and Burt Sprouse. Needless to say, the residents of Buttonwood, a town she'd not even known existed a few days ago, made a better impression than the men who'd traveled alongside her for weeks on end. Who, but for God's grace, she'd still be catering to.

The burly blacksmith and his sons unloaded things quickly, until everything she and Aunt Doreen owned stood in the backs of the buckboards.

"I'll drive it over," the youngest of the three

Burns volunteered for the job, shooting a smile toward Clara.

She gave him a light nod in return. Encouraging his attention would do no good, since she and Aunt Doreen would be leaving come spring. Instead, she needed to focus on the task at hand. "What can we do about the oxen?"

"I'll take the wagon over to the shop," Mr. Burn explained, "and Matthew will take the oxen over to the Fossets'. Frank's a reasonable man and will probably be glad to take them on for a while. We'll strike some kind of arrangement."

"Perhaps I should speak with Mr. Fosset." Clara spoke softly but tried to remind them just whose oxen they discussed—and who would be obligated by whatever arrangement was made.

"No need for that." Burn shrugged off her concern. "We'll see to it while you and your aunt settle in. Folks look after each other around Buttonwood."

With that, the men were moving again, leaving Clara and Aunt Doreen with little choice but to follow the buckboards back to the dugout. With two of the men looking after the wagon and oxen, it took considerably longer to unload everything.

As the men hefted heavy items into the soddy, she and Aunt Doreen sorted things. The two women set aside any boxes, crates, trunks, and bags they remembered as having things they'd need. Any cookware they hadn't seen counterparts to in the kitchen went in one pile, along with produce and foodstuffs. Their clothing and toiletries sat in trunks, ready to be carried to the house. Almost everything else, from dishes to the rocking chair, went to the soddy.

Another mound of items sat next to her aunt, so Clara went to investigate. Sure enough, she found a stockpile of things obviously squirreled away for the house.

"We don't need this." Clara retrieved a quilt from the pile Aunt Doreen kept adding to. "Or this." She picked up a framed sampler and tucked it under her arm.

"We can put them in our room," Aunt Doreen protested. "It's good to have a touch of home around you."

"That's just it." Clara set down the items and perched on a trunk. She lowered her voice so it wouldn't carry. "This isn't home for us. We have to remember that."

"I know." Aunt Doreen pulled a handkerchief from her sleeve and dabbed her forehead. "But a few things are a good reminder."

"This?" Clara held up the sampler, a verse stitched across the face. " 'As for me and my house, we will serve the Lord,' " she read aloud before looking at her aunt. "This isn't our household, Aunt Doreen. It's Mr. Reed's."

"I don't know what I was thinking." The older woman sighed. "The last thing I'd want is for that kind man to see it on the wall and be offended."

"Yes. I'm more concerned about you growing attached to Buttonwood." Clara stood back up. "It's a nice town, but in spring we'll be heading out to Oregon. If we settle in, well, that'll make things more difficult when it's time to leave."

"Makes sense." Her aunt replaced the lid on a crate. "This winter might be a good time to work on your drawing." The hopeful suggestion made Clara wince. "Mr. Reed says we'll be snowed in a great deal of the time after November, and it'd be nice to leave him something to remember us by."

"We'll see." Clara grudgingly added her own art set to the last mound of things they'd take inside. Why she'd never been able to capture the likeness of things in charcoal was an irksome mystery. She'd learned every other lesson quickly—cooking, sewing, managing a household, dressing appropriately, engaging in light conversation, and playing both the pianoforte and flute—but her list of accomplishments ended there.

"Don't look so glum, Clara." Aunt Doreen smiled. "Try to think of it as another form of expression, like writing in your journal or playing your flute." She cast an anxious glance around. "Have we found it?"

"Right here." At the start of their journey, Clara had taken it out and played a little tune, only to be told by a glowering Hickory McGee that he couldn't abide 'screeching through a metal tube.' He advised her to put it far back in her wagon and leave it there until they'd reached Oregon.

"Oh, good. Mr. Reed seems the type to enjoy fine music." Aunt Doreen braced the small of her back. "Is that everything?"

"I believe so." Clara gathered her flute, sewing kit, and art set before snatching the quilt she'd put aside earlier. If it made her aunt happy, a simple thing like a quilt shouldn't cause any problems. She waited while Aunt Doreen gathered her own art and sewing supplies then walked with her back to the big, empty house.

How awful it would be to have no family nearby. She snuck a glance at her aunt. If Doreen hadn't taken her in after her parents' accident, she'd know that deep loneliness firsthand.

Which is why it's so important to get to Oregon, where the land is fertile for gardening and we can make our own way taking in mending and so forth. Aunt Doreen took care of me; now it's my turn to look after her. She squelched the reminder that she'd already experienced failure. Hickory kicking them off the wagon train made for a harsh blow.

Which was exactly why she had to protect her aunt from further heartache. The more rooms they spread their things about in, the more settled they'd feel. Just like a mother bird tucking bits of fluff into her nest, Aunt Doreen would make herself at home.

Looking around, Clara had to stamp down her own urge to make her mark on the place. It took a stern reminder—the same one she gave her aunt when they packed the wagon. *The more we bring, the more we stand to lose along the way.*

If Clara could prevent it, her aunt wouldn't lose so much as a hairpin during their stay in Buttonwood.

Midge watched as the patch of sunshine grew longer, slanting toward her bed. When it crept up to where her toes made tiny lumps under the blankets, she threw back the covers and leaped onto the bedside rug. Arms over her head, fingers waggling, she gave a mighty stretch on her way to the washbasin. Her new yellow dress hung on a peg by the door, bright and clean.

And just for me.

She pulled it on carefully, tugging it into place instead of yanking it over her head like she had with her old one. That dress didn't exist anymore. Mrs. Henderson said it fell to pieces in the wash, not even fit for the rag bag. Midge didn't miss it.

When she really thought about it, she didn't miss much from her old life. Not the sour-smelling dark room, not the way Rodney slapped her for being in his way, not the way she'd huddled on the cold ground outside while Nancy worked. She only missed her sister.

Her nose tingled like it did when she was about to cry, so she rubbed it. Hard. *Crying never makes no difference.*

Besides, she didn't want to get her pretty new dress all wet. That'd be a fine thank-you when Mrs. Henderson made it special for her—coming downstairs all wrung out and mopey. She gave a great sniff and reached for the apron she'd sewn while Mrs. Henderson worked.

She liked Mrs. Henderson but didn't like the way the woman would look at her sideways, all worried. Mrs. Henderson thought Midge didn't see, but she did.

Those glances started when Midge said she

didn't want to go to church. Maybe it would be easier to go. Making Mrs. Henderson and Dr. Reed happy was real important. She nodded. That's what she'd do—tell them over breakfast that she'd changed her mind. If it meant so much to them, it couldn't be that bad. They were some of the good'uns.

Ready for the day, she moved to the small, circular window of her attic room and opened the shutters wide. No matter how bad things got, she could always count on the city to be busy. So full of noise and movement, the streets used to beckon to her to lose herself in them until darkness fell. Today she looked over them as though surveying her kingdom. She still claimed the city but stayed out of its reach.

Soft yellow light flooded her room now, resting on her new dress like she was part of the sunbeam. Midge gave a quick twirl before going to make her bed. She never had a real bed to make before, so she did it extra careful, folding the corners and fluffing her pillow just so before she finished.

Then she made her way down the back stairs to the kitchen, going slow so she wouldn't trip in the dark.

Dr. Reed and Mrs. Henderson were already in the kitchen. She could hear their voices. Midge started to speed up but stopped herself. Adults didn't take kindly to interruptions, so she'd wait a bit.

"You plan to go, then." Mrs. Henderson's words made Midge suck in her breath.

Who? Who was going? Not Dr. Reed!

"If you'll take Midge. . ." Dr. Reed didn't say where, but it didn't matter. Not really.

They're getting rid of me. She plunked down on the stairs, not even caring that her dress might get dusty. What did she do wrong? Was it church? She had to tell them she'd go. Maybe it would change their minds!

Midge bolted to her feet and burst through the door. "Please don't take me away. I'll go to church. I promise!" She grasped Mrs. Henderson's skirts. "Please?"

"What do. . .oh, child." Her hand came to rest on Midge's head, stroking her hair. "You don't understand."

"I came down the stairs and heard you." She hated the quavery sound of her voice, but she'd let them see her cry if she had to. Dr. Reed had already seen her do it once.

"Midge," Dr. Reed knelt beside her as he spoke, "I have to go to the Nebraska Territory for a little while to watch my father's store."

"I don't want you to go." She transferred her hold from Mrs. Henderson's skirts to his jacket sleeve. "Stay here."

"Even if Mrs. Henderson brought you to Nebraska once I had things ready?" His words took a while to sink in.

"You mean. . .we'd still be together?" She darted a glance at Mrs. Henderson. "All of us?"

"I'd bring you to him, dearie, but I wouldn't stay in Nebraska unless absolutely necessary. You'll see me when you both come back."

"We'll come back?" She tugged on the doctor's sleeve.

"Yes. Going to Buttonwood will be like an adventure."

"Buttonwood?" She wrinkled her nose. "That's a funny name for a town.

"It's a very tiny town by a river, with lots of land around it." He straightened up, but she still kept her grip.

"And we'd come back here," she repeated. "Do you promise, Dr. Reed?"

"I promise." He looked like he meant it, so she let go.

"All right then. When do we leave?"

"A couple of days after I go. Because you'll take the stage, it will take weeks for you to catch up, though. Would you want to start out later?"

"The sooner the better." She decided not to tell them what her sister used to say, "The sooner things get started, the quicker they're done."

CHAPTER 5

A motley group of folks pushed toward them after church the next morning. Not that Josiah thought himself one to judge, but even he could tell that the residents of Buttonwood would seem like an odd mishmash to his new guests.

The fact that everyone had gaped at them all through the service hadn't helped any, either. Despite the Burns swiftly settling into the pew behind him, Josiah had to employ his best scowl to keep the worst offenders at bay. Even so, the time of reckoning—one could even say judgment—had come.

Appropriately enough, it began with the parson walking up to them. "Nice to see new faces in the congregation this morning." He waited expectantly for an introduction and, it seemed to Josiah, an explanation.

"Mrs. Edgerly and Miss Field are my new staff," he began. "They'll be taking over my housekeeping, cooking, and lending a hand at the store as needed. They share the downstairs room." Josiah made sure to put a little extra emphasis on the words *share* and *downstairs*, just to be clear.

"Pleased to meet you." The parson gave a small bow. "How did you come to Buttonwood?"

"We ran into some trouble on the trail and"— Miss Field paused before finishing—"had to separate from our wagon train."

"Trouble?" Lucinda Grogan shouldered her way into the conversation, eyes agleam with speculation.

"One of our oxen wandered off at an inopportune time, so we fell behind," Mrs. Edgerly elaborated on her niece's statement. "When we arrived in Buttonwood, we met Mr. Reed. He mentioned his need of help, and our axle gave way. It seemed best all around for us to stay. Today's our first full day in town."

"A convenient solution." Lucinda's eyes narrowed as she turned her attention to Josiah. "Though, Mr. Reed, if you needed help, my Willa would have been glad to take on some odd jobs."

Interfering old buzzard. He inhaled sharply before answering. "I figured you needed her at home."

"Mrs. Edgerly? Miss Field?" Kevin brought Frank Fosset to the forefront of their group. "This is Frank Fosset, who's agreed to look after your oxen until spring."

"Thank you, Mr. Fosset." Miss Field looked the man over, and Josiah wondered if she noticed what he always had—with a thick chest, short legs, and a lumbering gait, Fosset resembled nothing so much as the oxen he sold to travelers.

"No trouble," he grunted. "This is my wife,

Nora, and my eldest daughter, Sally."

"Welcome to Buttonwood!" Sally reached out to clasp Miss Field's hand. "Opal and Amanda and I are so glad to have another girl here."

"And Willa." Lucinda Grogan all but spat out a tooth with her words. "My Willa will be a good friend to you." Bitter determination edged the statement as she yanked Miss Field's hand away from Sally and pulled her toward Willa.

Josiah stepped back. The women may be new to town, but they'd have to navigate the other hens on their own terms. It'd take a man with less between his ears to step into the path of a warring Grogan. He made a note to tell Mrs. Edgerly and Miss Field about the Grogan-Speck feud that night.

If they hadn't already learned firsthand.

"Those wretched Specks and their friends think they own this town," Mrs. Grogan muttered darkly as she tugged Clara away from her aunt. Obviously, the woman bore ill will toward that sweet Sally Fosset and, Clara decided, some family with the unfortunate surname of Speck.

"Where are you off to in such a hurry, Ma?" One young man broke away from the group they passed and fell into step beside them. He spoke to Mrs. Grogan but kept his eyes on Clara.

"I thought I'd introduce Miss Field here to our Willa." Mrs. Grogan's already-firm grip tightened when Clara tried to pull away. "Miss Field, meet my son, Larry."

"We're always glad to see another pretty gal in town." This, paired with something of a smirk, came out loudly enough for the entire town to hear. Larry went a step further by trying to take Clara's arm, but they'd already arrived.

She took the opportunity to pull away from both mother and son to approach the daughter. Miss Willa Grogan wore a patched calico dress and a wary expression. She seemed long used to her family's overbearing ways and tried to fade into the background so she'd be overlooked. Clara's heart immediately went out to this girl who reminded her of a young Aunt Doreen.

"You must be Willa." She gave a heartfelt smile, ignoring the way Larry puffed out his chest when he saw it. "I'm Clara Field. Your mother thought you might be able to help me get settled into things around Buttonwood?"

"Of course." The girl's eyes widened. "Everyone wants to meet you, hear where you're from, and such forth."

"Exactly." Sally Fosset, another young woman in tow, huffed up to them. "It's good for the town to have new blood."

"Maybe put aside old differences," Sally's friend added. Like Willa, she wore a patched, sun-bleached calico dress. There, the resemblance ended. This girl stood straight and tall, a smattering of freckles marched proudly across the bridge of her nose, and she met Lucinda Grogan's hostile gaze without flinching.

Clara liked her immediately, though she sensed

this girl's presence was the root of the tension between Sally Fosset and Lucinda Grogan. When they'd walked up, Lucinda had drawn back, her breath sucking in a rapid hiss. Larry alternately leered at Sally and glowered at her friend, while Willa proved Clara right and somehow began to blend into the background.

Clara couldn't resist trying to get to the bottom of the problem. "Old differences?" She echoed the words as though confused, hoping for an elaboration.

"Another Speck trying to stir the pot again." Lucinda all but growled the words, and one of the missing pieces fell into place.

Clara eyed Sally's friend with new understanding. The girl belonged to the Speck family then. *What is the story there?* Wracking her brain for a way to find the answer without deepening the rift, she ran out of time.

"Opal isn't doing anything wrong," Sally defended. "I had to practically drag her over here to meet Clara!"

"Not that I didn't want to welcome you to Buttonwood," Opal Speck hastily added.

"I appreciate it." Clara could barely bite back her smile at the contrast between Sally's indignation, Lucinda's ire, and Opal's exasperation with the entire situation. If the whole mess—whatever it was— weren't tearing people apart, it would be downright funny.

"You should have let her stay with her kin." Larry stopped leering at Sally to frown at her. He jerked his head toward Opal as though she were a feral animal and spoke slowly. "Specks should stay where they belong." This didn't sound like petty sniping any longer. Larry's tone held a note of warning, perhaps even threat.

Clara's amusement fled as an angry flush colored Opal's cheeks, Lucinda gave a self-righteous nod, and Willa shrank into herself even more.

Clara fought to keep her tone light but didn't bother to hide the conviction behind her words. "I'm pleased to meet Miss Speck and glad to see Miss Fosset again. In fact, it seems to me that all of us young ladies probably share a lot in common and should spend some time together." Who was this man—who didn't even have the pretext of family connection—to order Opal around?

"That sounds like a fine idea." Sally tilted her nose in the air and linked arms with Opal. "Let's go."

"Just a moment." Clara turned back to the Grogans. "Willa, why don't you come with us?"

"Really?" A glint of hope shone in the girl's dark eyes as she looked from Clara to the other girls. "Well, I. . ."

"Have supper to get on the table." Her mama gripped her elbow and began to steer her away. She directed a fulminating glare at Opal. "We won't have slothful ways rubbing off on our Willa."

"Opal ain't lazy." An adolescent boy of about thirteen rushed to her defense, his scowl growing more fierce when his voice cracked and Larry chuckled at him. "She's worth more than a whole passel of Grogans any day."

"Easy, Pete." Opal put an arm around his

shoulders, making Clara think he must be her brother. "This is the Lord's day."

"I know it." He squirmed away, his mussed-up hair sticking straight on end. "That's why I said *any* day."

"Watch what you say, boy." An older man pushed his way through. A sagging hat brim hid his eyes, but Clara could see the set of his jaw beneath a grizzled beard. Mean—just like Uncle Uriah. "There's a price on every word."

Clara shifted, placing herself more fully between the man and the boy. Her head spun with trying to sort out the identity of these people. The only thing that helped was the hair color of everyone involved. From what she could tell, the fiery Speck family boasted varying shades of red locks, while the stormy Grogans sported pitch-black tresses. Something brushed her sleeve, and she was surprised to see Opal moving next to her. The other girl didn't say a word, didn't push her away, just stood beside her.

"Don't threaten my brother." An older version of Pete shoved Lucinda away from the older man, who Clara assumed was Mr. Grogan. "Your wife insulted my sister first."

"I didn't so much as speak her name." Lucinda sniffed before abandoning her show of refinement to reveal the malice beneath. "Why waste my breath on a Speck?"

"Why waste air on breathin'?" A man Clara would have taken as twin to Mr. Grogan, were it not for the fact he stood half a foot taller and a considerable amount of stomach larger, jumped into the fray. A closer look revealed coppery hair that seemed a mark of the Speck family. "Seems like if you kept your trap shut, things would be easier for everyone."

"Don't insult my wife, Speck." Mr. Grogan's hands clenched as he took a step forward. "Even a mongrel like you should know to show respect to a lady."

"I always show respect to a lady." Mr. Speck tipped his hat toward Clara in a show of fine manners before folding his arms over his chest. "Anytime I see one."

By now, folks from town had recognized the disturbance. Clara tried not to be too perturbed that while they gathered round the fighting families everyone else kept a healthy distance. Everyone, that is, save her and Sally. Now that she looked, she realized Sally was stealthily edging away from the fray, and Clara wondered if it would be prudent to do the same. Even Lucinda had wandered toward the fringes with Willa. Only she and Opal stood in the eye of the storm.

"You're gonna eat them words, Speck." Larry began to shrug out of his coat, an ominous sign at best.

"Nope. I'll have a healthy appetite come suppertime." Speck started loosening his collar. "Opal, darlin', why don't you go and check on that while the boys and I take care of this?"

"It's not right, Pa." Opal's voice quavered on the last word, but she stood firm. "This is the Lord's day, and we have new folks in town, and I can't get out of the way so it's easier for you to have a brawl."

"Honor your father, heathen." This from Larry, who looked like he would've said more but stopped when a lone figure rode up on a mammoth horse. The self-satisfied smile on his face didn't make Clara feel any better.

"I knew it would be nothing good when you were late." A tall young man dismounted and stalked into the middle of everything. He gave a swift glance around as though assessing the situation.

Clara didn't have to wonder which family he belonged to. The dismay on Opal's face spoke as eloquently as the smug expression on Larry's. Still, she clung to hope. This man seemed like he might have a smidge of good sense and reason amid tempers.

"Miss Speck," the man took off his hat as he spoke, "I suggest you get out of the way. You, too, miss." His words obliterated Clara's hope. . .and her last shred of patience.

"This is ridiculous." She planted one hand atop her hat and fisted one on her hip, staring at each one of the Specks, the Grogans, and the assorted crowd of do-nothings. "There's no cause for any violence here today."

" 'Blessed are the peacemakers!' " The parson called. . .from afar.

"Ma'am"—the newcomer took a deep breath—"with all due respect, this is about more than you can know. So you and Opal need to get out of the way and let the men settle things."

That did it. Even though Clara had wondered the same thing just moments before, no man would order her around—especially when they hadn't been so much as introduced. And particularly not so he could use fists instead of reason.

No gentleman would engage in fisticuffs with women in the midst of the fray. At least, not with her there. With the animosity between families, she couldn't be so certain about Opal's safety. Fact of the matter was, Clara's presence kept things in check—if only just barely.

"I'm not moving. You're all going to have to be gentlemen enough not to endanger a lady, fight publicly, or break the Lord's day." She lifted her chin. "I'll have to assume that the first one to start the fight represents the family whose reputation has the least to lose."

"And it won't be the Specks," Opal announced loudly. "We're God-fearing folk. Right, Pa?"

After spluttering for a few seconds, he agreed.

Not to be outdone, Lucinda pushed her way forward. "Don't think it will be the Grogans!"

"Excellent." Clara put on a wide smile. "Now, Mr. Speck mentioned supper, and I'd suppose everyone here is more than ready for a good meal at home." She waited a moment, locking gazes with Lucinda and raising her brows meaningfully.

As the crowd broke up, Opal turned toward her. "Thank you."

"It was the least I could do." Clara shrugged. "I gather your families bear tension from a while past but typically avoid each other. Sally wanting to introduce you to me is what caused the entire mess, so I had to try to fix it."

"I've been trying to fix it my whole life." Opal sighed. "I can't seem to get through to my father and brothers though."

"That's the other thing," Clara confided. "When that other fellow told me to move, it set my back up. He doesn't so much as know my name! What makes a man think, no matter what the circumstances, he has the right to tell a woman what to do?"

CHAPTER 6

Fort Laramie, Oregon Trail

Why did women never listen? Saul Reed refused to consider the lack of logic behind his frustration as he tried to reason with the frazzled mother in front of him.

"Now, Mrs. Geer, was it?" He waited for her to nod. Saul only asked to get her to agree with him. If he could begin that pattern, it would bode well for the rest of the visit.

"My name don't matter." She crossed her arms and stood in the small doorway of the narrow room in the far corner of Fort Laramie, where the officers had put her and her children. "You're not going to so much as step inside this door. Last one—army doctor, he was—came in for two minutes, told me I was doing everything possible already, and wanted me to pay him. Threatened to have us kicked from the fort." Her thin frame shook with indignation—or exhaustion—as she spoke. "Go away."

"I don't care about money." He shifted his

saddlebag, with its specially designed medical compartments, to his other shoulder and maneuvered closer. "Let me see your son."

"No money?" She blinked. "We got nothing to trade."

"That doesn't matter." Saul heard the sounds of far too many people crammed into a small space. Tiny whispers hurriedly shushed told him that, if what he'd heard was true, more than one child was in danger. "Your children matter."

"Mama!" A sudden jerking of the woman's skirts had her twisting around. "Billy's worse."

"Come on then!" Mrs. Geer threw open the door and hastened to the far end of a miserably hot room, where a small figure lay beside a fire.

"Get the rest of the children out of here immediately." Saul didn't bother softening the order as he knelt at the sick child's side. Billy, a boy of about six, lay on his back, rasping for air. His face flushed with fever; his chest worked desperately for each breath. "Diphtheria. Croup," he clarified, using the more common name for the contagious ailment, which struck without warning, leaving dozens of children dead.

"That's what the other doctor said." Mrs. Geer reached for a small pot of steaming liquid, dipping a quill into it. She tilted her son's head back and prepared to drop the mixture of what Saul already knew would be boiled sulfur or brimstone into his nostrils. It would do no good.

"Stop. That never helps."

"Neither did the earthworm mash." She sat

back on her heels, disconsolate, as Saul brushed her aside and inspected the patient's throat.

White membranes blocked the boy's throat almost entirely, the obvious source of his difficulty breathing. This, the most urgent threat, would have to be dealt with immediately. Billy, lost in his fever, hadn't begun to turn blue. The heat in the room suffused his skin with color, but that wouldn't make a difference if it was too late.

"How old is your eldest son?" Saul hadn't made a thorough inspection of the troop rushing out the door, but he thought he'd seen a tall adolescent. The mother, so obviously weakened by exhaustion and worry, wouldn't be strong enough to help.

"Fifteen. Do we need him?" At Saul's nod, she yelled, "Amos!"

He came in so swiftly Saul knew everyone hovered just outside, waiting to see whether or not little Billy would make it. Saul offered a prayer that the child would survive.

"Mrs. Geer, I'll need an empty bucket. Amos, you are to help me hold your brother upside down over the bucket." He picked up the now-abandoned quill. "Amos will hold Billy by the legs while I brace his shoulders and use the feather to tickle his throat. We're trying to make him cough up the blockage. Ready?"

No one asked questions, and in just a moment, Amos held his brother over the bucket Mrs. Geer held below. Saul braced the unconscious youngster's shoulder with one hand and clutched the feather with the other. In this position, the boy's mouth fell open, so it wasn't too hard to hit his gag reflex.

He couldn't do any more to dislodge the membranes than make the boy retch. At first, dry heaves. Then the thin, sour stream of bile. Saul prayed and tried again. If the blockage didn't come out, the boy's chances of survival were slim. This time, a deep, wracking cough produced the desired results.

"That's it!" Together, he and Amos lowered the child back to his pallet on the floor. Saul inspected Billy's throat once more, satisfied to see almost none of the white patch remaining.

Already, the child breathed much more easily.

"You cured him!" Awe filled Amos's voice.

"No, I didn't." Saul shrugged out of his coat, now that Billy wouldn't suffocate before his eyes. "Bank the fire, and bring plenty of cool water to help bring his fever down. We need a hearty broth to keep up his strength, too."

"He's still sick?" Mrs. Geer stroked the boy's hair.

"Yes. The blockage in his throat is one symptom, the fever another. Now that Billy can breathe, we have to bring down the fever." Saul gentled his voice. "Otherwise, his heart will stop."

"No." She turned a stricken face toward him. "Cool cloths, hearty broth. . .what more can I do?"

"Don't keep the room so hot anymore, and give him as much water as he will hold to flush out the sickness."

"Calomel?" She named a well-known diuretic.

"No, nothing harsh. He should wake up as the

fever goes down, so no laudanum or opium. Those will keep him asleep so we can't gauge his progress." Saul opened his bag and pulled out a package. He measured some of the leaves into a twist of paper. "This is slippery elm. Boil the leaves into a tea and give it to him to help with the soreness."

"Yes, Doctor." Respect and gratitude warred with worry.

"I'll go check your other children. They need to be kept separated from Billy. If any of them begins to feel ill, starts coughing, or has any symptoms, isolate that one as well. Amos is probably old enough he's not in as much danger, but it's best he stay away, too, unless needed."

"This is our only place." She wrung her hands over her apron. "I have seven children."

"The fort's commanding officer will give you an extra room after I speak with him." Saul could see three other rooms next to the small one occupied by the Geers, none bearing any signs of activity. Fort Laramie's status as a military outpost meant few children—the Geers presence here was temporary. Most importantly, though, it meant Billy's illness wouldn't cause an epidemic.

"Thank you, Doctor."

"We'll see." Saul gathered his things. "I need to look over your other children, and Billy isn't out of the woods yet."

It took the rest of the day to sort out the Geer family, who'd lost their father a while back. None of the other children exhibited symptoms, but Saul knew all too well that by the time diphtheria made its presence known, there was little anyone could do. In truth, there wasn't much to do in any case.

He took care of a bruise from a nasty fall, a cut that should have been stitched but hadn't been, and a rash plaguing a few of the youngsters before he set off to talk with the commanding officer of the fort.

It didn't take long before he was ushered into Major William Hoffman's office. The commanding officer of Fort Laramie sat behind a massive wooden desk, thoughtfully chomping the end of an unlit cigar. No ashtrays or spittoons littered the orderly room, leading Saul to wonder whether Major Hoffman ever actually smoked or if the cigar was for effect.

"Major." Saul waited until the man gestured for him to sit.

"Diphtheria, was it?" He stopped chewing as he waited for the answer. "Hate to think that assistant surgeon is right but hate to think he's treating my men if he doesn't know what he's about."

"Diphtherial croup, yes." Saul considered his words carefully. "The boy almost suffocated today, though he's breathing well now. I managed to expel the membranes blocking his airway, so he has a fighting chance if the toxins don't stop his heart. The main concern, now, is the other children."

"Not a problem, Doctor." The chomping resumed. "We don't have children here now. Some of the officers have wives with them, but this is an operational military facility. Any children belong to the laundresses and stay in the tents outside fort walls. The contagion should not spread."

"Were you not made aware that the Geer boy has six siblings?" He leaned forward to impart the severity of his meaning. "The eldest bears little risk, but the other five could well become afflicted."

"Do you want me to separate the family?"

"I noticed several rooms in the corner. If you could allow the Geers use of another two, the children would be spared further exposure." Saul saw little concern in the mannerisms of the man before him. "Of course, while diphtherial croup most often strikes children, some adults have fallen prey to it. We want to do everything possible to minimize any possibility of outbreak."

"Of course." Blustering, the major got to his feet. "We do all we can to ensure safety at Fort Laramie." He waved his mangled cigar in a dismal arc. "One spark and all the cottonwood would catch aflame, you know. It happened with one of my predecessors, so I only smoke outside. Major William Hoffman, commander of the Sixth Infantry, won't be known as a failure, by heaven!"

"Your men must appreciate that." Saul grinned and made his way toward the door. "I know the Geers will."

"There you are, Amanda." Clara passed the young woman the flour she'd just bought. "I'll see you soon."

"I've yet to hear you get a name wrong, even though you've only been here for a couple of weeks."

Josiah Reed came alongside her. "You and your aunt have a way with folks."

"Buttonwood is a small town, Mr. Reed." Clara bit back a smile. "There aren't too many names to get confused."

"Fair enough, but I still say you notice things other people don't." Mr. Reed walked around the opposite counter. "I could see you were worried that Miss Dunstall ordered so little flour."

"She and her mother depend on that café, and I know business is slow now that wagon trains aren't passing through. Everyone hereabouts seems to do for themselves." Clara couldn't suppress a small frown. "They're good women who work hard."

"Mrs. Dunstall makes sure to put funds aside during the busy time of the year, so they muddle through."

"Amanda mentioned that business this year trickled slowly." Clara polished a scuff on the counter. "I wonder if it isn't that folks feel they have to order a meal anytime they step foot in the place."

"Could be." Mr. Reed raised his brows. "Doesn't mean there's much we can do about it."

"Well"—Clara gave a little cough to clear her throat—"I was wondering if maybe there wasn't a deal to be made." *Please, Lord, let him be receptive to this suggestion. If I approach it right, he won't feel like a woman is telling him what to do.*

"Oh?"

She had his full attention now. "When spring comes around again, you could speak with the Dunstalls about carrying some of their baked goods in the store. People on the trail always come in here, even if they bypass the café." She kept rubbing at the counter, even though she'd removed the scuff long ago. "I'd guess they wouldn't be able to resist some sweets if they're already in the store. Especially something like fruit tarts and the like. After weeks on the trail, travelers are ready for something other than stew and biscuits."

"Miss Field"—Josiah swiped the rag from her so she had to meet his gaze while he spoke—"you come up with wonderful ideas. It'd be another attraction for the store and increase revenue for the café. The only problem I foresee is that I might eat everything myself." He grinned. "Though it's not such a problem so long as you and your aunt keep feeding me like a king."

"Then you might well be adding to the sales." Clara kept her voice gentle as she reminded, "Aunt Doreen and I will be moving on when spring arrives. Oregon awaits."

"We'll see." He all but shrugged off the thought. "There's always hope you two won't want to leave our small town."

"When we came, you kindly offered to put us up until we found another wagon train to join." Clara started sweeping the hardwood floor to keep busy. "We never intended it to be anything but temporary, and we certainly can't stay permanently. At some point in time, we'll need to establish ourselves in our own home."

"Don't see the need." He gave what sounded close to a snort. "I've got all that room just going to waste, and the two of you more than earn your keep. This is one old man who won't be happy to see you leave."

The arrival of the monthly stage saved Clara from answering. Mr. Reed made his way outside to pick up his catalog orders and mail while Clara cleared a space for the goods. Once they inventoried what came, she'd put it away, but her mind was on Mr. Reed's comment.

Reminding Aunt Doreen that they'd be leaving Buttonwood in a few months took a toll, and Mr. Reed's open-ended invitations didn't make things any easier. When she got right down to the heart of things, she and her aunt couldn't rely on a man—however generous—to take care of them. They needed a home and a living of their own.

"Not much this month." Mr. Reed put a few small boxes on the cleared counter before drawing a handful of envelopes from his pockets. "The Burns and Fossets will be in for their special orders, so the packages stay behind the counter."

Clara slid the paper-wrapped parcels into the storage area before he handed her the unclaimed mail. People knew to come to the general store if they missed the stage. Until then, the envelopes would wait in a small basket atop the counter.

"Hmmm." Mr. Reed opened a letter and perused it. "My son wrote back. Says he'll come to Buttonwood for a spell."

"The doctor?" *He should be with his father. Mr. Reed deserves to be surrounded by his family.*

"Yep. Saul's agreed to come watch the store

while I go welcome my first grandchild into the world." A smile spread across the old man's face. "I wrote him before you and your aunt came to Buttonwood."

"We'd gladly watch the store for you."

"I know you would, but I couldn't leave the two of you alone and unprotected."

His words made her straighten her shoulders. "We can take care of ourselves. Aunt Doreen and I made it this far." *Though no farther.* Clara swallowed past a lump in her throat as she acknowledged how bad things would be if Mr. Reed hadn't needed their help.

"You're very capable women." His easy agreement let some of the starch from her spine. "All the same, I'm glad Saul's on his way. It'll do him good to get away from city life for a while, and a man can hope his son will decide to settle nearby."

"Buttonwood could use a doctor. It's in the perfect place for him to be able to tend to the sick on wagon trains, too." Clara decided to add Saul Reed to her prayer list. If he came for a while, maybe he'd abandon his stubbornness and stay to give his father some companionship. *That would certainly make it easier for me and Aunt Doreen to leave when the time comes.*

"I'll trust you to bring that up while he's here." Mr. Reed grinned. "Best thing that could happen to Saul, now that he's finished his education, is for him to find a good woman and settle down to raise a family. Of course, I'm selfish enough to want him to do it here."

"It's not selfish to want good things for your family."

"And myself," he acknowledged.

"Yes." Clara smiled. "Joy is always greater when it's shared."

"And burdens lessened." The old man stroked his beard as though thinking. "You know, Miss Field, there's nothing I want more than to have Saul set up practice here. When you get to be my age, you'll know how important family is."

"We all have dreams." Clara resisted the urge to mention Oregon once again. Mr. Reed already looked wistful enough without a reminder that she and Aunt Doreen planned to leave him. "Pray about it."

"I will." He turned a suddenly intense gaze toward her. "Though I wonder if perhaps God hasn't already given me the answer."

"I'm afraid I don't follow."

"Miss Field," a crafty smile spread across his face as he asked, "what do you know about romance?"

"Not much." She could feel her eyes widen. "I'm not in the market for a husband, Mr. Reed." *The last thing I need is another man making decisions for me.*

"The right man will change your mind." He chuckled. "You can stop backing away, Miss Field. Although I'd be proud to have you as my daughter-in-law, I wouldn't try to pressure you into marrying my son."

"Good." The word escaped in a rush of air, and Clara belatedly realized she sounded far too relieved. "Though I'm sure he'd make an excellent husband."

"What I wondered was whether or not you'd make a good matchmaker." Mr. Reed planted his elbows on the counter and leaned toward her. "You know every eligible gal in Buttonwood, and you'll be here while I go to the birth of my grandchild."

"You want me to find your son a bride?" She raised her brows. "I don't even know him."

"He's twenty-five, God-fearing, educated, and he inherited my good looks." Mr. Reed's expression didn't become any less serious. "Any woman could count herself fortunate to snag Saul. Trouble is he's got blinders on when it comes to marriage."

"What do you mean?"

"He's so busy establishing his career, he hasn't taken time to court any girl he comes across. It'll take extra help to nudge him in the right direction. That's where you come in."

"You want me to tell him he should get married." Doubt threaded the words. "Why would he listen to me?"

"You're young, kind, pretty, and hardworking. You can show him what he's missing by not having a wife."

Clara shook her head. "I don't know about that."

"I do." Mr. Reed leaned farther forward. "And you can invite the other girls from town over, dangle them under his nose. Saul just needs to realize he wants a good woman. Once he's gotten that far, it won't take him long to settle down."

"Playing matchmaker isn't one of my skills. I'm going to have to refuse."

"I'd make it worth your while."

"You've done more than enough for me and my aunt." She sighed. "So of course I'll do my best to point the girls out to your son, but I dislike scheming."

"God blessed you with a sharp mind—look at your idea about the café." Mr. Reed straightened up and slapped the countertop. "I have faith you could come up with something to get my son to the altar. All you need is the right motivation."

"Mr. Reed"—she gave an exasperated laugh—"I already said I'd do what I could. Nothing you say will motivate me to push your son into marriage." *No woman should be pushed into a union when the man who holds the power doesn't have a heart softened by love.*

"Listen to my offer before you make that decision." Mr. Reed gestured toward the windows at the front of the store, which looked out onto the house. "If you can get my son married and settled here in Buttonwood, I'll move into the room over my store and give you the deed to my house."

CHAPTER 7

Saul Reed rode faster as he spotted the buildings. *Buttonwood.* It had to be. The trip took less time than he'd anticipated, considering he couldn't wait for the next stage run and had been held up at Fort Laramie. With his saddlebags packed full of medical supplies, food, water, clothing, his Bible, and a bedroll, he traveled as light as possible.

His horse chuffed tiredly. Saul understood. He would be glad to sleep beneath a roof tonight. He wouldn't turn up his nose at a hot bath and a home-cooked meal, either.

The flat planks he led Abe over served as a rough bridge, a convenient way to cross over the sludge of the Platte River. Up ahead stood a small settlement, boasting no more than half a dozen buildings—a church, a smithy, a café, and Reed's General Store among them. The outlying area seemed dotted with fields, so Saul assumed that farmers made up the bulk of the community.

He steered Abe toward his father's business,

surprised by its fine construction of wood and brick with storefront windows. Nearby stood a house built with the same materials but created with graceful lines no one would expect to see in the midst of the prairie. *Looks like Dad's done well here.*

Saul smiled as he hitched Abe to the post out front and shouldered his heaviest bags—those containing his medical kit and Bible. Two steps up and he made it through the door, a tinny clang cheerfully announcing his presence. His eyes didn't adjust immediately after the bright day outside, but he could make out the shape of a woman at the counter as he strode forward.

"Good afternoon." He swung his bags onto the counter and rubbed a crick at the back of his neck. When he looked back up, he caught the full view of the young lady before him.

Golden hair caught glints of light, soft tendrils curling about a face too strong for conventional beauty. Her brows arched finely over brilliant green eyes. Her skin bore the tinge of time spent outdoors in the sun. Delicate hands with tapered fingers quickly finished oiling the eggs on the counter.

"What may I help you with this afternoon?" Her gaze lit on him with reserved curiosity, as though she was taking his measure but didn't want him to know it. Her findings remained a mystery to him as she waited for an answer.

"Can you tell me where I can find Josiah Reed?" He watched as her expressive eyes widened, as though she'd fit another piece into the puzzle of his identity.

"Saul." She breathed his name but blushed immediately when she realized he'd heard her.

How does she know my name?

Surprise must have registered in his expression as she quickly corrected herself. "I mean, you must be Dr. Reed." A slight dip of her head, and she clarified, "Your father isn't expecting you for a few days yet. He's over at the café. Says it's his duty to sample everything the Dunstalls bake."

"Sounds onerous." The corner of his mouth kicked up.

"Your father isn't one to shirk his duty." A smile blossomed on her lips, revealing straight teeth. "He's particularly responsible when it involves pie."

"Sounds like I should join him." Saul reached for his bags. "I didn't know Dad hired anyone to help with the store." He waited for her to introduce herself. Such a pretty girl should have a delicate name to match.

"I'm Clara Field. Your father hired my aunt and me to keep house, cook meals, and help out at the store when needed." She made an expansive gesture. "We only. . .arrived. . .recently."

He noticed her slight hesitation and decided to ask his father about it when he got to the café. Obviously there was more to the situation than met the eye. "Nice to meet you, Miss Field." Saul used the title of an unmarried woman though she hadn't used it in her introduction, illogically rejecting the thought she might have a husband somewhere.

"My pleasure." She laid a hand on the strap of his nearest saddlebag. "I'll watch these for you, if you like. The café's right across the street, next to the church. Amanda said today's pie is rhubarb, if that appeals."

"After riding for so long, I'd eat wet leather if someone slapped it on a plate." Saul smiled. "Rhubarb pie sounds far better."

"Amanda's a wonderful cook." She spoke hastily, with an odd intensity. "With a soft spot for your father, since he compliments her baking."

"I'll be sure to thank her for the pie. I'll take my bags with me so I can purchase my slice." He hefted the bags once more. "Thank you."

"You're welcome." Her gaze followed him as he left the building, and Saul got the impression she was waiting for something. He decided Dad must really be looking forward to going to see Hannah and had told Miss Field as much.

He moved across the large stretch of dusty earth marred with the grooves of wagon and stage tracks, coming to a stop before a single-story whitewashed building. The sign proclaimed to the empty street that this was Dunstall's Café.

Saul stepped inside, this time waiting in the doorway for his eyes to adjust. The café's smaller windows didn't let in much light, so it took a moment before he could make out his father. Dad sat with his back to the door, nodding as the young girl beside him offered more milk.

"Afternoon, Dad." Saul clapped a hand on his old man's shoulder when he walked up.

"Saul!" His father shot to his feet and drew him into a big bear hug. "So glad to see you, son. Early, too."

"It doesn't feel early to me." He sank onto one of the wooden chairs and shot a tired smile at the young lady holding the milk. "I'd like some of whatever he polished off."

"Rhubarb pie," the girl answered. Her straight, dark hair fought to slip loose of its pins as she turned and headed for what Saul assumed was the kitchen. She brought out a generous wedge of the pastry and a steaming mug of coffee.

"Thank you. It smells perfect." His words caused her to duck her head in a shy nod. Saul sank his fork into the flaky crust, through the soft filling, and raised the bite to his mouth. "Heavenly." He didn't waste any more time with words but saw a smile spread across the girl's face before she left them. Saul decided to make a note of the fact that good manners went a long way in little Buttonwood.

"That's Amanda." Dad jerked a thumb toward the back room. "She and her ma run this place. Sweet gal with a way around a stove, but times are hard. Her pa passed on a year ago."

"Good to know." Saul frowned at the thought of such hardship then frowned at the thought that followed. "Why are you telling me all that? She can't be more than sixteen."

"Sixteen last month," Dad acknowledged. "If you're going to run the store in my absence, you need to know about the townsfolk. No sense putting your foot in when I can give you the basics before I head out." He gave a grimace. "I learn from my mistakes."

Saul almost asked what he meant, but Dad

kept talking. "Besides, I just made a deal with the Dunstall women, so they're business partners of a sort."

"They're buying part of the store?" Saul took a swig of coffee, finding it strong enough to stand without the mug. "This is the way coffee should be." He drained the cup and went back to his pie, debating whether or not he should ask for another piece.

"No. Come spring, I'll be carrying their baked goods in the store, so even the travelers who don't stop by the café can have a taste of home." Dad nodded toward Saul's now-empty plate. "I like to think it'll be very successful."

"Smart thinking." Saul's stomach gave a growl, half-content at the fare, half-disgruntled there wasn't more of it. He cast a glance toward the rear of the store. "Did they come to you?"

"Naw. Whole arrangement was Clara's idea." Dad leaned forward. "Did you look for me at the store first?"

"Yes." Saul straightened when the girl came back, a plate of chicken in one hand and the pot of coffee in the other. He snatched his fork from the dirty pie plate as she moved to clear it. "Thank you, Miss Dunstall."

"You seemed like you came a long way and had an appetite to match." Amanda Dunstall watched with obvious approval as he tucked in. "Just give a call if there's anything more you need."

"So you met her." Dad snagged a chicken leg and bit into it.

"You just saw me meet her." Saul shot him a look. "She cooks just fine, but sixteen's too young for me even if I were in the market for a wife."

"She's not sixteen." Dad's glower disappeared as suddenly as it had shown itself. "I meant Clara. If you stopped by the store, she's the one who told you to find me over here."

"The pretty blond," Saul acknowledged. "She knew who I was the moment I asked after you. Clearly, you've told her about me. I can only hope what she heard is good."

"Almost." Dad wore his sly look—the look that meant he was up to some sort of scheme. Like as not, he probably meant to wrangle Saul into the middle of it.

"Almost?" He injected warning into his tone.

"I just told her I wished you lived nearby." Dad widened his eyes. "It's only natural that a father wants to be close to his son. I can't help it that you're so set on Baltimore."

"You're the one who moved from Baltimore." Saul set down his fork. "Hannah and I still live there, and it wouldn't be hard to find a place to rent if you want to be close."

"I've established a store and a place right here in Buttonwood." Dad leaned back in his chair. "Town could use a doctor."

"My office will be cleared out and ready for me to move in soon." Saul downed some more coffee, the heat energizing him. He thought of Midge, bouncing around on the next stage out here. "I have responsibilities in Baltimore."

"Patients?" Dad tented his fingers over his growing stomach. "You can have every patient in town if you stay here."

"Not patients." Saul slapped his hand on the table. "I came here so you could go be with Hannah, not so you could try to talk me into following you to the middle of nowhere."

"The middle's the best part." Dad stood up and plunked his hat on his head. "But I won't push it." He didn't say anything more, but the final, unspoken words of his statement hung in the air between them.

For now.

As soon as Saul Reed disappeared into the café, Clara grabbed a pencil and a sheet of scrap paper. She folded it in half, writing Saul's name at the top of one column and leaving the other side blank for the moment. Now that he'd arrived, she could start watching him, learning about him. Specifically, learning what kind of woman would most appeal to him.

Beneath his name, she wrote the few things she knew about the man—doctor, handsome, polite. The list would grow as she spent more time around him. Frowning, she added, *Baltimore?* It might take some prying to determine just why the young doctor was so set on staying in the city, but Clara would do what she had to.

She looked through the window to the house beyond. All she had to do was marry off this handsome young doctor and she and Aunt Doreen wouldn't have to go to Oregon. No more weeks under a relentlessly hot sun baking the earth, only to have a sudden rain change the land to mud sucking at their wheels and their progress.

Memories of her aunt trudging alongside the wagon day in, day out for weeks on end, only to go collect dried buffalo dung and cook supper before falling onto a meager pallet made Clara's chest ache. Aunt Doreen shouldn't have to face the trail again—not if there were any way possible to avoid it.

If Clara succeeded in this bargain with Mr. Reed, they wouldn't have to face the Rockies. Her aunt could settle in, bring in every item from the old dugout, and never have to say good-bye to Buttonwood. It wouldn't take much to open a few rooms to boarders, and running a sort of seasonal ordinary would bring enough money for them to live on.

No more wagon. No more failure. I can do this. Clara shifted her attention to the empty column and began listing names: Sally Fosset, Willa Grogan, Opal Speck, Amanda Dunstall. She hesitated over that last one. While she could see Amanda being enamored with Saul Reed, at sixteen she seemed a bit young for the twenty-five-year-old.

She added a question mark next to Amanda's name—not counting her out but acknowledging that she was a long shot. By the same token, she wrote Vanessa Dunstall at the bottom of the list. At thirty-one, Amanda's mother might make a better match, and Clara couldn't afford to rule out any prospects just yet. The top three women were eighteen and nineteen, much more appropriate ages and all single. Well, unmarried, at least.

In tiny script, she scribbled *Matthew Burn* beside Sally's name and *Nathan Fosset* beside Willa's. Though neither couple officially courted, that seemed the direction the wind blew. Saul's competition would need to be taken into account.

Opal Speck. She circled the name of the girl whose backbone helped divert the fight on the day they met. Opal's glowing hair and hazel eyes should draw any man out, but there wasn't anyone special at the moment—probably because of the tension between her family and the Grogans. The only woman amid her father and three brothers, Opal should be comfortable around men, too. *Yes, I like that. Opal deserves to have someone appreciate her, and Dr. Reed would be the type to notice all she gives.*

With that settled, she folded the paper into a tiny square and tucked it in her pocket. When news of Saul's arrival hit town, everyone would come to welcome him—same as they had welcomed her and Aunt Doreen. Clara resolved to stand back and watch as the doctor met each of the girls so she could pinpoint who he liked best. From there, it shouldn't be too hard to have the girls over to the house. Visits to the store for little things and weekly church meetings would round out his exposure to them.

Saul Reed's dark, windswept hair and pene-trating gaze would make him a sensation in the town. His dark suits and lean frame would stand out against the rougher clothing and more hulking presence of the local men. Clara could scarcely believe her good fortune. Once the girls met him, they'd fall for him and all she'd have to do is let nature take its course. This wasn't going to be nearly as difficult as she'd thought.

As soon as Mr. Reed and his son came back, she all but flew out of the store to go get things ready at the house. "He's here!" Clara rushed through the kitchen door, only to realize her aunt must be upstairs. She found her waxing the banisters of the stairwell.

"Is something wrong?" Doreen clutched her rag close, her brows slanted in worry.

"No. Dr. Reed—Mr. Reed's son—arrived this afternoon." Clara gestured up the stairs. "We'll need to ready the room for him right away."

"That won't be a problem." Aunt Doreen went back to polishing the banisters. "I dusted everything upstairs already, so we'll just need to put fresh linens on the bed and then all will be ready."

"I'll do it." Clara made a beeline for the linen cabinet, only to realize her aunt abandoned the banisters to follow her. "Did you want to help?" Clara didn't remember the bed in the room they'd chosen as being particularly high, but perhaps she remembered incorrectly.

"Why are you so anxious?" Her aunt peered at her, suspicion lining her brow.

"I'm not." Clara filled her arms with sheets and pillow slips before shutting the cabinet. "Everything should be ready, that's all."

"Clara, did you meet the doctor already?"

"Of course." She shrugged then compensated as some linen slid toward the floor. "Mr. Reed had gone for some rhubarb pie at the café when his son came to the store. I told him where he could find his father."

"I see." Aunt Doreen's brows nearly reached her hairline now. "Anything I should know?"

"He's here." Clara headed up the stairs. "So we need to make his room as welcoming as possible. You know how important it is to Mr. Reed that his son wants to stay in Buttonwood."

"We owe it to Josiah to make his son comfortable." Aunt Doreen walked into the spare room behind Clara and went to open the window. "You're right."

"Josiah?" Clara deposited the bed linen on a chair and turned to her aunt. Since when did Aunt Doreen call Mr. Reed by his first name?

"Mr. Reed and Dr. Reed sound so similar." Her words belied the blush creeping up her neck as she stripped the mattress. "I, for one, want to know more about the doctor."

"You know as much as I do." Clara moved to the opposite side of the bed and flicked her wrists, sending the sheet billowing across to her aunt. "He's twenty-five, studied in Edinburgh to become a doctor, comes from Baltimore, and Mr. Reed wants him to settle in Buttonwood."

"Facts don't make a man." Aunt Doreen smoothed out a wrinkle in the quilt they laid over the top. "You met him, so tell me your impressions."

"He's tall, dresses like a doctor, seems the serious

sort, and apparently works up an appetite when he travels. I ran into Amanda on the way over, and she said Dr. Reed ate pie, chicken, potatoes, and drank a full pot of coffee. I suppose he'll be glad of a good night's sleep, too."

"Clara"—her aunt finished fluffing the pillows before folding her arms over her chest—"that's not what I meant."

"What did you mean?" Clara frowned. "I only spoke with him for a moment."

"Did you like him? Did you find him kind or demanding? Does he set his jaw as though displeased with the world?"

"No, he's nothing like Uncle Uriah," Clara hastened to clarify. "Dr. Reed asked politely after his father, looked around with curiosity, and spoke pleasantly." This much, she remembered clearly. "He's handsome, with dark hair, brown eyes, and a deep voice. Dr. Reed holds himself still, like he doesn't want to miss anything. You'll like him, Aunt Doreen."

"He's Jo— Mr. Reed's son." Her aunt smiled. "I already knew I'd like him. The question is. . .do you, Clara?"

"Well enough." Clara straightened the curtains before turning around. "He's the type to turn a woman's head."

"Has he turned your head?" Doreen's eyes lit with delight. "A good husband is a blessing."

"But a bad one. . ." Clara's gaze met her aunt's, leaving the thought unspoken. They both knew how miserable a poor husband could make a household.

"Do you think Dr. Reed will be a bad husband?"

"I scarcely know him, but he seems a good man." Unlike Uriah, who'd made Clara's skin prickle the first time she'd met the man. "He gives me no reason not to introduce him to Opal."

"Opal? So you're not interested in him for yourself?" Aunt Doreen's disappointment came through loud and clear.

"We're going to make our own way, Aunt Doreen. Neither of us needs a husband to provide for us out West. We'll establish a home and life without anyone ordering us about." She looked at the woman who'd done her best to raise her. "Just you and me and the land, remember?"

"Yes, Clara." A wobbly smile accompanied the words. "Remember, too, that plans can change. The last thing I want is for you to ignore opportunities because you're so set on one plan. Oregon isn't the only way."

"Believe me, Aunt Doreen"—Clara thought of her bargain with Mr. Reed, and a smile crept across her face—"I'm not ignoring any opportunities."

CHAPTER 8

"What's your arrangement with Miss Field?" Saul waited until he and his father were alone in the store before broaching the subject. As far as he could tell, a pretty young girl like that shouldn't be flitting around his father.

"Arrangement?" Dad cleared his throat and widened his eyes, signaling a secret all too clearly. "With Miss Field?"

"Yep." Saul took a deep breath. If Dad took to echoing him, things were worse than he'd thought. If the girl were planning on gold digging, she'd do better to head for California. Saul decided to probe gently. "When did she and her aunt come to Buttonwood?"

" 'Bout three weeks ago." A gleam of what Saul would have called relief lit his father's gaze.

Obviously, Saul had asked the wrong question. "Did you send for them to be your housekeepers?" Stranger things happened out West, and everyone knew women weren't exactly thick on the ground along the Oregon Trail.

"No. She and her aunt came passin' through on their own. Something needed to be done, so you could say I took them in." He gave a sheepish shrug.

"They're not asking you for money, Dad?" Saul's eyes narrowed. Dad's hand always reached out to give before he groped for help. These women wouldn't be permitted to take advantage of that. "You don't owe them anything."

"I raised you better." His father's thick gray brows met in the middle as a ferocious scowl. "It's every man's responsibility to help a woman fallen on hard times."

"They're in trouble?" His mind whirled with thoughts of sweet-talking swindlers on the lam.

"Ole Hickory McGee kicked those women off his wagon train." The scowl grew more intense.

"Their wagon train booted them out?" Saul slid from horror over this abandonment to suspicion over why anyone would leave two women behind. Sounded like trouble, all right.

"No good reason why he did it, either. He could've spared a few minutes to search for their missing ox." Dad thumped the counter. "Man won't show his face in my store again if he knows what's good for him."

"A missing ox? He abandoned them in the middle of the prairie to get lost or sick, bit by snakes, overrun with bison, or attacked by Indians. . .over an ox?" Disbelief made the words skeptical.

"Well, Simon's not your average ox."

"Simon. . .they named their oxen?" Saul's

opinion revised once more. It sounded like these women were one ox short of a team, all right.

"I said the same thing." A grin split Dad's face. "They say Simon eats leather and caused more than his share of problems on the trail." The grin faded. "Still no reason to leave the ladies behind. Not with all the dangers of the trail."

"Unthinkable," Saul agreed. "He could have waited until they reached town to cast 'em out. Leaving them on their own, days away from help... it's amazing they found that ox and made it here."

"Miss Field followed the wagon ruts so she didn't get lost. When she and her aunt came in here, I couldn't believe they were alone and asking after Hickory." He shook his head. "The starch left their spines when I told them they were two days behind."

"They knew they wouldn't catch up."

"Yep. When it looked like they were still going to try, I stepped in and asked them to lend a hand around the store and the house until the next wagon train came through."

"Which won't be until late spring." Saul raised a brow. "So they'll be here for the end of summer, all of fall and winter, and part of spring."

"Longer, if I can wrangle it."

"Why?" Doing his duty by a woman in need was one thing; keeping troublesome strangers around was another.

"Mrs. Edgerly—that's Miss Field's aunt—isn't up to taking the trail to Oregon. She's not one to utter a word of complaint, but Doreen's a delicate lady who deserves a stable home."

"Doreen?" These women worked fast if Dad already used their Christian names.

"Mrs. Edgerly." Dad cleared his throat.

"I see." So they weren't on a first-name basis. It didn't take much to surmise that Dad wanted to be, though. "In any case, I don't have any room to lecture anyone about taking in strangers."

"Oh? Did you find a nurse?"

"No. I came across a girl in trouble myself," Saul admitted. "There wasn't any way I could leave her there."

"A girl?" Speculation lifted his father's brows. "You're finally settling down?"

"Midge is thirteen." Saul shook his head. "Her sister's pimp was trying to turn her out since Nancy wasn't up to working that day. By the time Midge found me, her sister had died. I couldn't leave that little girl there."

"Absolutely not." Rage mottled Dad's features. "Where's the child now?"

"She's on her way here. Mrs. Henderson—she keeps the boardinghouse where I live—is bringing her. I thought it'd be good for Midge to get away from the city for a while."

"I'm sorry I won't be here when she arrives. We'll have to let the ladies know so they can ready a room." He pointed above his head. "I've got a bed in the storage area upstairs, along with a few other things."

"They won't mind having a little girl around? With Mrs. Edgerly in the house, Mrs. Henderson wouldn't have to stay." Saul thought aloud. "It'd be some extra work for them."

"Those ladies have big hearts and willing hands. They cook, clean, do the laundry, and Clara keeps an eye on the store when I need her to." Dad gave a brief nod. "They won't mind having a little girl around."

"Sounds like a good setup."

"Asking those two to stay just might be the best bargain I ever made."

"Might?" It sounded pretty good to Saul.

"Oh"—Dad rocked back on his heels—"time will tell."

From where Josiah stood, things looked promising. While his son walked the length of the store, getting more familiar with the setup, he thought of all the reasons why the bride bargain he'd struck with Clara Field should go well.

A deal was a deal, and Josiah wouldn't go back on his word if Miss Field managed to match Saul up with Sally Fosset or Opal Speck. But if all went well, it wouldn't come to that. No, he aimed to have it both ways—see Saul settled in Buttonwood and keep the house in the family.

With Miss Field taking note of what a fine catch his son was and trying to match him up, Josiah figured she'd have to get mighty close. The more time she spent with Saul, the more chance nature would take its course. It might not take much, either, since the girl had been so keyed up she flew out of the store the minute he got back.

Josiah hadn't missed how his son identified Clara, either. "The pretty blond." He had to swallow a snort of laughter. No doubt about it—Saul inherited his good taste in women. After the way Saul bolted down Amanda's chicken, Josiah could count on Clara's cooking to catch his attention, too.

Better yet, what woman could resist a man who saved a child from a life of poverty and degradation? Not many he'd met—especially not a woman who'd been orphaned at a young age, herself, like Clara Field. Yes, the little girl his son saved was another sign of Saul settling down.

Only thing left to worry about was whether Clara did her job too well—worked herself so hard Saul didn't have a chance to recognize all her potential. The girl already did more than she should. He'd heard her rustling around the house, organizing things late at night after putting in a full day at the store. She ran on pure determination, but exhaustion tugged at her strength.

*Maybe. . .*Josiah straightened up as inspiration struck. *The shadows under her eyes, the way she droops when she thinks no one sees her, how grateful she is to sink onto a seat come mealtime. Anyone could see she takes on too much. Surely a doctor would want to keep an eye on her.*

Decision made, he called his son back over to the corner where he kept the books during the day. "Saul? Now that you're here, I'll be leaving so I can spend as much time with Hannah as possible. This will also have to be a buying trip, since I rarely get to the city, and I know I can count on you to look after the store while I'm gone."

His son nodded. "Of course."

"While you're here, folks will ask for your help. There's no doctor around here for days, and even then the soldiers keep the man at Fort Laramie busy enough as is." Josiah took a deep breath and looked away, as though not wanting to add to his son's burden. "I don't want to ask any more. . ."

"Whatever you need, Dad." His son stepped right into the trap as he spoke. "Just tell me."

"Well. . ." This time Josiah's hesitancy wasn't a show. It seemed too easy to maneuver a son who meant well. *But I mean well, too.* "The thing is. . . Hickory pushed Mrs. Edgerly and Miss Field real hard on the trail. You know the journey already takes a lot out of a person, but these women showed up looking done in. Mind you, don't tell them I said so." He fixed Saul with a sharp stare. "They're strong women, but everyone has a limit. Mrs. Edgerly reached hers long before they made it to Buttonwood, and her niece took everything upon herself."

"I see."

"Since they settled in here, Clara Field hasn't stopped for a moment. Every time I turn around, she's dusting or sweeping or polishing something at the house or store, straightening displays, updating inventory, organizing closets, and the like. She pushes too hard."

"Sounds like a hardworking woman." Approval rang in his voice. "I take it her aunt rested up during that time?"

"Yes, she's in fine condition." Josiah didn't even stop to consider just how fine a woman Doreen Edgerly really was as he pressed onward. "Thing is it's taking a toll on Miss Field now. Months of hardship have her running on willpower, but every so often I see her wilt."

"What do you mean? Does she go pale? Any headaches? Dizziness?"

"She's not one to complain, but she'll sink down to sit for a while or leave the room for a moment." Josiah chose his words carefully so as not to lie but to get the point across. "She's not the type to admit anything's wrong. Even if she felt ill, she wouldn't want anyone making a fuss."

"It's good you told me." Saul clapped a hand on his shoulder. "I'll be sure to keep a close eye on her."

Josiah quelled the urge to smile. "That's all I can ask."

"I should have thought to ask what Dr. Reed's favorite foods are." Clara tossed the sliced cubes of meat into the mixture of flour and seasonings, deftly switching pans with Aunt Doreen. While the meat sizzled, she set aside the already-browned onions.

"Have you ever met a man who disliked steak and onion pie?" Aunt Doreen kept an eye on the meat while Clara rolled out the pastry crust. When her aunt judged the time right, she added boiling water and covered the pan.

The next hour flew by as they worked alongside

one another in the well-set-up kitchen. While her aunt chopped potatoes and carrots to add to the meat and gravy, Clara tackled dessert. Since both the Reeds ate dinner at the café, she wouldn't attempt a pie. Besides, that would take a little too long.

"Aunt Doreen, do we still have any of that milk left?" The Fossets brought in fresh milk to trade a few days ago, and Mr. Reed gave it to Clara for baking.

"Probably about a cup or so, but it'll have gone sour by now. The bucket's in the well."

"Perfect! I thought I'd whip up some sour milk coffee cake for dessert. The men both had pie at the café earlier." At her aunt's agreement, Clara made a quick trip to the well and brought back the milk. "This will do nicely."

She added the potatoes and carrots to the meat while Aunt Doreen stirred it all in. In fifteen minutes, she'd put the onions on top then pour it all into a casserole dish. For now, her aunt would watch to make sure it cooked evenly.

During that time, Clara worked on the coffee cake. It didn't take long to cream butter and sugar to blend with a beaten egg. Baking soda added to the sour milk dissolved on its own. She sifted together flour, salt, cinnamon, and nutmeg before mixing everything together. She poured the batter into a shallow greased pan, sprinkling brown sugar with cinnamon and melted butter over the top to form a crispy topping.

It went into the Dutch oven just as Aunt

Doreen stretched the rolled pastry over the steak and onion pie. She slid it into the heated brick alcove in the left corner of the hearth to bake golden brown. It should finish at the same time as the coffee cake. The next twenty-five minutes was a flurry of cleanup and setting the table.

Clara brushed the ashes from the top of the Dutch oven, using dishrags to remove the hot coffee cake. Then she passed the dishrags to Aunt Doreen, who swept the pie from the oven nook and went to put it on the trivet in the dining room.

After two hours of work, they had everything ready just in time to be eaten in twenty minutes flat. Well, the steak and onion pie, at any rate. The coffee cake still waited in the kitchen, along with a fresh pot of coffee.

"That takes the prize of best steak and onion pie I've ever tasted," Dr. Reed praised. "When my father told me how great a bargain he'd made with you ladies, I still needed convincing. Not anymore."

Clara put down her fork at his casual mention of a bargain. Her gaze flicked to Mr. Reed, whose subtle head shake told her his son didn't refer to the more recent deal they'd made. The fleeting hope that Dr. Reed knew and wanted to find a wife disappeared, leaving behind a nagging guilt. She chose to soothe it with coffee cake.

"Are you ready for dessert?" She rose from the table, gathering dishes to take back to the kitchen.

"I don't see how I can eat another bite."

"You'll manage." Mr. Reed held none of his son's qualms. "What're we having tonight?"

"Coffee cake," Aunt Doreen answered as Clara made her way back to the kitchen with all the plates and utensils. She came through the door behind her niece, arms loaded with the now-empty casserole dish. "I'll get the coffee." She bustled back out to the men, pouring fresh cups while Clara cut the coffee cake and took out four dessert plates.

"Here we are." She brought everything to the dining room, where she served up the treat. Generous wedges filled the small plates, the crispy topping tumbling to the very edges as she passed portions around the table.

"I take it back." Dr. Reed picked up his fork. "Now I see how I can manage." He sliced off a respectable bite and brought it to his lips with an appreciative smile.

"Good." Clara sampled her own piece. "We hope you'll find a lot of things to surprise you in Buttonwood."

"So far, I can't complain." He reached for his coffee. When a lock of his dark hair tumbled over his forehead, Clara almost moved to tuck it back.

Her guilt over planning to find him a wife eased a little more. *If he appreciates one meal so much, he needs a good woman to look after him. Any of the girls in town would be blessed to call him her husband, to run her fingers through his hair and share smiles every night.*

Polite chitchat filled the rest of the time as they lingered over their coffee, and it wasn't until Dr. Reed went to his room to settle in that his father asked Clara for a word.

She wiped her hands on her apron and abandoned the dishes, only to stop Aunt Doreen when she moved to take over. "I'll finish up in a moment." Clara couldn't answer the questions in her aunt's eyes, not when such an important one blotted out everything else in her own mind.

After tantalizing her with the promise of a good home and a way to provide for Aunt Doreen, would Mr. Reed retract his offer?

CHAPTER 9

"Yes, Mr. Reed?" She followed him into the parlor but didn't sit down until he gestured for her to do so. Even then, she busied herself smoothing out her apron. Her hands slid over the worn cotton, pressing out folds in the fabric and working through some of her anxiety.

"Since Saul's arrived, I'll be leaving in a couple days. A few things have changed, though, and I wanted to talk with you before I go."

"I understand." Clara took a deep breath to push down the tears. "If you've changed your mind, you've still done far more for my aunt and me than we could have dared hope."

"Changed my mind?" Surprise colored his voice. "Young lady, I'm too old to change my mind. I set it on something and move on, and that's that. The deal stands."

"Oh?" The exclamation held a world of hope. Incredible how attached she'd become to the idea of settling in Buttonwood.

"Yep." He gave her a slanted look. "Unless you're having second thoughts about your ability to see the matter through?"

"No. Any woman in town would be more than proud to call your son her husband." Clara lowered her voice. Just because Dr. Reed happened to be upstairs didn't mean she could afford to be overheard. "He's a fine catch."

"Thought so, but it's good to hear from a young lady." Mr. Reed grinned. "I meant to give you some specifics before he got here, but that's changed. We'll have to strategize now."

So that's what he meant. Relief almost made Clara giddy as she fetched pencil and paper. "I'm ready."

"First thing"—Mr. Reed shifted on the sofa as though uncomfortable, and Clara jotted down a note to fluff the cushions as he kept speaking—"is that a man has to be alone with a woman—or as close to it as possible—to cultivate a romantic interest."

"Absolutely, though the proprieties must be observed." Clara shot him a stern glance. While she wanted the house and everything it promised, she drew the line at compromising anyone's reputation for a forced wedding. Dr. Reed deserved to choose his own bride—from the selection at hand, of course.

"No question. So if it's possible to give the illusion of privacy, that's a good thing. Makes him feel as though he's moving things along instead of the other way around."

"Mmmhmmm." Clara bit her lip to keep from smiling at this obvious advice. "Perhaps you could tell me more about what your son would look for in a woman?"

"He wants a lady, but someone who's healthy. That's important, him being a doctor and all." Mr. Reed shifted on the sofa again. "Maybe there's a way to make the gals in town seem strong by comparison."

"I'm not sure what you mean." She tapped her pencil against the paper. "Most men don't like a woman who's overly active."

"That's to say"—he cleared his throat—"maybe you could mention having had a long day and needing to rest then go sit in the other room. Or that you'd love to work on your sewing or whatnot. Something to underscore how the other gal's full of energy and get them some of that feeling of being alone all at the same time?"

"I understand." She made a note of the plan. "That won't be difficult, to say I'd like to sit down after a long day. You're right. It's a good way to have him spend time with the girls and get to know them, too."

"Excellent. Just excellent." He beamed at her. "Now, for the other thing. If you could let the other gals in town know how much Saul loves apples, that'd be another step in the right direction. So for the church social or corn husking or whatnot, they can bake a pie or cobbler or some such thing that's sure to catch his eye. You and your aunt can make something different to round things out a bit."

"The way to a man's heart is through his stomach," Clara recited the maxim and jotted down the information about apples. "Does he have any other particular likes or dislikes?"

"Eyelashes. He likes to see long eyelashes on a girl. You know how some women can be all fluttery and shylike?"

"Yes." Clara suppressed the urge to roll her eyes and dutifully added the information to her list. While she found it ridiculous when women batted their lashes at a man in an obvious ploy for attention, some men found it appealing. "This information could be very useful, Mr. Reed."

"That's what I thought." A dull flush stained his cheeks, and he wouldn't meet her gaze. "It will all work out for the best."

Saul awoke the next morning with none of the stiff joints he'd found as his constant companion on the journey to Buttonwood. He sat up on the rope-slung mattress, spurred by the strong scent of fresh coffee wafting up the stairs.

Despite his initial doubts, Miss Field and Mrs. Edgerly proved to be welcome surprises. Tired as he'd been, Saul still recalled the taste of supper last night as being more than worth the day's ride. As he moved around the room, washing up and dressing for church, the light of day revealed small touches he also attributed to the women.

Fresh cedar planks tucked in the corner of his wardrobe chased away stale air and moths. Not so much as a speck of dust dared rest on the dresser or washstand, which also boasted a pitcher full of fresh water and clean towels. The windows shone with the morning sun, as though cheery from a good scrubbing, and the sheets he'd slipped under were obviously freshly washed.

He recalled his father's words about how hard Miss Field worked, and a frown crossed his face. The things he appreciated must have taken a lot of time and work then been multiplied to cover the rest of the rooms in the house.

As he deftly swiped his razor blade over his chin to remove the night's stubble, Saul refused to think too much about what state the women had found the house in after Dad had lived here alone for so long. *Worse, I'm asking them to take on more responsibility when Midge arrives.*

The idea of imposing made him uncomfortable, but Midge needed some time away from the grim realities of life in the city. That little girl deserved to enjoy some sunshine and relaxation while they stayed in Buttonwood. Besides, Midge didn't make any demands or cause trouble. He'd broach the subject at breakfast.

A few moments later, they all sat around a table heaped with fried slices of ham, stacks of flapjacks, and crocks of syrup and preserves. After Dad asked the blessing, Saul noticed the women still wore plain calico dresses—another example of how they'd risen early and worked hard to set the table. They wouldn't change for church until after everything was cleared.

As Saul slathered raspberry preserves on a flapjack, he pondered whether there was a way to have Miss Field help Midge but get more rest at the same time. Nothing sprang to mind, but he'd think on it.

"Delicious," Dad commented as he helped himself to another flapjack. "I can't say how much I'll miss waking up to these breakfasts when I'm on my way to Baltimore."

"It won't go to waste," Saul promised. "As a matter of fact, there's something I need to speak about with you ladies."

"Yes?" Miss Field put down her fork and gave him her undivided attention. The intensity in her green eyes sent a jolt through him, and he found himself hoping she'd approve of his decision to bring Midge to Buttonwood.

"When the next stage comes through Buttonwood, in about two weeks. . . ?" He looked to his father for confirmation of the time frame before continuing, "Two friends of mine will be arriving with it, Mrs. Henderson and Midge. I made these plans before knowing you ladies were in residence here."

"I see." Miss Field straightened her shoulders. "With a little time, we'll have cleared out of your way. Since you've already arranged for housekeepers. . ." A slight tinge of doubt crept into her tone.

"No!" Saul realized he'd bellowed the word and lowered his voice. "That is to say, you misunderstand the situation. Midge is a young girl, recently orphaned, who I've taken in. Mrs. Henderson, a respectable old widow, runs the boardinghouse where I live in Baltimore and is bringing Midge out to join me here. She agreed to stay as a favor to me, but with the two of you ladies already here, I hoped you would lend a hand with Midge so I can send Mrs. Henderson home." He took a breath and watched as the two women before him exchanged astonished glances.

"We're to understand you've taken in a young girl? An orphan?" Miss Field, he couldn't help but notice, hadn't blinked in quite a while.

"I arrived too late to tend to her sister, and Midge had nowhere else to go." He purposely glossed over the less savory details. He saw no reason for the little girl to suffer the stigma of a background she couldn't control. "When we return to Baltimore, I'll need to send her to a boarding school," he added. "Midge just turned thirteen, but for now her loss is fresh, and I thought it would do her some good to be away from the city."

"What a wonderful idea!" Mrs. Edgerly exclaimed. "Clara and I will be delighted to look after her during your stay."

"We'll do everything we can." Determination showed in the set of Miss Field's jaw, but her eyes softened. "Thirteen is a tender age to lose one's family."

"I know, dear." Mrs. Edgerly reached over to pat Miss Field's hand, making Saul wonder whether the connection between the two sprang from more than the obvious relationship.

"Thank you both." He leaned forward in his

chair. "You should know Midge's upbringing was a bit rough. Her family fell on hard times. She hasn't seen much schooling. In fact"—the idea struck as he spoke, a perfect way for Miss Field to forgo hard work without feeling as though she shirked anything—"I'd consider it a particular boon if you could help with her manners and speech and reading and the like, so she'll have an easier time adjusting to boarding school." Now that he thought on it, Midge would really benefit from the arrangement, too.

"We'll do our best." Miss Field stood up to clear the table. "First, we'll need to set up a room for her."

"I've things in storage above the store," Dad offered. "We'll haul them over tomorrow so it's all in place before I leave." A flash of sadness crossed his features. "After rattling around here alone so long, seems a shame I'm going just when it's full."

No one said anything more, but the genuine longing in his father's voice stayed in Saul's thoughts throughout the morning service.

Unlike the barely avoided brawl caused by Clara and Aunt Doreen's unexpected arrival, Saul's appearance in town seemed easily accepted. This was due, at least in part, to Mr. Reed and Clara spreading word as folks came to the store.

At any rate, families came to worship the next Sunday prepared to welcome the new doctor. Makeshift tables near the church rapidly filled with food pulled from buckboards. Clara added a few dishes—butter-roasted potatoes, scalloped corn and tomatoes, and baked beans flavored with molasses and bacon—to the variety already in place. She and Aunt Doreen knew this impromptu town gathering would most likely occur and had prepared for it after supper last evening.

"So that's Mr. Reed's son?" Sally Fosset appeared at Clara's elbow. "He's better looking than I pictured."

Opal joined them. "Looks aren't everything, Sally."

"Saul Reed bears more than a handsome face." Clara jumped on the opportunity to talk him up. "You both already know he's a doctor. Not one of those self-taught shysters, either. He went to a university in Scotland for a medical degree."

"I heard about that." Opal raised a brow. "Sounds like the type of thing folks get uppity about, though."

"Dr. Reed doesn't care about things like that." Clara hastened to disabuse Opal of that notion. "As a matter of fact, after he arrived too late to help a woman, he took in her orphaned little sister."

"You don't say?" Amanda Dunstall set a berry pie on a nearby table, not even noticing it wobbled precariously close to the edge as she listened to the conversation. "A bachelor like that took in a child?"

"She'll be coming here on the next stage." Clara lowered her voice so they all leaned in. "The little girl just turned thirteen, and he plans to send her off to school when she's ready. I wonder if your sister wouldn't make a good friend to Midge while she's here, Sally."

"Tricia's turning twelve soon." Sally cast a glance at a trio of nearby girls. "I'll be sure to mention it to her, so she'll say something to Alyssa Warren and Lauren Doane. They're all about the same age."

"I'll tell Pete to behave himself." Opal sighed. "It's not much, but it's the best I can do."

Clara couldn't help but laugh at the rueful expression on her friend's face. "A little teasing should make Midge feel at home, I'd think. After the rough time she's had of it in the city, a place like Buttonwood could be precisely what she needs."

"Shame it sounds like the doctor is set on going back to Baltimore," Sally observed. "We could use a doctor around these parts, and I wouldn't turn my nose up at another handsome bachelor to add to the list." She cast a surreptitious glance toward Matthew Burn.

"We have a couple of months to change Dr. Reed's mind," Clara pointed out. "If we put our heads together, we can show him all the wonderful things about this town so he won't want to leave. Sometimes a man just needs the right incentive to settle down."

"Like a good woman?" Amanda's gaze took on a dreamy cast.

"Yes." Clara stifled a pang of guilt over encouraging the girl, who was a bit on the young side for Dr. Reed. "He's already taken in a child and is in the midst of setting up a practice. Now seems to be a good time for the right woman to step in."

"Hmmm." Sally eyed him with new interest.

"I like that he cares about folks beside himself."

Opal patted her hair to make sure it was in place. "That's a good quality."

"Dr. Reed carries a man-sized appetite, too." Amanda's voice rang with approval. "He'd appreciate a wife who knows her way around a kitchen."

"Not to mention he has the education and career to provide a fine kitchen for that wife." Sally turned back to face them all. "What do you say, ladies? I think we can convince Dr. Reed to think twice about settling in Buttonwood."

"Why don't you set your cap for him, Clara?" Opal's question cut through the chatter in an instant. "You're educated and don't plan to stay here, too, so why are you so set on having Dr. Reed settle in Buttonwood?"

"Well"—Clara struggled to find an honest answer she could give them without breaking faith with Mr. Reed—"it's because Aunt Doreen and I can't stay here on Mr. Reed's goodwill indefinitely, but he's always talking about how much he wishes he had his family nearby. He says having us around helps the house not feel so empty, and I don't want him to feel abandoned after all he's done for us."

"That's sweet, Clara." Sally gave her a hug. "While we're convincing Dr. Reed, though, we're going to use the opportunity to change your mind about staying, too!"

"Truth be told, I don't want to leave you all behind." Her nose stung as Clara smiled at them. "We'll see what God has in store."

"In the meantime"—Amanda nudged Opal

with her elbow—"how about you introduce us to Dr. Reed. Since God already brought him to town, I mean."

"Of course. You know," Clara whispered as they made their way over to where Mr. Reed stood, introducing his son to the other members of the town, "I've been thinking we should have a quilting bee over at the Reed place, since the parlor's so large. It'd be a good reason to have all of you come to visit."

"You're a sharp one, Clara Field." Brushing a speck off her skirt, Sally added a suggestion of her own. "Threshing will start soon, too. Everyone gets together for that."

"Yes." Opal looked back at a point Clara couldn't follow. "You will invite Willa to the quilting circle, won't you, Clara? She always turns down any invitation from Sally or me."

"Shouldn't be so snobby then." Amanda scowled. "I don't understand why she goes out of her way to avoid you when you're always so nice, Opal."

"It's because I'm a Speck. That's all." Opal brushed away Amanda's anger. "I think maybe her mother makes her stay away, too."

"Of course I'll invite her, Opal." Clara didn't mention that she'd already planned to.

"Since Mama passed on so long ago, there's no one for Mrs. Grogan to squabble with." A shadow of grief passed over Opal's face, and Clara reached over to squeeze her arm. The pain of a lost loved one never completely went away.

"I'd say she brings trouble on herself." Amanda's

brow furrowed as she nodded toward where Lucinda barged in front of Dr. Reed and waved her arms in the air, pointing toward Willa. "Could she be more obvious in her attempts at matchmaking?"

"Perfect. This gives us the opportunity to rescue him. Smile," Clara directed as they edged within hearing distance.

"You simply must meet my Willa," Lucinda simpered in a high pitch. "I've always said the girl has a healing touch."

"Dr. Reed," Clara raised her voice, not bothering to hide a wide smile. From the look on his face, the doctor knew he'd made a narrow escape. Good. It couldn't hurt to have him owe her a favor. "I'd like you to meet some of my friends. . . ."

Chapter 10

Midge kept her hand clamped around the money shoved in the pocket of her skirt, hidden beneath her apron. She darted suspicious looks around every corner, keeping her head high and shoulders back so any thieves lurking around wouldn't think her an easy mark.

With her free hand, she tugged the brim of her straw boater low over her eyes so no one would recognize her. Not that anyone would, what with her being all clean and dressed so nice now, but it was smart to be careful about these things. Fancy clothes, a bath, and a few miles between her and her old life only amounted to so much when a body got right down to it.

She darted across the street after a carriage passed, narrowly avoiding a coal cart. Two more blocks and she reached the open market where a mishmash of sounds, smells, and sights assaulted her. Shrill wives hawked produce, reed-thin voices wavered offers of matchsticks or flowers, and a muddle of accents made it impossible to understand most of them.

Midge wound her way past a shifty-eyed hag rubbing wax into old apples to make them shine, a thickset man who tried to pinch her bottom when she passed his stall of spittoons, and a greasy-haired fisherman who smelled as though he slept near his wares. In times past, she'd dawdle around the market, waiting for an inattentive stall owner to turn away so she could nab a bite to eat.

Wandering around the stalls, looking at everything from pocket watches to manure carts, whiled away many an afternoon when she couldn't wait inside the room with Nancy. The market offered a place to lose herself in a crowd, to become part of the heartbeat of the city until she forgot about how alone she really was. For a while, at least.

Today, though, she'd come to buy salt pork for her trip with Mrs. Henderson to go meet Dr. Reed. Midge ignored the meat stalls closest to the outside, where everything became coated with street dust and soot, and twisted through the rows until she reached old Finnergan. Here, smoked sausages roped along the high beams in merry streams, hanging down just far enough to tease her nose with good smells.

She bought the salt pork and some of the sausages as Mrs. Henderson asked. Many times before, she'd watched him wrap things for other customers but never for her. Sometimes he'd pass her a sausage, not saying a word about it, but never bundling it up like a present. She watched over the counter as, for the first time, he did it for her.

Midge liked the rustle and tear of the thick, brown paper, the way it creased so straight and sturdy until tied off with a bit of string. She slipped the packages into her apron pockets with a muttered, "Thank you," and went back the way she'd come.

Navigating the twisting alleys of the market always seemed to take longer on the way home, and this time was no different. The wind picked up, making Midge wrap her shawl tight around her shoulders so she wouldn't lose it. She ducked her head against the dust as she rounded a corner, clipping a passerby as she moved.

"Sorry," she mumbled, blinking the dust from her vision. Midge started to move on, but the man reached out and put a heavy hand on her shoulder. She went rigid.

"Can't be runnin' into folks, luv." A familiar voice sent chills down her spine, and she kept her head bowed. He shifted, and Midge could see his big brown boots.

"Sorry." She rasped it this time, staring at the scuff mark on the toe of his left boot. The one Rodney'd gotten when he kicked in the door after Nancy locked it against him and the doctor the night before she died.

"You can apologize better'n that, a pretty little thing like you." He leaned over her, and when his hand moved from clamping her shoulder to reaching for her chin, Midge sprang into action.

"No!" She jammed her elbow into his doughy

middle, slapping his hand aside and leaping away. Midge didn't look back to see if he bent over double. The sound of his wheezing breath spurred her to run and keep running.

She dashed around corners, cut through the park, and circled back in a sideways scuttle to make sure he hadn't crept up behind her. Then, only when she was sure he couldn't have followed, did she run home.

Did he recognize me? She didn't think so but had no way to tell for sure.

Midge lifted the latch on the gate and walked around to the back, where she gulped air in quick pants until her breaths came normal again. Then she went inside.

"Glad to see you've returned, Midge." Mrs. Henderson gave her a big smile as she took the packages. "All ready now for our trip out West?"

Midge gave a tight-lipped nod. *If you only knew. . . .*

"How you brought so many things out here, I'll never know." Saul stepped over an upended crate to enter the rooms above the store. "Halfway to nowhere, and you've a storage area full of items!"

"Wait until we find everything we need," Dad huffed. "Then you'll be singing a different tune."

"It looks as if we could spend the day unearthing treasures," Miss Field agreed. "Though I'm glad you asked Aunt Doreen to watch the store. The dust up here would make her sneeze."

"We'll take frequent breaks." It didn't escape

Saul's notice that Miss Field already rubbed her nose. He looked around at dressers, washstands, and bedsteads leaning against each other in no sensible order. "What made you decide to order all this furniture, Dad? Shipping it out here must've cost a solid sum."

"No. Most everything up here I took in exchange from pioneers when their wagons came through." Dad shrugged off his own generosity even as he explained, "If they were low on cash or had to lighten the load to make room for supplies and had something too fine to go to waste, I stashed it up here."

Miss Field stared at his father with admiration. "You're a blessing to many, Mr. Reed."

"I just couldn't stand the thought of all those heirlooms dusting the mountains when the going got too rough." Dad rubbed the nape of his neck. "Twice, someone came back through to buy something back. Had a fellow this year who dug through everything to find his great-grandfather's clock in the corner. That probably made both our days, to tell the truth."

"What about the other time?" Miss Field asked the question Saul wondered.

Dad squinted as though it helped him think. "Most of these things aren't necessities around here, so folks don't buy them and I don't bother putting them in the store. I took a fancy spice chest once. Pretty thing. Put it in the store, and the Warrens snapped it up the same day. Well, that lady's son came looking for it. Said his father had made it special."

"Oh!" Miss Field gripped the edge of a nearby server as though anxious for the family to recover its heirloom.

"I sent him to the Warrens'. They sold it off to him for a fair price, and everyone went their way happier for the deal."

"As the town grows, there'll be more need for bigger items." Saul followed his father's lead and shrugged out of his coat, hanging it on a hall tree shoved against a corner. "Keeping these things represents a solid investment as well as a way to help folks right now."

"Well, for now I'm thinking we'll be able to fill one of those rooms in the house with things for Midge." Dad stomped over to a trunk and pushed it aside. "Big things first. She'll need a bed, washstand, and dresser."

"This bedstead looks good to me." Saul shifted a headboard with wooden slats so the others could see. "It has a matching footboard."

"Oh, yes!" Miss Field came over and traced the floral carving on the center slat. "It's perfect for a little girl."

"These iron bars fit into the joists, and here's a bed box that should fit." Saul nudged it with the toe of his boot. "I don't see any mattresses, though."

"Aunt Doreen and I will make one for her." Miss Field stepped out of the way as he and Dad started moving the pieces toward the door. "We don't have feathers, but there are cornhusks aplenty to use for the time being."

"That sounds good." Saul raised the headboard

high to avoid hitting a leather trunk. It took them three trips to get all the pieces for the bed down the stairs and to the house. When they came back upstairs, he found Miss Field scooting a chest of drawers toward the door.

"This seems like a good match for the bedstead," she puffed, obviously out of breath.

"I'll get it while you sit down for a moment." He closed the distance in two strides, noting her relieved expression as she moved out of the way and perched on the edge of a crate. *Dad's right. She does take too much on herself.* Saul frowned as he moved the dresser toward the door, realizing it might take more than he expected to get Miss Field to rest.

"If you don't like it, there are others." The nervous lilt in her tone told him she'd seen his frown.

"You picked the right one," he assured her. "I'm just thinking I should remove the drawers so they don't slide out and bounce down the stairs."

Without a word, she waited until he removed them, then she led the way down the stairs with two long drawers while he and Dad took the heavier outer shell. By the time they had it out to the house, she'd brought the two smaller drawers, as well. With the addition of a washstand, they were ready to haul it up to the room they'd earmarked for Midge.

"We'll take it all up." Dad motioned toward the house, where the furniture lay heaped in the parlor. "If you and your aunt want to put up the closed sign and poke around upstairs to see if you can find anything a little girl might like, go on ahead."

"I'd love to!" Mrs. Edgerly's eyes shone with excitement. "It'll be such fun to sit there, going through boxes and seeing what we find. If we run across anything for the store, we'll set it aside, too."

"Or the house," Dad encouraged. "Anything that captures your fancy, ladies. It doesn't do anyone any good gathering dust up there."

Saul didn't say a word, content with the idea of the women settling down to go through boxes. They shouldn't overtax themselves that way, but the two would still feel useful.

Time flew by as he and his father lugged the furniture up the stairs. Sliding the drawers back into the dresser and assembling the bed frame took longer than anticipated, and it was a while before they returned to the store.

"Ladies?" he called, expecting they would be back downstairs by now. A soft thud sounded from the floor above, so he headed for the stairwell. What he found when he made it upstairs made his jaw drop.

"Oh, Dr. Reed." Clara swiped a lock of hair from her forehead, trying to push it back into her bun. "We didn't hear you come in." She straightened from where she'd just set down a crate of china in the section they'd reserved for kitchenware.

"What have you. . ." He seemed to be experiencing difficulty getting the words out. "What. . .happened?"

"While we went through everything, we decided to organize." Clara beamed. Obviously, the man appreciated their hard work. He was so bowled over by what she and Aunt Doreen had accomplished while they'd been gone, he could scarcely believe it. "Bed frames are in the corner over there, along with the rest of the furniture. We left all that, for the most part." She gestured as she spoke. "You know how heavy it is."

"I've an idea." His voice came out sounding strangled.

His father appeared behind him. "Would you take a look at this place!" Mr. Reed looked around with obvious enjoyment. "You've worked wonders."

"Clara did most of the real work," Aunt Doreen demurred. "I mostly sat here, looking through the contents of trunks and crates and the like. She moved things around."

"Nonsense." Clara waved away her aunt's modesty. "It took both of our efforts." She took a deep breath and tried to ignore the way dust coated her throat. She'd been meaning to go downstairs for a dipperful of water for a while now.

"Furniture in the corner then?" Mr. Reed walked across the room. "What's this lot?"

"Those are things you might want to put out in the store come spring. There's a wagon repair kit, two travel cooking boxes, and the crate has a few lanterns and lengths of rope in it." Clara led him to the next grouping. "These hold finer merchandise— china and silver. People might come back for these or may ask as folks marry or the town grows."

"Excellent." Mr. Reed grinned, while his son still looked stunned.

"These two small crates hold books." Excitement had her lifting off the lid on the top one. "Some have water damage, but altogether they're in wonderful condition. This next to them is a portable writing desk. You lift the top and it has clever compartments for ink, pens, nibs, paper, and wax. It'd be perfect for Midge to work on her penmanship."

"I don't remember trading for that," Mr. Reed admitted.

"Aunt Doreen found it beneath some clothing in one of the trunks. Clothes are over here"—she gestured to one large wooden chest before moving on—"and quilts there. In the portmanteau you have some shoes."

Tears clogged the back of her throat as she finished speaking. The clothes, blankets, and shoes were best clothes. The clothes, families packed away to be worn only when they reached Oregon or California. These items belonged to unfortunate souls who'd been buried in their Sunday best but hadn't survived the trail to wear their finery.

"I never could go through those things." Mr. Reed swept his hat off his head. "It seemed disrespectful."

"Folks can get some use out of them," his son spoke up. "There's no shame in that. By taking them, you helped their families and took away a painful reminder, Dad."

"He's right." Aunt Doreen gave an encouraging nod. "You don't have to sell them unless you want to."

"Did you come across anything more for Midge?" Dr. Reed's attempt to lighten the subject worked.

"Yes!" Clara seized the opportunity. "We found some school supplies to help her get caught up." She opened a box to reveal a slate, chalk, and a primer. "This leather trunk would look good at the foot of her bed to store extra blankets and whatnot, but the best part. . ." She exchanged a glance with Aunt Doreen. "Show them."

"Look!" Aunt Doreen flung open the trunk with a dramatic flourish to unveil a hand-painted tea set too large for a small child but not standard size, either. "Have you ever seen the like?"

"That's something." Mr. Reed hunkered down next to Aunt Doreen. "I recall this, vaguely. The family intended it as a gift for someone in Oregon, but they needed money for a broken axle."

"At thirteen, will Midge feel too old for this?" Clara looked up at Dr. Reed for his opinion.

"She'll love it, I'm sure." His hand dwarfed a tiny cup and saucer. "Midge hasn't had the chance to enjoy the fun little things in life much. I'm glad Buttonwood will help remedy that." His smile when he handed back the cup made Clara's breath catch.

"Buttonwood is like that." She managed to remind herself of her purpose in making Midge and Dr. Reed comfortable here. One glance at Aunt Doreen strengthened her resolve. "We aim to please."

CHAPTER 11

"Please sit down." Saul spoke firmly, reaching to pull his father's saddlebags away from Clara, but the woman batted his hands away and kept on rummaging around.

"I'll break my fast once I'm certain Mr. Reed packed everything he needs. Now where"—her voice grew muffled as she all but stuck her head in the leather—"did he put that. . .ah, here it is." She emerged with a smile and checked something off what seemed to Saul an inordinately long list.

"You've been up since dawn making breakfast and double-checking everything, Miss Field." He gripped her elbow and steered her toward the table. "Those delicious biscuits and gravy are going cold."

"I misspoke when I said I'd break my fast. You see, I nibbled a biscuit earlier and can always eat another later." She turned into the kitchen, out of his grasp, and toward the pantry as she spoke. "Though I do believe your father could use a few more provisions for the journey. . . ."

Saul leaned on the doorjamb to the larder to see her bundling apples, jerked beef, a loaf of fresh baked bread, a crock of preserves, and a chunk of cheese to go with cold chicken and hard tack she'd packed already. Saul barely held back a chuckle, since he'd already seen Mrs. Edgerly flit back and forth, doing much the same thing.

"Between you and your aunt, Dad will be lucky if his horse can walk, much less carry him along with his bags."

"What do you mean?" Miss Field drew up short, arms laden with provisions and green eyes wide. If it weren't for the purple smudges beneath those eyes, she'd be the picture of health. "Is something wrong with the horse? I'm certain Mr. Burn would loan him another—"

"The horse is fine." Saul couldn't stifle his laugh. "Your aunt already added a few bacon sandwiches and extra biscuits to his pack. With all that"—he nodded toward what she carried—"plus what you two packed before, the horse won't be able to budge."

"Oh, that's an exaggeration." She attempted to sidle past him through the doorway but lost the apples in transit. Dismay crossed her features as they tumbled to the floor. "Well, perhaps he won't need those."

"Good thinking." This time, he hid a grin. While she looked at the fallen fruit, he reached out and shifted the load into his own arms. "I'll get this." He carried it out to the entryway, where Dad's saddlebags rested on the big hall table.

Before Miss Field could catch up and reevaluate, he stuffed all the food together. "That ought to do it." Saul struggled to fasten each of them shut before shouldering the lot.

"Perhaps I should check one last time." Mrs. Edgerly bustled down the stairs. "Just in case we overlooked something."

"Your niece has it well in hand," Saul assured her, making his way for the door. "Though maybe now you can convince her to take the time to eat a good breakfast!"

"Clara!" The disapproval in Mrs. Edgerly's tone made the packs seem lighter as Saul walked outside. "You've not eaten?"

"Thanks, son." Dad grabbed a pack, and together they situated everything so the horse was ready to go. "Think you can handle everything?"

"Those two are more than I bargained for," Saul admitted.

"You have no idea." Dad's grin didn't exactly ease his mind. "They're good women though."

"I know. Getting Miss Field to slow down her pace and rest"—Saul whistled—"that's a task more suited to Hercules. The woman seems determined to wear herself out."

"I get the feeling she thinks she has something to prove." Dad's jaw clenched, and his Adam's apple worked hard before he got the next words out. "Mrs. Edgerly raised Clara, but neither of them talks about Clara's uncle much. I get the impression he was a mean sort. Left them both high and dry."

"They do seem extremely close." Saul cast a

glance over his shoulder. "Setting out for Oregon after he passed on says a lot about them trying to leave their old life behind."

Miss Field came out on the porch. "Is it time to leave us already?"

"Afraid so, ladies." Dad walked over, and Saul tried to hide his surprise when the women both enveloped his father in a simultaneous embrace. "I'll be back in a couple of months."

"We'll miss you." Mrs. Edgerly's whisper carried to where Saul stood by the horse.

"The time will pass quickly. Remember. . .I'm trusting you to make sure Saul doesn't step between a pair of spitting Specks and Grogans." Dad's smile, when he turned around, bore more than a touch of sadness. He swung into the saddle and took one last look at the three of them. "Knowing you're all here will make coming home a trip worth taking."

With a wave, Dad took off. Saul joined the women on the porch as they watched him until he faded in the distance; then they went inside.

"Strange how I've only known him a few weeks, but it feels like I'm losing family." Miss Field's whisper floated past Saul, sending a prick of guilt through his chest that he ever thought these women might have set out to take advantage of his father.

"We'll make him proud while he's gone," he promised. "That reminds me. . .Dad said something about how you'd started taking inventory since he'd fallen behind. You probably know as much about where everything is as he does."

"I wouldn't say that." Rose tinged her cheeks.

"All the same, I'd appreciate it if you'd show me the ropes, so to speak. Muddling around on my own doesn't appeal."

"Certainly. Aunt Doreen? Will you need help making dinner this afternoon?"

"I'll bring it over to the pair of you." Mrs. Edgerly shooed them on. "I made sure she ate well, Doctor. Clara, you go on ahead and show Dr. Reed how things work. If you can have everything in order and inventory done by the time Mr. Reed comes back, so much the better."

Miss Field pulled a shawl off the peg by the door, although the sun had already burned off the morning dew. "Ready?"

"Absolutely." In a moment they'd crossed to the store. It seemed strange to unlock the door without Dad. The counters running the length of the store opposite each other seemed bare without him bustling behind one of them.

"The whole place feels different." Miss Field's comment so closely echoed his thoughts, and Saul glanced at her. A fond smile graced her lips. "Your father has a way of bringing life to a place. I remember my father having the same gift." The smile wavered but held.

"Your aunt raised you?" He made it a question, open enough for her to tell precisely as much as she wished and nothing more.

"Yes." The glow vanished abruptly. "My parents died after I turned twelve—just about Midge's age."

"If you feel comfortable, you might tell her that.

Shared grief makes the burden lighter, and Midge doesn't know anyone who's lost her parents." *And I've never told her about my sister.* He drew a sharp breath at the connection but shoved it away. This wasn't the time to examine it.

"God blessed me with Aunt Doreen, just as He's blessed Midge with you." Her gaze seemed to cut right through him.

They'd moved on, Miss Field showing him the drawers and bins built into the counters which held spices, flour, sugar, coffee, and the like. She seemed eager for the distraction of the store, but he tried to steer the conversation back. He meant to discover more about the shadowy figure of her uncle.

"Your aunt was married when you joined her?" He spoke casually in an attempt to hide the awkward nature of the question. "Mr. Edgerly was already in residence, I mean?"

Miss Field's gaze shot straight to his face, her expression shuttered. "No." The single word fell between them as she turned away.

"The coffee grinder sits here. Just measure in the beans, turn the crank, and the grounds collect here." Clara spoke quickly, retreating into the minutia of running the store. His close proximity made her anxious, and the brush of his shirtsleeves against her shoulder seemed to whisper a warning that she couldn't afford to waste any time. "You see?" They'd already looked over the books, writing supplies, and lamps displayed in the left-hand window and moved on to the grocery items.

"Simple." His breath fanned warm against her ear. "Do we use pokes, bags, or gunnysacks for the coffee?"

"That depends on how many pounds the customer orders." She pushed away from the counter—away from him. "It works the same way as the other dry goods, but folks usually order a lot of coffee, so it'll be bags. Gunnysacks are used if they want the beans whole. The only time you'll need pokes is for fine sugar, spices, or candy."

"Good." He pulled away from the large grinder to follow her. "I'm still not convinced I can make a cone out of brown paper and not spill spices everywhere—even if the bins pull out of the counter so handily."

"Don't you put medicinal powders in twists of paper?" She shot him a quizzical glance. "It's the same thing."

"Folding the paper seals it off. Shaping it into a cone leaves a loose end." He looked at the shelves behind one counter, then turned to and surveyed the other length of the store. "That reminds me. . . where are the pharmaceuticals?"

"On the other side, with toiletries and razors and tooth powder." She directed his attention back to the area directly in front of them. "Behind the grinder is the display of dishes and silverware. According to your father, people rarely ask for them, so they're tucked away. She moved farther down the shelves lining the wall to the canning jars, skillets, pots, and other cookware. "Any questions?"

"He displays produce on the countertop, and smoked and cured meats sit on the shelves along with eggs, canned goods, and preserves." Dr. Reed leaned back against the counter as he took stock. "Candy's in the glass jars up front to tempt all the customers."

"You don't need me to go over all this." Clara sidled around the counter. "Everything's arranged in sections. Tools and hardware along the back wall." She inclined her head toward the jumble of tubs, buckets, barrels, tools, rope, and lanterns to make her point. "The shelves beneath the other counter hold men's hats, work gloves, and boots leading up to the display of women's bonnets, Sunday gloves, and shoes. The wall behind holds all the yard goods and trimmings for any sewing needs."

"What about this corner?" He moved behind the counter to peer at the shelves in the far corner. "Ah, yes. The toiletries?"

"Yes. Here you'll find soap, combs, and brushes next to the irons and washboards. Your father was clever to put those next to the fabric, I think."

"Hmmm?" He'd plucked a small bottle from the shelf and squinted at it. The morning light didn't reach through the windows to the far wall yet. "I suppose so. When I asked, I meant these liniments and things. Is this all the town has for a pharmacy, Miss Field?"

"It must be."

"We'll start that inventory list right here then." He crossed the store to take the biggest lamp from the window display and bring it back to the dim corner, dropping that bottle in the trash along the way. "Please fetch pen and paper, Miss Field. We'll need to place an order at once so the town doesn't continue to lack essential medical supplies."

"All right." Surprised by his switch from easygoing shopkeeper to intense physician, she hastened to get the logbook. When she had what she needed, she skirted around him, laying the ink and records on the counter. "First, shall we record what we do have?"

"It won't do much good." He pulled away from the shelf and raked a hand through his dark hair. "Most of these aren't worth the bottles they're in. We'll have to dispose of them."

"Why?" Clara caught herself nibbling on her lower lip and immediately stopped. Dr. Reed knew medicine better than she.

"Some are out and out quackery. Look at this." He passed her a small box.

" 'Colden's Liquid Beef Tonic,' " she read aloud, " 'for treatment of alcoholic condition.' Well, I'd think that could be useful to some people, Dr. Reed."

"Look here." He moved to stand beside her, his hand closing over hers. "Read this small print at the bottom of the box."

"Twenty-six percent alcoholic content." She gasped. "Surely that's a mistake! You don't drink spirits to overcome a dependence upon them!"

"Precisely." He swept the box from her hand and plunked it on the counter. "This goes, as does anything proclaiming miracle cures or bearing a high alcohol content. They temporarily mask symptoms and prevent the patient from seeking treatment until it may be too late."

"Look at all of them!" Dozens upon dozens of small boxes and bottles marched in neat rows upon the shelves. "Will any remain?"

"Some." Dr. Reed rolled up his sleeves, exposing strong forearms lightly dusted with dark hair. "We'll make three piles. One for things I'm certain are genuine, one for hoaxes, and the last for tonics to evaluate later."

"Oh." Clara tore her gaze from his arms and snatched the first box she saw. " 'Hostetter's Celebrated Stomach Bitters.' " She turned it over, scanning over promises until she came to a shocking number. "Forty-four percent alcohol by volume!" It started the garbage pile.

They worked in silence, dust motes dancing in the glow of the lantern and the increasing light stretching from the window as time passed. Occasionally they'd stop to read a particularly overblown or ridiculous claim.

" 'Dr. C.V. Girard's Ginger Brandy, a Certain Cure for Cholera, Colic, Cramps, Dysentery, Chills, and Fever,' " Clara mused. "With a wonder like this, it's incredible we even need doctors nowadays."

"That, Miss Field"—an amused sparkle in his eyes belied the gravity of his tone—"is because we of the medical profession wage a war on poor health. And no one understands this better than the estimable Mr. Scott." He whipped a box off the shelf, holding it up as though it were a pistol yet carefully leaving the side free so she could read the print on the side. Dr. Reed announced, " 'Scott's Emulsion: A cough or cold is a spy which has stealthily come in the lines of health: SHOOT THE SPY.' "

Clara clamped one hand over her mouth to muffle her laughter. Between his antics and the dramatic script, the Scott's Emulsion box proved the best entertainment she'd seen in months. "Oh, can we keep that one? Even if we don't sell it?"

"As a matter of fact"—Dr. Reed tapped the box—"it's made with lime and powder, which can temporarily help clear the airways in case of a cough or cold. It's not a cure but could provide some relief." He placed it in the disgracefully small pile of boxes they'd be keeping.

"At a guess, I'd say Pink Pills for Pale People probably don't work so well." Clara held up the light pink box and gave it a shake, the tablets inside crashing against each other.

"Do you know anyone particularly pale?"

"My uncle Uriah used to be so pale it seemed as though the colors ran away from him." She gave a strangled gasp when she realized she'd said it aloud.

"It's all right, Miss Field. You're a truthful sort."

"Yes, but it's never proper to speak ill of the dead, Dr. Reed." She pushed the pills onto the counter and clasped her hands together. "He passed on a little over a year ago."

"Is that what made you decide to go to Oregon?" He leaned close. "To leave behind the memories?"

"How did you—" Her head snapped up and she stared at him for a moment, wondering how he knew she and Aunt Doreen sought to leave the dreadful memories of Uncle Uriah behind forever. Then she realized the innocent nature of the question. Many people felt haunted by good memories when someone died, that a house carried too many remembrances of happy times long passed. She chose her words carefully. "It's always difficult when a family member dies."

"Should you ever need to discuss it, Miss Field—"

"No, thank you." She softened her words. "It's still too fresh."

He looked as though he wanted to press further, but the tinny brass bell over the door jangled.

The tinkle of that bell sounded the death knell to Saul's fledgling interrogation. Just when he'd gotten her talking about her uncle, a customer had to come striding into the store. That rankled. Particularly since Dad's suspicions seemed correct.

The way Miss Field paled at the thought of her uncle—something was wrong there. Saul didn't know what, but when the sparkle in a woman's eyes died like a doused fire, something caused it. He hadn't missed what she meant by leaving behind the memories, either. Despite her cautious words about fresh pain and difficulty losing a family member, she'd not said a thing about a loved one.

The man striding up to the counter didn't know what he'd walked into. Trouble was, Saul couldn't be exactly sure himself. Only Clara knew, and guarded as she'd been, it might be a long time before he'd be able to get her talking again.

"What can I get you today?" Saul recalled meeting the tall man at church the Sunday before. "Mr. Grogan, isn't it?"

"Call me Adam. I need some baking powder."

"Sure." Saul moved across the store, tore off a strip of thick, brown paper, and rolled it into a cone. Then he shoved in the tip for good measure before opening the baking powder bin. "Say when." White powder poured from the scoop for a good while before Adam Grogan was satisfied.

"Do you need anything else?" Miss Field had risen from the low stool where she'd been sitting, digging through bottles of tinctures and cure-alls.

"No, ma'am." Adam hastily removed his hat. "Except to apologize for that hullabaloo when you first arrived. If I'd been around when the whole thing started, maybe I could have put a stop to it. As it was. . ." A shrug finished the statement.

"Yes." Miss Field held herself ramrod straight, and Saul wondered at the "hullabaloo" Adam referred to. "I did wish you would've made more of an effort, but I also understand you have family loyalties and the situation goes deeper than I know. All that matters is we averted the crisis."

"For the moment."

"What crisis?" Saul decided not to wait until dinnertime to ask the ladies. The longer trouble brewed, the stronger it became and the more people got hurt.

"There's bad blood between us Grogans and the

Specks, you might say." Adam shifted his weight. "Sometimes it boils to the top and spills over on unsuspecting folk like Miss Field."

"Opal Speck and I averted a minor scuffle on my first Sunday in town," Miss Field clarified. "Mr. Grogan here came into the picture too late to avoid trouble altogether."

"I'd stayed home from church that morning when Sadie first showed signs of being ill." Adam reached for the poke of baking powder. "I hope this'll settle her stomach."

"She's been sick for weeks?" Saul snapped to attention. "What are her symptoms?"

"Sadie's always been energetic, but she got real tired, eyes went dull. She stopped eating and didn't want to drink much." Adam sighed. "It seemed after a while she was on the mend, but it started all over again, and now she's starting to bloat."

"Why didn't you come for me sooner?" Saul headed for the door. "I'll grab my kit. We'll go right away."

"You don't mind, Doc?" There was no mistaking the hope in Adam Grogan's tone. "I thought it'd be beneath a college-educated fellow like you.

"Dr. Reed," Miss Field interjected, "you might want to stop a mo—"

"No time to stop now." Saul could scarce credit her interruption. "Not if the girl's been without treatment for so long. Of course I'll help Sadie, Adam."

"I'm sorry I doubted you, Dr. Reed." He followed him toward the door. "I sure appreciate you taking a look at Sadie."

"Every life is sacred." Saul grabbed his jacket from the peg beside the door.

"Sadie's special, too. She's our best milking cow."

CHAPTER 12

Fort Laramie, Oregon Trail

After days on end of being cramped in the bumpy stage and endless stretches of grassy plains taunting her from the small cutout windows, Midge needed to stretch her legs.

She itched to tear off her bonnet and go racing across the earth, leaving her boots and all their buttons behind her so the long grass tickled her toes and cushioned her feet. Midge wanted to run until she gasped for breath, taking great gulps of wind and sky until she forgot the feeling of being trapped in a tiny coach, bouncing over every rock hidden on the prairie.

"We'll stop by Sutton's General Store for a few supplies while the stage trades horses." Mrs. Henderson swept toward the wooden structure, obviously intending for Midge to trail along behind.

Instead, Midge edged along the uneven, gapped cottonwood walls and buildings of Fort Laramie until she reached the far corner. Here, no soldiers marched or drilled or yelled. Mrs. Henderson, bless her for the caring soul she was, kept a gimlet eye fastened on every move Midge made unless Midge took the opportunity to break away from the scrutiny. No, this area away from the bustle of the store suited her better. It seemed quieter, as though not as much in use. Farther off, behind another structure, she heard the giggles of children.

Children? I thought only soldiers lived at forts. Her immediate reaction was to pick up her pace and head toward them, hopefully have some fun before the stage changed out horses and she had to leave again. Something caught her eye—most doors were thrown open in the heat as though trying to tempt a breeze.

Only one stood shut, as though guarding a secret. A furtive glance showed nobody about, so Midge headed to explore the mystery. Her hand closed over the knob, the door gave beneath her slight pressure, and she moved to step into the darkness within.

Just then, a strong arm roped about her middle from behind, pulling her against a wiry body while the man slammed the door shut and dragged her away, toward another. Toward danger.

Midge did as Nancy taught her long ago and went limp, letting the full weight of her body sag against her attacker's arm. Sure enough, the unexpected tactic caused him to falter for a moment—long enough for her to grind her heel into the fleshy part of his foot, dig her elbow under his ribs, and jerk away in a swift movement.

She lunged for the door, shoving it open with all the force of her escape, determined to slam it against her assailant and wait him out. No such luck. He caught her before she could get behind the wood, this time wrapping his arm around both of hers and heaving her away.

To her surprise, he didn't hold her but let go, leaving her to spin like a top with the strength of his movement while he yanked the door shut once more. Midge caught her breath and backed away, taking his measure before she budged.

Tall, the boy had more years than she'd seen and verged on manhood. The anger in his hot gaze didn't translate to his stance. He'd already proved his strength, his speed, but nothing about him suggested he'd pounce on her if she ran. Which meant he wasn't interested in hurting her so much as defending whatever hid behind the door.

Now that she had her breath back, and Midge could be fairly certain her heart wouldn't burst from her chest in panic, she could recognize the heat enveloping her as anger. "Do you normally go around grabbing girls like that?"

"Do you normally go off on your own to snoop?" His voice came out deeper than she expected.

"The other doors are open." She shrugged. "Gentlemen don't manhandle ladies."

"That wasn't manhandling." He gave a snort but eyed her like he might know what she meant.

"You came up behind me, grabbed me, and dragged me backward." She huffed. "What's a girl supposed to think?"

"She should be more careful where she pokes her pretty little nose." He crossed his arms over his chest and leaned on a wooden post. "And I didn't hurt you any. You can't say the same."

"You're lucky." His lack of apology rankled, in spite of that offhanded "pretty" remark. "I could've given you a bloody nose."

"You could've come out much worse." His frown made a wrinkle between his eyebrows. "And I would've just told you not to go there, but when I came around the corner you'd already opened the door. It was too late."

"Oh." The small concession took her aback. "What's in there?"

"Nothing at the moment." He shrugged. "But my brother Billy got sick, and then Dr. Reed came and saved him, and—"

"Dr. Reed?" Midge moved closer. "You saw Dr. Reed? When?"

"Couple of weeks ago." The boy smiled for the first time, showing a slight gap between his front teeth. "He saved Billy's life."

"Then why can't I go into the room?" Midge planned to ask how Dr. Reed saved Billy's life, but first things first.

"Billy's sickness was catching, and the fort doctor hasn't cleaned out the room yet."

"Oh." She moved a little closer. "Thanks, then, and I'm sorry I stomped on your foot."

"And elbowed me in the ribs?"

"That one you deserved." She gave a little smile. "I'm Midge. I'm going to Buttonwood to meet up with Dr. Reed."

"I'm Amos Geer, and I'm sorry I grabbed you without warning. Your Dr. Reed saved my brother's life, and probably my sister's, too."

"Seems like there's no one he won't save. . . ."

"Cow?" Saul stopped, still gripping the door handle. "Did you say this Sadie is a cow?"

"Yes, sir." Adam plunked his hat back on his head.

"Their best milking cow." Laughter underscored Miss Field's helpful reminder from behind the counter. "Remember. . .you don't have the time to stop since she needs treatment right away." She bustled down the length of the store as though to shoo him along. When she came close, a mischievous glint shone in her green eyes.

"You meant to tell me—"

"That's right." She gave a sage nod, letting him know that if he'd just listened he could have avoided this whole mess.

"Now, Mr. Grogan"—Saul tried to maintain his dignity—"you do realize I'm not trained in bovine medicine or veterinary arts?"

"I appreciate it." Adam Grogan couldn't look more serious if he tried. "A fancy doctor like you coming to look after a milk cow is a favor I wouldn't have thought to ask."

"We're blessed to have a man like Dr. Reed who honors his word." Miss Field brushed past to open the door. "I hope everything turns out all right."

With that, Saul couldn't back out. Not with Miss Field talking about his honor, Adam Grogan full of hope and respect, and a sick creature suffering out there.

In under ten minutes, he stood in a small, musty barn, looking at a decidedly unhealthy cow. The manger stood full of hay. Green slime spreading up the sides of a full trough told of water standing for too long. In the dim light, Saul could see the cow's dangerously distended abdomen. "Let's get her outside so I can take a better look."

It took both of them to coax the listless animal outside. Eyes dull, coat lackluster, stance placid, Sadie didn't so much as bow her head to inspect the grass at her feet. Flies settled on her face, but she couldn't seem to muster the energy to flick her ears and chase them away. Her pink nose, cracked and dry, told of dehydration.

"It's gotten worse since I left," Adam remarked after surveying the cow's bloated stomach. *Stomachs,* Saul reminded himself. Cows have four.

"Last time she seemed sick, did she look the same?" If so, Saul decided they'd start from what worked before.

"She was tired and dull like this, but no bloat." Adam thought a moment. "And she had the slobbers all over the place."

"How did you treat it before?"

"Shut her up in the barn so she could rest, brought her hay and silage so she'd bulk up. In a couple of weeks she seemed better, so we let her out again." Adam patted her side. "Now she's worse."

"If she continues to bloat, her heart will stop." Saul shook his head. "I've heard of baking powder for humans and horses, but not for cows. At this point it's worth a try."

"We've tried it, but it hasn't helped yet. Do you have any other ideas?"

"Since we don't know what caused it, it's harder to treat."

"Since she got better while in the barn and worsened when she went in the open, Pa's taken to the notion that the Specks are poisoning her." Adam's eyes narrowed. "It hasn't happened before, so there has to be a solid reason."

"I doubt they're poisoning your milk cow." Saul tried not to sound like he discounted the idea out of hand but stayed firm that it wasn't likely. "She's probably eaten something that disagreed with her. Right now she needs to release some of the gas."

"If she dies, Pa will take it out of a Speck's hide." Adam's warning came low and grim, a revelation that Saul might save more than a cow.

"Best thing I can suggest at the moment is elevating her front end." Saul looked around for a good spot. "Put her on a hill so her front legs are higher and hope the gas rises out. Unless you know another way to make a cow burp, that's about the only advice I can give you."

"There's an old wives' tale that if you scare a cow, chase it around, it can help release bloat." Adam hooked his thumbs in his suspenders. "I never thought it held much truth."

"Wait." Saul considered it for a minute.

"Walking Sadie might not be enough to get things moving, but running might jostle her into it. The idea makes sense, if you think about it."

"Would chasing her uphill help any?"

"I don't see how it could hurt." Saul grinned then looked at Sadie, who stared at him with big, dull, brown eyes. "She doesn't look like she's going to move for anything less than a butcher knife."

"Here." Adam disappeared behind the barn and came back with a spade and a hoe. "Bang these together and on the ground to direct her toward that western rise. I'll come at her from this end."

"All right." Saul ignored the thought that his fellow doctors would howl with laughter if they could see him now. "Go!"

In a burst of movement, they rushed the cow. A tangle of waving arms, banging implements, flying dust, and hoarse shouts, the pair of them would have terrified a pack of wolves into running over that western rise.

But all their efforts didn't budge one exhausted cow. The entire Grogan family, armed with skillets and spoons, pots and lids, earned no more than a quizzical glance. Mr. Grogan's whip, a last resort, got her to shuffle to the side a few paces before heaving a beleaguered sigh.

"I know!" One of the children, a young boy with more gums than teeth, raced out of sight. A flurry of indignant cackles told Saul the youngster went to the chicken coop, and sure enough, the boy returned with a rooster tucked beneath each arm.

"Here!" The child thrust one of the birds at

Adam then gifted Saul with the other squawking mass of feathers and spurs.

"Sadie's scared of 'em since that one flogger got loose and tore up her flank."

Sure enough, once Saul had his bird under control, he noticed Sadie stealthily putting distance between herself and the roosters. He exchanged a single nod with Adam before they moved in tandem.

A glorious cacophony of shouts, shrieks, squawks, and frantic lowing sounded as men, roosters, and one long-suffering cow made a mad charge up the western hill.

"It worked!" Clara announced as she came through the door. "Lucinda Grogan didn't want Willa to come over while Opal was here, but when I told her we were all pitching in to make things ready for Midge, she yielded."

"Wonderful!" Aunt Doreen clasped her hands together. "With all the help, we'll have everything ready within the day."

"Midge will be tickled when she hears her arrival has folks laying aside grievances to work together." Dr. Reed grinned, and Clara shoved aside a stab of remorse for the real reason she'd invited all the young women over to the house.

"Lucinda's reasoning had more to do with you than Midge," Clara admitted. "Even Willa said after the sight of you and Adam brandishing roosters and chasing that cow over the hill, her mama wouldn't be able to deny you anything."

"I hold out hope Sadie will prove one of my most difficult patients." The doctor reached for his hat, clearly on his way to the store. "Though I can't claim much of the credit for her recovery, a doctor won't argue with success."

"You're overmodest, Dr. Reed," Aunt Doreen chided. "Be prepared to tell the tale over dinner, too. The ladies will ask."

"I wouldn't want to get in your way. Should I eat dinner at the café?"

"No!" Clara blurted then softened her voice. "Sally, Opal, Willa, and Amanda agreed to spend the day working on Midge's room, and it'd be a poor return to deny them your company."

He frowned. "I'd only thought to spare you the task of making a large meal, but you're right. It could be perceived as ungracious."

"We'll send someone over this afternoon, when it's time to eat."

A breath of relief escaped her when Dr. Reed left. For a moment, her plan had teetered on the brink of ruin. How would she ever convince Dr. Reed to marry one of the local girls unless he got to know them? She'd schemed to invite all the prospects over so he could spend some time with each one, and the man almost evaded them!

Clara rubbed her temples, reminding herself of the brilliance of this day's work. Not only would Dr. Reed see Opal, Sally, Willa, and even Amanda, he'd see the best of what they had to offer a husband. The comfort a wife would bring to a home and her willingness to love his children should prove appealing lures to someone like the good doctor.

A knock sounded on the front door, announcing Sally and Amanda's arrival. Clara ushered both inside, gesturing for them to set their sewing kits in the parlor. No sooner had they removed their bonnets than Opal and Willa appeared.

"Morning, Willa." Opal made the first attempt at conversation. "I like your shawl."

"Thanks." The other girl gave a tentative smile. "I've always admired your pin."

"Oh?" Opal's fingers fluttered to touch the carved jet bar on her collar. "It belonged to Mama."

Sensing that faint note of grief, Clara stepped in. "Every girl should have something pretty. That's why I'm glad you're all here to help make Midge's room welcoming."

"Oh yes." Aunt Doreen rested a hand on the first banister. "Would you like to see it before we get to work?"

"Please!" Sally moved forward. "We've never really seen the inside of this house, you know."

"It's beautiful," Amanda breathed. "Even if I lived in a regular house instead of a soddy, I'd still think this one was special."

"Yes." Clara followed everyone up the stairs, her gaze lingering on the small details carved in the banister. *Special because it represents a home we can be proud of, a way to support ourselves, an end to the searching and struggling. All it takes is one of these girls marrying Dr. Reed. . . .*

She pushed back the thought that her new

friends weren't surveying the house out of polite interest or idle curiosity—it was only reasonable to assume that Dr. Reed's wife would become mistress of the home. Though Clara disliked the idea, she misled them by not directly admitting her bargain. The deal was to be held in strict confidence between herself and Mr. Reed.

Besides, any girl who married Dr. Reed might well expect to go back to Baltimore or to help him build a home and a practice here in Buttonwood. There's no use making assumptions.

While the girls admired the spacious room and carefully selected furniture, listening as Aunt Doreen explained the projects planned for the day, Clara reminded herself that Dr. Reed would build a fine house for his bride. She needn't worry about him providing for his family.

An odd clenching sensation in her stomach sent her back to the kitchen for a drink of water. The rumbling of footsteps coming downstairs gave her enough time to smile before everyone appeared.

"Look at all this space!" Opal hung back at the door, taking it in.

"Perfect for baking." Amanda ran her hand lovingly across the worktable. "Though I'd keep the pie tins below with the pots. . . ."

"It was arranged differently before we arrived." Clara rested her hand protectively atop the shelf, where she'd placed the pie tins beside the measuring cups.

"*Arranged* might be a kinder word than strictly truthful," Aunt Doreen admitted with a smile. "But

I've never seen a finer kitchen."

Clara noted the speculative glance on Amanda's face as she eyed the worktable anew, as well as the curiosity behind Sally's fascination with the expensively carved hutch. One of these girls could be the way she'd succeed.

Her gaze returned to Aunt Doreen. *Then you'll never have to leave this kitchen.*

CHAPTER 13

"Good morning," Saul greeted the older Speck brother as he wandered into the store just before noon. "What can I get you?"

Elroy meandered about for a while before selecting a spade and some lard. By the time Saul finished the transaction, Matthew Burn strode into the store. While they pored over a catalog, choosing a new leather apron for the young blacksmith, the Speck boy lingered. Not one to make assumptions, Saul decided Elroy must be waiting to meet someone. But who?

"Yep, Doc." Matthew thumped the ad with a work-roughened hand as he chose the largest apron available. "That one."

"A fine choice." Saul wrote up the order for Burn. "The leather should offer excellent protection."

When Larry Grogan sauntered in, the store went from busy to crowded. Too crowded. Instead of backing out to let Speck pass or moving out to return later, Larry blustered inside as far as he could. Eyes slid to slits as Elroy sized up the invading Grogan.

Granted, Saul couldn't claim an overabundance of experience in feuds or fights of any kind, but common sense revealed Larry's mistakes. What man, unprovoked, strutted up to a long-standing adversary, ignored his only exit, turned to cut himself off from it, and trapped himself between the two counters of a general store filled with an abundance of sharp and breakable items?

Saul already moved from behind the counter, ready to minimize the damage as best he could, when the bell over the door clanged again.

Nathan Fosset assessed the situation at a glance. "If you're about to get into it, go outside."

"He's not." Adam Grogan bypassed Fosset, fisted his hand around his brother's collar, and jerked him backward. "Larry's got things to tend to at home."

"I'm just going to check on Willa," the whelp whined, pulling away from his older brother. "And maybe stay for lunch, if the ladies ask me to."

Ah, that's his plan. Saul swallowed a grin when Elroy became very interested in his boots. It looked like Larry wasn't the only one angling for an invitation to lunch with the town's marriageable ladies. Of the men in town, they'd all know since their sisters made up part of the group. Which meant Fosset probably didn't have an urgent need for that coffee he stared at so blankly.

"What ladies?" Suspicion colored the blacksmith's tone. "What lunch?"

Adam looked around the store at the assorted

bachelors, giving Saul the missing piece. "He's the only one who doesn't have a sister."

"Some of the ladies in town, including all of the sisters of these good fellows"—Saul made a wide gesture—"generously agreed to spend the day helping Miss Field and Mrs. Edgerly prepare a room for Midge, who will be arriving on the next stage."

"The orphan," Larry muttered.

"The young girl I've taken as my ward," Saul corrected. There was to be no mistake—everyone would treat Midge with respect, not pity. "The women are sewing and such forth at my father's house today."

"All of them?" Burn's eyes were wide as he processed this. "Miss Fosset, Miss Speck, Miss Grogan, and Miss Dunstall, all over with Miss Field?"

Elroy gave a brief nod. "Yep."

"With Mrs. Edgerly," Saul added to be fair.

"So you all showed up around noon." Burn's eyes narrowed as he looked at the men around him. "You didn't even tell me?" This last he gave in a loud whisper to Nathan Fosset, who Saul assumed to be a close friend.

Nathan managed an unrepentant shrug before pinning his gaze on Saul. "Guess we've been caught hoping for an invite, Dr. Reed."

Embarrassment gave way to purpose as heads came up, shoulders went back, and jaws squared. Every bachelor in Buttonwood eyed Saul as Larry gave voice to the challenge in the air. "So what do you say?"

~~~◈~~~

"The more, the merrier." Clara could hardly believe her good fortune.

"Are you sure?" Mrs. Dunstall set down the pan nervously. "I only meant to bring by the raisin bread, not stay for lunch."

"You've said yourself the diner's not seen a customer since Dr. Reed arrived," Clara reminded her. A striking young widow of only thirty-one years, Mrs. Dunstall had married and borne Amanda very young, which left her in the ranks of eligible women for Dr. Reed. This golden opportunity wouldn't slide out of Clara's hands. The more women, the better. "We'd be more than happy to have you at the table! Please join us."

"I suppose it wouldn't hurt." A smile spread across Vanessa Dunstall's face. "Let me run back to the café and bank the fire."

"Absolutely." Clara returned to the parlor, where the newly repatched quilt lay folded on a table and the women worked on a matching sham. "How goes the project?"

Aunt Doreen sifted through the remaining squares. "We'll need more yellow and green fabric. Would it be any trouble to pick out a little when you fetch Saul for dinner?"

"I'll come with you!" Sally stuck her needle in her corner of the quilting and rose to her feet. "It'll be a good chance for me to look over the fabric in stock anyway."

"The same thought crossed my mind," Amanda admitted.

168

"That tea set cries out for a tablecloth," Opal added. "If we can add that to the list. . ."

"And napkins to match!" Willa's shy smile blossomed. "I could help pick out the material, if you want."

Every one of them wants to fetch Dr. Reed and catch his eye. It's working!

"All of you go." Aunt Doreen made shooing motions. "Dinner's all ready, and I can put it on the table. Bring back what we need, and we'll enjoy a nice meal."

"Vanessa Dunstall will be by in a moment to join us," Clara announced. "She brought raisin bread."

"Ma's raisin bread could make a stubborn mule behave," Amanda promised. "You'll love it."

"Would it work on a stubborn ox?" Thoughts of glove-eating Simon danced in Clara's mind as she led the troop of girls to the store.

Her small flock of women patted their hair, angled their bonnets, dusted tiny specks of lint from their bodices, and studiously avoided any damp spots in the street as they made their way to the shop. Their obvious preening told Clara more clearly than any words could that any one of her friends would be happy to marry Dr. Reed. Each woman would make a good wife.

Distracted by the thought, Clara opened the door to the shop before realizing she'd never seen it so full. . .

Of men. Tension crackled in the place.

"Elroy?" Opal moved past her to stare at her

brother. "What are you doing here?"

"Larry?" Willa slid over to implore her brother. "You're not causing trouble?"

Clara shot Dr. Reed a pleading glance. Hostilities between the Specks and Grogans couldn't erupt now—not when Willa and Opal were getting along, and especially not when she was so close to pulling off this crucial luncheon!

"We were having such a nice day," Sally fretted, drawing close to Matthew Burn and looking up at him through her lashes.

"They won't ruin it, miss." Mr. Burn puffed out his barrel chest and lowered his voice. "I won't let them."

"Neither will I." Nathan Fosset moved to stand in Willa's line of vision. "Don't you worry, Miss Grogan."

"Larry's on his way back to the farm." Adam Grogan's gaze found Opal's and held fast, a silent promise not to double-team her brother even Clara could read.

"We have things well in hand," Elroy Speck directed his assurances to Amanda.

Just like that, Clara watched every young woman she'd rounded up for Saul's selection be claimed by a Buttonwood bachelor. Admiring glances flew in coy exchanges across the store. Men cleared their throats and straightened their posture while the girls patted their hair and smoothed their skirts. They paired up as though facing the gangplank to Noah's ark.

No. No, I can salvage this. Clara's thoughts raced

past the avoided fight, the almost catastrophic interlude unraveling before her very eyes, and straight to the one stronghold in her plan. *Dinner*. Just Saul and the ladies and *no other men*.

"Your assistance was greatly appreciated, gentleman." She spoke loudly enough to garner everyone's attention. "I'm afraid the store must close for a brief while. We came to tell Dr. Reed it's time for dinner."

"Dinner does sound good." One of the men put a hand over his abdomen, and several swiftly followed suit.

"Had they known there'd be such an"—Dr. Reed glanced around, obviously taking note of the same things she had—"influx of business, the women would have been glad to make extra food and invite everyone. As it stands, there surely won't be enough for so many strapping men."

"No." Clara fought to look regretful of the fact. "I'm afraid not, gentlemen."

"I reckon I'll go to the café." Elroy Speck's tone matched his hangdog look, which should have made Amanda bristle at the implied insult.

"Oh, you can't!" A wide smile spread across her face. "Ma's joining us for dinner. Isn't that right, Miss Field?" She didn't wait for Clara to answer before adding excitedly, "We keep extra food on hand and can rustle things up really fast when needed. With Ma's help, we'll be able to have everyone over."

A chorus of eager agreement sounded from the men—sung in round by the women, who seconded the "fine idea."

Clara searched desperately for a way to veto the suggestion. "Such a generous suggestion, Amanda, and I know you don't mind the trouble"—she paused while every one of her potential matches promised to help in the kitchen—"but we can't take the business away from your mother's café like that if these men planned to be paying customers."

She relaxed at the remorse on the faces surrounding her as they took that into account. By hook or by crook, she'd get things done, and business was the one thing she could fall back on as an excuse.

"Oh, I'll gladly pony up for a fine meal and better company." Matthew Burn stepped forward. "There's no reason for Mrs. Dunstall to miss dinner with her friends or the business to her café if we can bring them together."

"Couldn't have said it better m'self." Nathan Fosset nodded.

"My brother and I will pass, if it's all the same. We've got a lot of work on the farm." Adam Grogan, the one who'd rode up late that first Sunday and told her and Opal to move, caught his troublemaking brother by the arm.

"Surely you can stomach a meal with a Speck, Adam Grogan?" Opal's voice held quiet determination. "Your sister's strong enough to be civil."

Adam froze, his grip tightening on his brother's sleeve as Larry tried to whirl around. "Go." He shoved Larry out the door. "Tell Ma I'm staying to have dinner with Willa while you see to things at home." Only after Larry stomped off did he turn around and give Opal a quirked smile. "We'll see what I can stomach."

"Two Specks, two Grogans, one big meal." Opal seemed to belatedly realize she'd taken the arrangements for granted. "If it's all right by you, Dr. Reed?"

"So long as Mrs. Dunstall doesn't mind." Dr. Reed's approval brought smiles all around. . . .

Except for Clara. No sense trying to deny it— she'd be eating her plans for lunch.

"That worked out well," Saul commented to Miss Field as everyone headed toward his father's house, arms laden with dishes from the diner.

A strangled sound came from her throat, causing him to look at her in concern. Dad's talk about how the woman wouldn't be one to admit to feeling poorly flashed through his mind. "What's wrong?"

"Oh, nothing." She stayed back while everyone tromped through the mud room and into the house. "My throat went dry for a moment. I'll be sure to drink some water."

"With Mrs. Dunstall adding to the meal, and the other women helping, you should take a moment to rest." He held the door for her. "Since you've done so much to arrange everything."

"How could I let my invited guests work in the kitchen while I laze about?" She shot him an incredulous look.

"Mrs. Dunstall will be reimbursed for her

efforts," Saul pointed out. "Besides, only so many women can cook in a single kitchen."

"I'll be one of them. In addition to which"— she lowered her voice and leaned toward him, green eyes snapping—"I invited Mrs. Dunstall. Her willingness to work on what was meant to be a respite is a favor. I'll come alongside her."

An unsettling suspicion wormed its way into his thoughts. "Miss Field," he, too, spoke quietly, as if the loud group spread out in the parlor and kitchen would overhear them, "would you have preferred I sent the men home?"

"I'd rather have kept the day simple." The admission cost her a bit of resolve. "But there weren't many options."

"They were rather determined." Saul chuckled. "I couldn't see any other way to earn Mrs. Dunstall some much-needed business and keep myself and my father's store in good standing with all those gentlemen. Dinner seemed the easy way to avoid ugliness between the feuding families and also set up a happy arrival for Midge this next week."

"You're right." She moved past him to the doorway. "If you could make a special effort to let the women know you appreciate all they've done, it would be wise."

"Of course." Saul went to join the men as she disappeared around the corner.

"Nice place your father built here, Saul." Matthew Burn, the one man Saul knew from childhood, steered the conversation to deeper waters. "He built it hoping you'd come set up your practice in Buttonwood and fill the place with grandbabies to dandle on his knee."

"Dad knew what he gave up when he left Baltimore." Regret tugged at his heart, and resentment boiled from his stomach as Saul made his decision clear. "I've a practice to finish setting up and plans for back home."

"I'm not sure he's convinced." Burn shrugged. "I offered to buy the place if he was interested in selling, but he turned me down flat."

Nathan Fosset goaded his friend. "Looking to settle down, eh, Burn?"

"Don't spit in the wind, Fosset," Adam Grogan spoke up from where he leaned on the mantel. "You pushed for an invite to lunch with the ladies, too." Ignoring the dirty looks cast his way by a few other bachelors, he directed his next statement to Saul. "Doc, you could do plenty of good here. You traveled the trail and saw the graves. Wagon trains come all through late spring and summer with everything from ailments to epidemics. We've been all right so far, God be praised, but the day can't be far off when Buttonwood's gonna need a doctor."

"My decision stands, gentlemen." Saul wouldn't discuss the matter any further. The poor of Baltimore lacked medical care just as much as the pioneers traveling West, who'd chosen the treacherous trail. Hannah and his niece or nephew-to-be lived in the city.

Then, too, he'd promised Midge they'd return, and he wouldn't rob her of the scant comfort of familiarity. She'd go to school close enough so he could visit her regularly. No, his resolve couldn't be frittered away like dust on a breeze. They'd return to Baltimore, as he planned.

My jaw hurts. Clara raised a hand to rub the soreness before she resumed brushing her hair. Gnashing may be too strong a term, but she'd ground her teeth all through dinner yesterday and beyond. Otherwise, the smile dropped from her lips, and she couldn't explain her frustration over what seemed such a *successful* gathering.

Successful. Clara didn't consider herself the sort to dwell on unpleasant matters, but there came a time when every woman needed to reevaluate. She thrust her hairbrush back on the bureau hard enough to make a dull thud. The loose bun she'd worn at breakfast proved too loose, so she settled on a strict style. Clara divided her unruly golden waves into sections, twisting them with short, hard jerks into a tidy French braid. If only she could direct Dr. Reed as easily as she ordered her hair. After tying off the end with a jaunty blue ribbon that would peek from beneath her bonnet, she set about buttoning her shoes.

A perfect plan. Dr. Reed enjoying a fine meal with four—five, with Mrs. Dunstall joining them—prospective brides the day before the whole town would go to the Fossets' for threshing. He'd get to know the ladies one day, have the opportunity to see them among the community next, and with each visit he'd grow more involved until he settled on one. Having five unmarried women at the table with one bachelor was the marital equivalent of trying to hit the broadside of a barn.

What Clara presumed impossible turned out to be merely improbable. Not only could the plan miss, so to speak, but it also backfired spectacularly. How else could she explain hosting the most successful matchmaking meal ever seen in the Nebraska Territory? Not one of her friends, sweet young maidens all, caught Dr. Reed's eye, while focusing instead on the town bachelors.

Dr. Reed, unlike the other men, seemed no closer to courting any of the women. The thought of her failure made her swipe at her nails until the buffer squeaked and her fingertips glowed.

With a deep breath and a prayer for patience, she left the room to join Aunt Doreen, who'd been wrapping a loaf of bread, a plate of biscuits, and a bowl of sweet potato pudding to take to the threshing today. The Fossets would provide the heartier fare, and the women in the town would help cook it once they arrived, but baking took more time and finesse than the occasion allowed.

"If you're both ready, the wagon's waiting outside." Dr. Reed ducked inside, the open door revealing early morning's shy glow.

With her cloak snug around her shoulders and the pudding bowl in her arms, Clara followed Dr. Reed to the wagon. She settled in the back with her aunt, cushioned by old blankets and surrounded by dishes.

A cleverly designed saddlebag, unhooked from

its accompanying harness, rested beside them. Clara knew from Dr. Reed's descriptions that it held his medical instruments and powders in small compartments that would fold out when needed. Sturdy brown leather and the ability to convert from portable bag to weatherproof saddlebag made its versatility unmatchable.

He'd paid the princely sum of twelve dollars for the convenience of his unconventional "little black bag"—a detail Clara needed to work into the conversation among the women of the town to underscore how well Dr. Reed would provide for his family. Discussing financial details bordered on vulgarity, but Clara was in no position to overlook any marital incentive when it came to finding Dr. Reed a wife.

They pulled to a stop near the Fosset house, where other wagons dotted the area. Women in full skirts flocked to the house with hurried steps, eager greetings, and home-baked goods. Small children raced around a hastily fenced-in yard. Others played jacks and took turns with hoops. The men gathered in clumps around the farm—some loading a deep wagon with loose sheaves of cut grain, most working to connect heavy iron tumbling rods or set up wooden sweeps to harness the horses who'd power the thresher all day. Frost softened to dew sparkling in the sun, leaving the farmers and helpful tradesmen to do the day's work without interference.

As Clara reached back into the wagon for one of the dishes, she noticed Sally and Opal heading toward the wagon. Toward Dr. Reed. Her first real smile of the day teased the corners of her mouth.

Another day, another chance to repay Mr. Reed's kindness and secure Aunt Doreen's future.

CHAPTER 14

"Glad to see you, Dr. Reed." Nathan Fosset clapped him on the shoulder. "Today we'll return a little of your hospitality."

"I don't recall making you work for your dinner." Saul grinned to take the bite from his words.

"Depends on what you call work." Adam Grogan strode up to join them. "They danced around the issue long enough to work up a sweat."

"You shouldn't be so keen to talk about dancing." Fosset's gaze held a glint of anger. "The way you and the Specks've been circling each other, I expect to see buzzards on the horizon."

"Mind you don't stir things up," Saul broke in.

"We all enjoyed dinner yesterday." Elroy Speck gave a nonchalant shrug. "I see no reason to forget that."

A short nod was all the approval he needed from Adam. Anything the Specks and Grogans agreed on put the other party squarely in the wrong.

"Right," Fosset muttered.

"We've got the power set up," Matthew Burn announced, gesturing toward where his father hitched the horses to the cylinder. "Band-cutting tables are hooked to the separator, and the straw carrier's ready. As soon as the horses set up a rhythm and everyone's in position, we'll be in business."

As one, they headed for their stations. Frank Fosset hopped atop the power, giving the cry of "Teams on!" The horses began to move, sending the rods tumbling with dull clangs like blunt wind chimes. Individual teeth in the thresher awoke and stretched, hastening until they became a steel blur keeping time to the cylinder's constant hum.

Saul, who'd never before seen the process, waited to relieve one of the men who sacked the threshed grain. Free to observe, he drank in the scene, reveling in its unexpected complexity. So many men performing various steps, all working in harmony to complete one job. He'd never seen anything close to it in the city.

Workers stood atop wagons filled with hay, forking bundles onto the band-cutting tables, where the burly Burn scooped the sheaves. One swift, graceful motion sliced the band and unrolled the wheat into an even belt entering the maw of the machine. This kept on in a constant course of cooperation, underscored by the whir of the power and the smothered snarl of the separator itself.

Saul heard both from where he stood. The strong yellow stalks entered the machine, where metal teeth ripped and slashed, spewing straw and chaff into the air for two younger boys to rake into some semblance of order. The pieces drifted everywhere, tickling noses and scratching beneath collars. Saul couldn't imagine trying to stack the itchy stuff.

All of this work, in addition to the plowing, sowing, and harvesting that came before the threshing, for something he'd taken for granted all his life. Saul watched as the threshed grain came pouring out of the machine, filling sack after sack, which were put to the side to be sewn shut. This would later be ground into flour to make bread. *So much work, and I never appreciated any of it.*

The time for mulling it over soon passed, and his arms and back soon appreciated just how much work threshing took. He hefted bag after bag of grain under the hot sun, breathing in the smell of his own sweat, the prairie dust, and the heady quality of the fresh grain. There weren't words to describe the grain, exactly, though it had an earthy feel much like some nuts and a hint of tang that made for good biscuits, but Saul would recognize it the rest of his life. The steady rhythm, sound, smell, and movement meshed into a smear of exertion until the gears ground to a halt.

Dinnertime. After the parson said grace, Saul headed for one of the metal tubs set out as washbasins for the men, choosing a far one that stood in the shade of the barn. He reached it first. The cool water closed over his arms, so refreshing that Saul followed the lead of other workers and dipped his head beneath the surface. Sliding down his face, dripping down the back of his neck, the water provided instant relief from the heat.

Saul mopped it up with his bandanna, finger-combing his hair before putting his hat back on. He surrendered the basin to the next man, moving to take a drink from the smaller bucket and lingering in the shade a moment more. The moisture trickled past his parched lips, a measure of coolness he felt clear down to his stomach, which gave a loud roar.

By the time he reached the tables of food, he brought up the rear. A second growl chided him for waiting in the shade, but Saul ignored it. He turned to move to the back of the line and just about ran into Miss Field. How a man could do that when she looked so fresh and pretty in her soft-blue dress, Saul didn't know, but he caught himself by placing his hands on her shoulders.

She stared at him, silent, with wide eyes.

"Miss Field?" When she still didn't speak, worry jolted through him. "Is something wrong?"

Clara almost walked right past Dr. Reed. The man barely resembled the man she sought, and then only in his face.

No, Dr. Reed wore dark slacks, a matching vest with pocket watch fob, a well-cut jacket, and collared shirt. On Sundays he added a silk tie. He stood a bit taller than other men without making one feel awkward, his dark eyes kind beneath severely parted hair that rarely strayed out of place.

This man, on the other hand, wore no jacket. No somber vest constrained his strength. A cotton shirt, sleeves rolled up and collar slightly unbuttoned, stretched across shoulders far broader than Clara recalled. His time in Buttonwood lent golden color to his skin, and for the first time, his hair kissed his brow in a bid for freedom.

When her hand moved to brush it beneath the brim of his hat, Clara fisted her fingers and moved her gaze away from his face, staring fixedly at her own eye level to regain composure. Unfortunately, her eye level reached the base of his throat, exposed by the two undone buttons of his shirt. The sun lavished radiance on a lone drop of water clinging to his collarbone.

The words caught in her throat as that droplet winked at her, the heat of his hands on her shoulders spreading down her spine. She watched in fascination as his Adam's apple moved, and the rumble of his voice washed over her.

"Is something wrong?"

You look different. She kept the thought to herself, not through any prudent decision but because her mouth wouldn't form words. A dry swallow didn't loosen her tongue, but the weight of his gaze made her flush with embarrassment.

"Is the heat bothering you?" He ran the backs of his fingers over her forehead and down her cheek, the light pressure making her tingle with intensity.

"Yes," she managed to croak over her own mortification. "It is overly warm."

"Let's sit you down." He tucked her arm into the crook of his and steered her toward the leafy cover of the cottonwood tree.

Since that's where Aunt Doreen and all the girls waited for her to bring Dr. Reed so he could sample their cooking, Clara didn't protest. The area beneath the tree cooled her hot cheeks, and she hoped her blush faded as she sank to the grass near her friends. She kept her head bowed, waiting for everyone to distract him while she regained her composure.

"The heat's gotten to her."

"Clara, are you all right?" Aunt Doreen's concern prompted her to give a nod, but it seemed she wouldn't escape further scrutiny.

Dr. Reed hunkered down beside her, one large hand reaching beneath her chin to tug the ties of her sunbonnet. He ignored her muffled squeak of objection but used her surprised movement to glide the bonnet off completely. Its ribbons danced in a breeze she barely felt as Aunt Doreen put it to the side.

"Is that water?" He spoke as he reached for a mug, the cotton of his shirt brushing her hair and sending shivers dancing across the back of her neck. "Drink this." His grasp folded over hers.

She swallowed every drop before registering he'd given her a command, not a kind offer of refreshment. Dr. Reed didn't look after her as a gentleman concerning himself with a lady's comfort but with the determination of a physician caring for a patient. Curiosity surged to replace awkwardness as Clara considered the difference.

He let go of the cup and continued to study her.

"Thank you." She turned the empty cup in her

hands. "I feel much better."

"Any dizziness?" The intensity of his gaze made her breath hitch for a moment. "Shortness of breath?"

A wry smile tilted her lips as she shook her head. "I'm quite recovered. There's no need for agitation any longer."

"Let me be the judge of that." Words that might have made her bristle came with no browbeating, only determined humor. "You'll eat something before I'm persuaded."

"I'll get something light to start, along with more water." Amanda took the cup and left.

"You took on too much." Opal rested beside her. "There wasn't any need to take Mrs. Warren's turn at the cookfire just after your own."

"Her babe needed attention," Clara pointed out. "I'm fine now, thanks to Dr. Reed's swift treatment." She made sure to fix in everyone's minds how thoughtful he'd been. It didn't take much to see what a considerate husband he'd make.

"Honestly, I don't know how you men work the thresher for hours on end with the sun beating down on you." Clara noticed Sally eyeing Dr. Reed's shoulders and knew her comment had succeeded in drawing attention not only away from her little difficulty but also toward Dr. Reed's manly contribution to the day's work.

"We don't battle the constrictions of women's fashions." His response alluded to the corsets they all wore, tightening their lungs and shortening their breaths. Thankfully, he'd too many manners to humiliate them by mentioning them directly. "Heatstroke is a threat to be taken seriously by all."

"After so much hard work, you deserve a hearty meal." Willa passed him a plate heaped with food.

"Thank you." Dr. Reed accepted it and looked around. "Where are your plates?"

"The men eat first. We go after, since we've had the opportunity to taste all morning." Sally handed him a fork. "We knew the others would storm the tables, and since this is your first threshing, we wanted to be sure you got some of everything. You're the only one who doesn't have anything to gain by being here today."

"I wouldn't say that." He started to eat. "The Burns don't have a farm for folks to return the help, nor do the Dunstalls."

"No, but the Burns repair the thresher and shoe the horses and take part in the community same as everyone else," Opal reminded.

"And everyone pitched in to build our café." Amanda said as she returned with the water and gave it to Clara. "Were they telling you why we saved you a plate?"

"Yes." Dr. Reed smiled at everyone. "I'm so glad you did. Ladies, I've never enjoyed a meal more."

"Good." Clara handed him the water. "Let there be many more."

CHAPTER 15

"Y ou gotta stop hoggin' the ladies, Doc." Larry Grogan's nasal tones invaded their haven scant moments before he plunked down beside Miss Field with an overblown grin.

"He does no such thing." Her indignation made her fine brows beetle slightly. With her chin raised, clear green eyes flashing, Miss Field made up for Larry's irritation. "Dr. Reed merely sought to help when I didn't feel well." A faint hint of rose swept her cheeks at the admission of her own weakness.

Dad's assessment of Miss Field's reluctance to let anyone trouble himself over her couldn't prove more accurate. Here she sat, moments after suffering from the heat, rising to his defense like a mythical Valkyrie. Dappled sunlight flirted through the leaves to gleam in the gold of her hair.

"Grogan's words may be blunt as a mallet," Matthew Burn settled next to Miss Fosset, carefully balancing two plates as he spoke, "but you can't fault him for wanting to join you." What Saul assumed to be fodder for the blacksmith's huge frame turned out to be pure cunning. His old acquaintance silently held out one of the plates, along with a fork, to Miss Fosset.

"Thank you, Mr. Burn." She accepted the offering with a delighted smile. "How thoughtful!"

Saul smothered his amusement as he watched the fallout of Matthew's courting. Miss Dunstall and Miss Grogan both gave small sighs at the gesture, which didn't go unnoticed by the two other bachelors approaching their group. Nathan Fosset and Elroy Speck, each holding only one plate, headed back to the tables to rectify their mistake.

Most interesting, though, was the reaction of his fellow observer, Miss Field. She watched the entire proceedings first with an obvious air of approval at Matthew's gesture then apparent disgust at Larry's gaping mouth. These swiftly faded to a soft look of seeming wistful disbelief warring with frustration.

Two facets captured his curiosity. Could the wistful shine be a longing for a sweetheart of her own? He'd not seen her encourage any man's interest. And that hint of frustration he glimpsed, so uncharacteristic from what he'd seen, could only be ascribed to Larry's intrusion. Even as he deciphered the expression, her eyes changed again, slanting a concerned glance toward Miss Speck.

The only one of Miss Field's friends not to have a steady admirer present, Miss Speck would be left to fetch her own plate. With the problem pinpointed, Saul immediately stood up.

"Miss Speck, I plan to claim another biscuit and some of that honey if there's any left. Is it true your family cultivates it?"

"Yes." A smile flitted across her face, transforming her for a brief moment. "I keep the bees."

"Fascinating. Would you accompany me to the tables and tell me about it?" Saul didn't miss the pleased look on Miss Field's face as he extended the invitation to her friend.

"Certainly."

From there, the respite of lunch passed quickly. Saul stood at the thresher once more, now in the heat of the afternoon with the weight of a full belly. His muscles groaned until he found the rhythm again. Fill, close, haul, repeat, all to the steady drone of the machine. Everyone moved to the same pulse, shifting and pulling in a seamless pattern as hours melded to bushels filled.

When the golden brown tones of grain turned darker, the metal chutes glowing orange then blue, everything scraped to a halt. The final bag held more air than grain, and Saul asked if he should put it aside for tomorrow.

"That's it." Nathan Fosset slumped on a stack of sacks sewn shut. "We didn't just quit for sundown. We're finished. Since we raise oxen, we grow more in the way of corn for fodder and silage than we do grain."

Saul trudged to the washbasin before supper, cleaned up, thanked God for the meal and the parson for a short blessing, and sank onto the nearest bench with a plate full of whatever had been within reach. No one spared the energy to talk, focusing solely on the food.

After the first plate, Saul's aching muscles had gone blissfully numb. He helped himself to a mug of coffee strong enough to fell an ox, downed it in two swallows, and filled it again before going back to refill his plate. Only now could he appreciate what the women worked on all day.

Every man in town had already gobbled several heaping plates worth of food today, and these tables still swelled with bounty. Fried chicken, roast duck, ham hocks, beef stew, thick gravy, and platters of chops filled one makeshift table. Another bore biscuits, rolls, sliced sourdough, cornbread, and more salads than he could describe, from potato to coleslaw. The final stand held pies, cookies, puddings, and cakes to tempt any appetite.

Saul drained the coffee again, revitalized and ready to enjoy this fine cooking instead of bolting it down. He helped himself to another plateful and refilled his mug before swiping an empty seat next to Adam Grogan.

"You put in a hard day's work," the farmer commented between bites of his own feast.

"Everyone did."

"This is different work than you're used to." Adam's gaze held respect. "And nothing you profit by."

"I'm glad to help."

"Are you handy with a needle?"

"Are you injured?"

"No. Old Mr. Doane's slower than he was last

year, and we've got a lot of sacks to sew shut before we leave." A grin stretched across Adam's face. "Think you can ply a needle through burlap?"

"Figures you'd be trying to arrange a sewing contest, Adam." Scorn dripped from Larry's tone as he addressed his older brother.

Saul itched to teach him some respect. He left Adam to handle his own business, as he'd more than proved himself capable of reigning in his scoundrel of a sibling.

"Sewing takes a great deal of skill." Miss Field shot Larry a look of reproof. "After a long day of threshing, your brother and Dr. Reed are to be admired for volunteering to work into the night."

Several girls sent both of them appreciative glances to punctuate that statement then turned expectantly toward the men with whom they'd shared lunch.

Saul shifted uncomfortably.

"I don't know what Larry's thinking, making knuckleheaded comments like that." Matthew Burn held up his ham-sized hands. "Needles seem to stick in all the wrong places, if you ask me, but I'm game to try."

"He probably doesn't want to compete." The jeer came from Elroy Speck, who hastened to add, "I won't back away from the challenge."

"The more of you who sign on, the fewer bags left for me to stitch shut." Fosset grinned at his lessening workload but spared a grimace for Larry.

"I never said I wouldn't do it," Larry muttered the words but maintained a mutinous scowl. "Contest usually means there's a prize for the winner."

"Shut your mouth and listen to my father's announcement," Nathan Fosset warned, "before you say something even more foolish."

Frank Fosset stood before the wall of the barn, a large fire casting his shadow into prominence over the sacks of grain, the two looped off corners of each bag sticking out like a set of cow's ears. "You all know we got to such a pace today we fell behind sewing the bags shut. For those interested, we're fixing to have a contest to see what man can sew 'em off the fastest."

"What's the winner get, Pa?" Nathan hollered the question, shooting a smug glance at Larry. Silence fell as the entire town awaited the answer.

"The team, and yes, I said team—one man to stitch the bags, one man to haul 'em to the barn— that does the most earns a summertime treat from my daughter, Sally. The very last of our stockpiled ice from last winter will make ice cream for those hardworking men, to be enjoyed fresh at the next threshing."

His stomach might not be able to hold another bite right now, but Saul knew without a doubt that come noon the next time he worked a threshing, he'd want that prize. He wouldn't have thought anyone had an icehouse. And even if someone did, every last shard usually vanished by August.

Just imagining the sweet coldness sliding down his throat, a welcome relief after inhaling scratchy bits of hay and grain dust all day, practically made his mouth water. He looked around for a partner and found Matthew's eyebrows raised.

Saul gave a nod. His stitches would save Burn his clumsy jabs with the needle, while Matt's strength would spare Saul from hauling the sacks to the barn. A slow smile spread across his face as he gauged the other teams. There was nothing like a little rivalry to bring out the best in a man.

So many men couldn't compete without things getting ugly. Clara suppressed a groan as squabbles over partners broke out, followed hard with bickering over who would sew and who would carry.

"You take the haulin'," Larry directed his brother. His obvious attempt to squirm out of the heavy lifting, particularly after his derision of sewing, made Clara turn away.

"I'm rooting for Matthew," Sally confided. Color bloomed high on her cheeks as she looked at the young blacksmith, who spoke with Dr. Reed. "Even when he's not threshing, he spends the day beside a blasting furnace. If anyone deserves some ice cream, it's one of the Burns."

"I see." Clara didn't need to mention that Matthew's father and brother made up a separate team. After witnessing the fledgling couple over lunch for two days in a row, she saw how the wind blew.

Though she hated to lower her own odds of success, Clara no longer listed Sally among Dr. Reed's prospective brides. A wedding loomed large in her friend's future, but it would be a matter strictly between bride and groom in that case. No house would make Clara stand in the way of Sally's happiness.

Which made it a blessing the two men formed a team. "I'll be cheering them on, as well." She'd encourage Matthew and Sally's budding romance but expected the focus of this contest to fall on Dr. Reed. Outdoing every other man in town would go a long way toward recapturing the attention of the remaining ladies.

After his kindness to her this afternoon, Clara would have cheered him on even if there were no bargain. He'd put in a hot morning's work then focused on taking care of her. Sally was wrong. If any man in town deserved a treat, it was Dr. Reed. Clara craned her neck as the teams took their places.

The "haulers" stood next to the stash of bags, each one loosely wound shut with twine. Any dropped sack resulted in a penalty. Any lost grain cost the team two sacks from their final count. The "threaders" sat on benches arranged horseshoelike around a jumping fire so they could see what they worked on.

At the call of "Ready. . ." the whole town caught its breath, causing a stillness broken only by the pop of the fire, until "Go!" made the men spring into action. The haulers grabbed sacks, moving them to the threaders as fast as they could.

The weakest lifted their bags like large children, clasping them to their chests and waddling forward to deposit them before their teammates. Others scooped the sacks up, using their arms like shovels to get the job done. Some swung a sack under each of their arms and hustled toward the fire as though ready to knock down anyone in their paths. These men moved the fastest and grabbed the most sacks, but they dropped the most, too.

Clara processed all this scrambling, cheering along with everyone else, but swiftly turned her attention to Dr. Reed. Sitting on the end of one of the benches, boots planted firmly against the ground and a sack of grain braced between them, he looked to have a good start.

The firelight flickered reddish orange over his shirt, lending his skin a golden cast as he deftly threaded the large needle, knotted the end, and pinched the edges of the sack. Concentration furrowed his brow, bringing his hat down to block his eyes from her view as he pushed the needle through the burlap. He moved with grace, skill, and careful expertise.

Slowly.

Shaking her head, Clara looked again to be sure. Dr. Reed eased the blunt needle through the rough weave of the burlap as though expecting more resistance from the fabric. As though time didn't concern him and this wasn't a competition. As though precision mattered more than finishing and a neat row of stitches held importance.

Understanding flooded her. He stitched like a doctor suturing a wound. Others moved on to bags four or five, and her chosen contestant finally looked up after accomplishing his first. Shock flitted across his features as he witnessed the burlap butchery practiced by the other contestants, who jabbed their needles in and out without bothering to pull the thread taut or attempt any semblance of straight stitches.

Only intense pressure from her teeth sinking into her lip kept Clara's giggles from spilling out as she took in the scene. Matthew, the only man to master the fine art of carrying three bags at once—one over each shoulder but both held at the base of his neck with one hand, and a third sack slumped in his free arm, had all but built a fort around Dr. Reed. Only the area before him, needed for the firelight, remained open.

Beyond the makeshift structure, the elbows jabbed the air and needles punched through bags as though chasing personal vendettas. Haulers shifted from claiming more sacks for their teams to piling sewn bags in the barn, smirking at Matthew as he cradled the sole mark on his tally sheet and made his way to the barn.

Her smile faded at those smirks. Matthew toted more bags than any one of those men, and while Dr. Reed lacked speed, he did a fine job. Were she to purchase a bag of grain, she'd choose his over any other, certain no bugs would have wormed their ways inside between slapdash stitches.

Clara noticed she wasn't the only one to resent those smug glances. Dr. Reed took the next sack, readied his needle, and tipped off his hat. He pointedly set it atop the vast mound of bags Matthew earmarked for him and fell to stitching with renewed vigor.

His moves became sharper, less fluid. The stitches lengthened but remained strong and rigid as he thrust the needle in and out in a more steady rhythm. Gaze unwavering in the dancing light, he tied off the sack and reached for the next. He still made more stitches per bag than any other man, and kept them firmer and more even, yet Dr. Reed exhibited great determination.

"You can do it, Matthew!" Sally cheered loudly as Mr. Burn hefted another bag.

He gave her a saucy wink as he toted it toward the barn, a hint of a strut in his step as Saul's sewing steadily caught them up. His economy of movement, deftness, and skill more than made up for his scruples over quality. The indiscriminate techniques so arrogantly displayed by the others became more haphazard as the contest wore on and they sought to save time.

"Hurry up!" A red-faced Larry shoved a bag of grain at his brother, who'd been waiting for him to finish. The slipshod stitching ripped apart from the strain, spewing the contents of the bag all over his feet. The acrid smell of burned wheat tainted the air as some hit the flames licking farthest from the center of the fire.

Saul didn't so much as look up from his work while the other teams halted to jeer at the Grogans' misfortune. Tempers raised as paces slowed, eyelids drooped, and shoulders slumped. When the fire burned low and the men finished, consulting the numbers seemed more a formality than anything else.

Clara made a beeline to congratulate Dr. Reed, only to find that Amanda Dunstall and Willa Grogan, who'd shot Larry a haughty glance at that final embarrassment, had beat her to it.

She pulled up short. *It worked!* She watched as several other townspeople blocked him from her vision. *He's recaptured the attention of the girls!* Success couldn't be far behind.

CHAPTER 16

"Mornin', Dr. Reed." Adam Grogan greeted him as they set up to thresh the Grogan grain. "I'm glad to see you're on hand to help out."

"After working the Fosset place, you should've dropped like a fly," Larry grunted as he toted two water pails past them. "If you don't have to work, why keep showing off?"

"Showing up ain't the same as showing off." The rebuke came in a tone low enough to rival a growl. Elroy Speck jerked a nod toward Adam. "Your brother knows it. After the way you flapped your gums last night then couldn't stitch two sides of a sack together, you should have learned the difference."

"Sewin' ain't the test of a real man, Speck." The jeer slid from Larry's face as his brother rounded on him.

"No, but his behavior sure is." Adam loomed over his brother. "Stuff your pride or I'll tan your hide to remind you."

The threat stole some of the swagger from Larry's step as he walked away—the first sensible thing Saul had seen from the young man. At his defection, everyone else breathed easy until the real work of the day began.

The thresher whirred to life, a heady tempo that pulsed in the veins of every man on the job. Sheaves rained down, bands burst apart, straw belched through the air to mingle with dust and sweat. One task flowed to the next, an unbroken cadence sending grain surging down the chutes to the bags below.

A mighty screech pierced the rhythm, wrenching them from their tasks as everything scraped to a stop.

Saul stepped back, tilting his hat brim to better gauge the problem. Mr. Speck, Opal's and Elroy's father, crouched on the platform and peered in the opening. He shifted to the right then the left before straightening again.

"Feeder's blocked." He yanked on thick work gloves before hunkering down again. Nothing happened while men got the horses under control, ensuring no power fed into the machine whose powerful jaws could snap off a limb or mangle a man so badly he bled to death.

Saul edged closer as Mr. Speck assessed the workings before him and reached in, drawing out a hunk of chewed straw wound into a lump dense enough to clog the machine. A few more cautious swipes assured Saul that the man bore enough respect for the power of the contraption to exercise great caution, and some of the tension left his neck.

"Try 'er now." Upon Speck's order, the horses were let go, the great rods starting their slow dance of climb-and-plunge until the gears of the thresher kicked into action. For a moment, it seemed to function properly. Then a second screech, louder than the first, ruptured their hopes.

Desperate to escape the sound, horses tried to buck free of their traces. Men who'd been leading the horses now dodged sharp-edged, flailing hooves. In a show of bravery and strength, these men kept hold and fought for control of animal and machine. Dust whirled around them, a brown mist shadowing every movement, hiding any injury.

Saul whipped off his gloves, edging around the chutes for a closer vantage point. He scanned for anyone on the ground, any men holding an arm, a shoulder, or limping away from the area. The dust cleared to reveal none of his fears.

Mr. Speck stooped on the platform once more, tilting his chin as though to explore every angle. "Looks like one of the wheels got tilted by the blockage," he announced. "I'll have to pull it back and realign it." He shifted his weight from the balls of his feet to his knees to gain more stability, taking another look before he did anything.

"Get on with it." Larry Grogan stalked up next to the platform. "Time's wasting, and we have more acres than most."

"Do a job right and you don't have to do it twice." Speck's wisdom came with the vigor of fighting words.

"Stop slowing us down." Larry jumped atop the platform and crowded the older man. "You're stalling so we Grogans don't get all our grain threshed, Speck."

"Careful." Speck held his ground as Larry tried to edge him out. "The belt attached to the wheel's stretched tight, and you have to know your way around what you're doing."

"Move out of my boy's way." Larry's father shoved his way forward, pitchfork jabbing the air as he spoke.

"I'll have her going in a minute." Speck rose to his feet, bristling at the order. "Tell your fool of a son not to mess with things he can't manage."

"Don't call me a fool." Larry shouldered Speck hard enough to make the man stumble.

"Stop right there." Saul gripped the center tine of the pitchfork and pushed it away from the platform. "Mr. Speck might have fallen onto this if he didn't have such a good sense of balance. This has gone far enough."

"I won't risk my neck for an ungrateful Grogan." Mr. Speck left the platform to Larry.

"And I'll show you that we could've been working this whole time." Larry squatted down, reached inside, and pulled back the wheel with a fierce yank. A victorious grin hadn't even stretched across his face when a loud *snap* sent something smacking into his chest with enough force to knock him clear off the platform. Larry flew over his father's head, landing facedown yards away. He didn't move.

Saul did. He made it to the boy's still form before most others processed what had happened. Blood seeped around a rock embedded in Larry's right cheek, high enough it might have struck his temple. Saul pressed his fingers against the carotid artery, finding the pulse strong and urgent even as he noted Larry didn't struggle to breathe. Cupping his hands, Saul checked to see if light pressure made the skull compress then quickly ran his hands along the arms and legs. So far no fractures, but ribs. . .that would be a different story.

Adam fell to his knees beside his brother. "What can I do?"

"Keep his head and neck steady while I turn him over." Saul waited until Adam was in position. Then dozens of calloused hands helped him get Larry on his back. Seeing no change in the boy's breathing, Saul murmured, "Good."

"Good?" Mr. Grogan croaked hoarsely as he surveyed the blood streaming from his unconscious boy.

"The stone wasn't high enough to crush his temple." Saul leaned forward, thumbing the patient's eyelids open. Larry's pupils constricted sluggishly beneath the onslaught of the sunlight, but they didn't remain dilated. "Pupils are responsive, another good sign. I'll need my medical bag."

"Here." Clara hefted his altered saddlebag to his side. "What else can I do?"

He flashed her a look of gratitude. "I'll need some cool water and a compress. . .as cold as you can possibly make it." Saul eyed Mr. Grogan.

"You'll need a well-sprung wagon lined with any blankets you can spare to get Larry to my father's house, where there's enough light for me to see to his wounds."

Several townspeople rushed to help carry out his orders, most remaining a respectful distance away as they watched him draw a thick band of cotton from his bag and fold it into a pad. "Adam, I need you to place this here," Saul laid it over the deepest part of the cut on Larry's cheek to demonstrate as he spoke, "and apply firm, even pressure against it."

With that in Adam's hands, Saul quickly checked Larry's chest. When he cautiously felt around the left side of Larry's rib cage, he could easily detect two fractures. Miraculously, they hadn't punctured his lungs because he wasn't gasping, turning blue, or foaming at the mouth.

"Larry!" Lucinda collapsed in the middle of the scene, throwing herself over her son's legs. "My boy!"

"Get her off of him." Saul still didn't know whether Larry'd done any major damage to his spine.

Mr. Grogan pried his wife from his son, but Lucinda continued to wail, making a mighty racket. It seemed as though nothing would get her to stop caterwauling, until Saul gave Adam fresh cotton and changed out the blood-soaked compress. At the sight of the gash across her son's cheek, Lucinda sagged against her husband.

"Take her out of here, and keep her away."

Lord, I can stitch the slash on his face, give him ointment for his bruises, rest for his body, and binding for his ribs, but the rest lies in Your hands.

Clara ran to the well. She leaned over the edge, lowering the bucket to reach the coolest depths before bringing it to the surface.

Willa rushed into the soddy and brought out freshly washed rags and a pail for the water when Opal sprinted forward to join them. Sally followed hard on her heels, apron folded up as though holding something.

"The ice," she panted. "Opal reminded me." She barely got the words out before all of the women hurried back to where Saul tended Larry.

Clara saw Aunt Doreen working alongside Lucinda to pad Mr. Burns's best wagon with hay and blankets so Larry wouldn't be jostled during transport. They passed several women clustered around the parson, heads bowed in fervent prayer.

Men busied themselves clearing the area so the wagon could pull up. Others unhitched the horses from the thresher, determined to avoid any more accidents. Older children marshaled their younger counterparts away from the scene both to spare them worry and to keep them from getting underfoot.

When they reached the doctor, Clara took the largest rag, dipped it deep in the water pail, and folded it around one section of the ice. Sally had already broken it into two chunks. Opal quickly mimicked her, layering cloths soaked in the cool water about the ice to prevent melting.

Saul took the first from her, the warmth of his

fingertips a fiery jolt as he brushed her hand. His gaze shot to hers at the cold of the compress.

"The last of Sally's ice," she explained, placing the second compress in the chilly pail for safekeeping. "As cold as we can make it."

"Excellent." He removed the blood-soaked cotton from Larry's face, laying the compress over the wound as he directed Adam, "Keep applying pressure to slow the bleeding."

"So much blood." Willa's face was pale as though she'd lost an equal amount of her own.

"Head wounds bleed more than others," Saul stated. "It looks alarming but isn't as bad as it seems. Adam's managed to slow it down enough that I'll be able to stitch the wound when we've carried him back to my place."

Clara stood back with the other women as the wagon pulled forward. She watched Saul lead Matthew and Adam, carefully lifting Larry into the bed and cushioning him around the sides to prevent movement. The compress blazed an angry red before they'd gotten him situated, so Clara brought forward the replacement.

"Matthew, drive the buckboard. Adam, keep the compress on his cheek and hold him down if he tries to stir. I'll ride here, too." Saul's commands came out crisp and clear. "Clara, who remembered the ice?"

"Opal."

"Mr. Grogan," Saul ordered, "take Clara and Miss Speck to my house. You'll make it before we do since we'll go slow. We can't jostle Larry around.

Ladies, I'm counting on your help. Clear off the kitchen table. Make sure there is as much light and as many clean cloths as you can find ready for use." Only after he'd finished his instructions did Saul realize Mr. Grogan hadn't moved. "Go!"

"She's a Speck." Grogan whispered the words almost apologetically, as though sorry to have to point out the doctor's mistake.

"I'm aware of that." Saul turned his back on the man, giving his attention to Larry once more. "Get going."

The wagon rolled away, slowly covering ground so as not to jolt Larry and worsen his injuries, leaving them no choice but to follow Saul's orders. Grogan stomped off, muttering to himself.

"Opal?" Clara didn't use more than her friend's name, but the question came out clear for all that.

"I'll come." A stubborn spark lit Opal's gaze. "Larry's as ornery a fellow as I've ever seen, but if I can help, I will. Mr. Grogan won't scare me off."

"Thank you." Willa put a hand on Opal's arm, unshed tears thickening her words. "For thinking of the ice. For ignoring Pa."

Then it was time to go. Mr. Grogan drove like a madman, which, Clara reflected, was as apt a description as any. The sole bit of consideration he showed was to veer wide around his son's wagon so as not to kick up dust. Otherwise, he showed no regard for rock, ditch, bump, or rut as he raced to the house.

She and Opal hunched low in the back of the wagon, clinging to the sides and riding it out until he jerked to a stop. Neither of them waited for any help out of the wagon, scooting to the end and making inelegant leaps for solid ground. They hit the earth running, burst through the doors, and set to work.

"We'll need hot water to clean up the mess and wash the bandages afterward. I'll draw and boil water and scrub the worktable while you get the rags and lamps"—Opal pulled two large pots from their storage places and hooked them over the hearth as she spoke—"since you know where things are and I don't."

By the time the men arrived, the women had done just as Saul asked. Clara opened the curtains wide to let in sunlight and lit lamps in any dark corner where no one would knock them over. Stacks of clean linen stood beside fresh-drawn water while the pots heated. For a brief moment, the kitchen shone.

Then everything became a blur of motion. Matthew and Adam carried Larry in and stretched him on the table. Matthew left the room to wait outside with Mr. Grogan—on Saul's orders, Grogan was to stay outside. Adam moved toward Larry's middle. He'd be ready to hold his brother down if he woke up or tried to move while Saul treated him. Clara and Opal retreated toward the hutch, prepared to bring cloths and water as needed.

"Ladies, I'll have to ask you to step outside for a moment." Saul began opening Larry's shirt. "I need to check for bruises from internal bleeding."

The next minutes were tense as they waited for

Saul to call them back, but he finally did. It seemed Larry had no hard spots on his stomach indicating blood rushing to the surface, and Dr. Reed could treat the cut on his face.

From where she stood, Clara could see everything. The gash in Larry's cheek still oozed blood, but nothing like before. Saul flushed it with cool water several times until the wound ran clear, mopping up the area with towels she passed him.

"He's got at least two broken ribs," Saul spoke as he took out needle, thread, and a bottle of Gilbert and Parson's Hygienic Whiskey for Medical Use. "Best thing is for him to stay out. If he wakes up or tries to move, grab him by the shoulders to keep him down. Stay away from his left side, but be ready." He uncapped the whiskey and held the bottle over the cut, which still sent a thin ribbon of blood down Larry's neck. "This will burn, and he might jerk."

"Wouldn't the liquor do more good inside him?" Opal's whisper to Clara carried farther than she intended.

"If he could swallow it under his own steam, I'd give him a belt for the pain." Saul peered at them. "There's some proof alcohol helps prevent infection." With that, he tilted the bottle.

Immediately, Larry hissed, throwing his head back and twisting to avoid what had to be a painful sensation. Adam placed his forearm across Larry's sternum—his elbow applying pressure against his brother's right shoulder—using his hand to immobilize his head. After a few moments, Larry stopped moving. Adam maintained his position as

Saul readied his needle and bent close, blocking most of Clara's view.

She considered it a blessing, as the first stitch tore a ragged moan from Larry. His head and upper body held in place, Larry began to kick, the movement radiating upward and making Saul stop his work.

"He's still unconscious; he won't keep calm by willpower." Saul didn't need to say another word.

Clara and Opal darted to the table, each grasping a worn leather boot and leaning their weight to still his thrashing limbs. Their efforts, combined with Adam's, held long enough for Saul's exacting stitchwork.

"I'll say this much," Saul mused as he washed his hands, "it seems he sustained no neck or spinal damage. No paralysis."

"He'll be all right then?" Adam's tone lay in odds to the question.

"There's no paralysis," Saul repeated. "His cheek should heal well, too. Beyond that, I can't say until he wakes up."

"What else could be wrong?" Opal moved forward, between Clara and Adam, to get a better look. "Beside his ribs, I mean?"

"That's the biggest problem. He doesn't have any big lumps or fractures to his skull, so I'd think he would wake up. The other big danger is if one of those broken ribs pierced any organs." The planes of Saul's jaw seemed severe in the bright light of sun and lamp. "If he's bleeding internally, I didn't sense it. There's nothing more I can do."

"Where's my boy?" An earsplitting shriek sounded outside the door as Lucinda caught up with them. "Let me in!"

Larry instinctively reacted to the soothing tones of his mother. His eyes fluttered open as he gave a piteous bleat. "Ma?"

~~~⧫⧫⧫~~~

"My angel!" Lucinda Grogan burst through the door and across the room to her son's side.

Angel? Saul didn't give voice to his doubts, instead standing his ground beside his patient as Larry's mother clucked over him. He shot a glance toward Mr. Grogan, who ducked his head and wouldn't meet his gaze. At least the man had enough shame to know he should've kept his wife out of the house. . .and sense enough to see he couldn't do it.

"What happened?" Larry struggled to sit up and immediately abandoned the effort. He winced and used one arm to brace his bandaged left side. His other hand crept up to gingerly trace the tenderness around his stitches. "I remember I fixed the thresher."

"That's right." His mother stroked his hair as though Larry were a drowsy cat. "You fixed the thresher when that useless Speck couldn't, but a strap snapped and knocked you off the platform."

Her conveniently abridged version of events didn't sit well with anyone. Adam snorted at his mama's doting, Miss Speck's hands—just moments ago wrapped around Larry's right boot to help hold him down—curled into fists at the affront to her father, and Clara's eyes shot green fire.

"No." Saul pulled Lucinda's hands away, stepping between her and his patient. He looked Larry in the eye. "Mr. Speck worked to clear the machine, but you grew impatient and all but pushed him off the platform. After you disregarded his warning about how tight the belt was stretched, you yanked the wheel loose. The belt snapped free, struck you in the chest, and sent you flying."

"No need to be quarrelsome." Lucinda weaseled her way forward. "He was just trying to help the farm and got hurt."

"Yeah." Larry's gaze clouded when he tried to shift his weight. The pain from his broken ribs and other injuries had to be getting to him. "What's wrong with me?"

"You've broken two ribs and taken a gash to the face from a rock you landed on." Saul measured drops of laudanum into a glass of water and held it out. "This will dull the pain."

Matthew and Mr. Grogan held Larry up. He downed it without asking another question, giving a faint gasp as he lay back down. His eyes drifted shut as he waited for the medicine to take effect.

"It will make him drowsy, Mrs. Grogan, but he'll sleep comfortably." Saul moved to his bag and poured some of the liquid into a smaller vial. "Mix a couple of drops of this in a cup of water and give it to him when he hurts. Try not to give it to him unless he truly needs it." He handed the medicine to Mrs. Grogan, whose eyes narrowed while she accepted the instructions.

"What's she doing here?" Her beady gaze stayed fixed on Miss Speck.

"I told your husband to bring Clara and Miss Speck ahead to ready things." Saul kept his tone light. "Miss Speck remembered that Miss Fosset brought ice to make ice cream. It was her quick thinking to grab it to help relieve inflammation and slow Larry's bleeding. She has a good head in a crisis, so I asked her to come assist me and help Clara."

"He's my son." The disagreeable woman rounded on him. "I should have helped."

"Your emotions would have clouded your judgment, Mrs. Grogan. I needed someone to help hold Larry down so I could stitch his wound. You wouldn't be able to do that for your son."

"I'd be able to do anything he needed." Lucinda raised her chin. "And better than that Speck gal. If her father fixed the block right the first time, Larry wouldn't have had to step in."

"Larry didn't need to step in at all, Ma." Adam shifted to stand alongside Miss Speck. "He shoved his way in and paid the price. After the way he treated Mr. Speck, we owe this woman special thanks for all she did."

"I ain't thanking no Speck." Lucinda all but spat out the words.

"You're welcome." Miss Speck looked only at Adam, head held high as she said the words. "I'll be going now."

"And I'll accompany you." Clara linked arms with her friend as they swept toward the door.

She stopped to address Mr. Grogan as they left. "I suggest you take your son while he won't feel the ill effects of the ride home, Mr. Grogan."

Saul bit back a grin at the flummoxed expression on Lucinda's face. "I'll second that prescription. It's time you take Larry home and keep him there until he's fully recovered."

"Yes." Matthew Burn looked solemn as he chimed in. "Even if it takes a long time. Peace and quiet are important."

"For any recovery." This time, Saul had to turn away. The grin just wouldn't stay hidden.

CHAPTER 17

I remembered what you said about how Dr. Reed likes apple desserts." Willa Grogan sidled up to the counter where Clara was looking over the condition of the bolts of fabric and slid a pan toward her. "This cobbler's to thank him for helping Larry."

Cinnamon teased Clara's nose as she nudged the dish back toward Willa. "How thoughtful of you!" She kept her voice low and encouraging. "Go on ahead and take it to him. Your appreciation will mean a lot."

"Couldn't you just mention I brought it by?" Willa darted a shy glance toward where Saul pored over catalogs, filling out orders for the medical supplies he deemed necessary for the town. "The last thing I'd want to do is disturb him."

"Nonsense!" Clara stifled a sigh, hovering halfway between amusement and exasperation. She settled for raising her voice to capture Saul's attention. "He'll want to hear all about how Larry's recuperating."

"Hmmm?" Saul looked up from the catalog, gaze focusing on Willa. "Miss Grogan!" A welcoming smile crossed his features before a businesslike frown slid into place. "How is your brother?"

"Same as ever." A dry note entered Willa's voice, signaling to Clara that Larry as a semi-invalid hadn't become any more gracious than his usual cantankerous self. "He says his stitches scratch, and he's got a powerful thirst."

"If he picks at those stitches, his scar will be worse. The wound might even become infected." Saul pulled his medical bag from behind the counter and began rummaging around. He scooped some salve into a small vial. "Use this gently, sparingly if it troubles him anymore. As for the thirst, it's a good thing. He should drink lots of water, and the more he's able to get up without overtaxing himself, the better."

"Thank you, doctor." Willa tucked the vial into a pocket and hesitated a moment. "Though. . .Larry ain't thirsting for water."

"Oh?" Saul's gaze snapped back to meet Willa's, and Clara wondered whether her friend could feel the heat of his intensity all the way to her toes. "I take it he doesn't want milk or coffee, either?"

"Whiskey. Ma gives it to him for the pain."

"I sent home doses of laudanum, which acts as a pain control and sedative." Saul braced both hands on the counter. "Larry doesn't need alcohol when he's dosed with a narcotic."

"Thank you. I'll tell Ma you said so." Gratitude shone in Willa's face as she turned to grab the cobbler then delivered it to Saul. "I baked this apple cobbler for you, as a thank-you for all you done for my brother."

"Thank you, Miss Grogan." Surprised pleasure painted his features as he watched Willa leave the shop, but he didn't so much as take a deep whiff of his treat. He went right back to his catalogs.

Clara didn't give it much more thought, since they'd had breakfast not long ago. She merely went about inspecting the bolts for water damage, brittle spots, pulled threads, faded areas, uneven weaves, and anything that might need to be sold as sale goods or quilting scraps. Yard after yard of fabric unrolled across the counter. Soft cottons, thick merino wool, bright ginghams, cheery flower prints, and bold solids all graced the area before her as she went through.

The bell on the door chimed to announce Sally Fosset, carrying what looked to be a pie in each hand. A smile played about the corners of Clara's mouth as her friend marched right up to Saul. Sally didn't claim a shy bone in her body, particularly now that she'd fixed her attentions on Matthew. All the same, the hints Clara dropped to the girls about rewarding Dr. Reed for his hard work with one of his favorite treats had obviously borne fruit.

"Apple," Sally boasted. "We can't replace the ice until winter, and by then you'll be plenty cold enough and wanting hot cider, instead of the ice cream you were due. So I made an apple pie for you and a peach pie for Matthew. I'll be dropping his off next."

"Thank you very much." Saul accepted the pie, sliding it on a back shelf along with Willa's cobbler. "I know Matthew will appreciate it just as much as I do—if not more."

"I hope so." With another smile, Sally sailed out the door and off to see the young blacksmith.

Clara hummed under her breath as she jotted down the lengths of cloths she cut away. If the way to a man's heart was through his stomach—though an educated doctor might disagree with the anatomical basis of the adage—then the ladies of Buttonwood were well on their way.

When Opal bustled through the door, Clara gave a final snip to the last bolt in the top row and set down her scissors with a merry little click. Sally might be earmarked for Matthew, but both of the other girls burst with potential. Willa's admiration for Saul's kindness and skill, and the way Opal had been spending time with him these past few days showed promise.

"Good morning, Clara." Opal spared her a smile as she passed the counter with a cloth-wrapped plate. "Dr. Reed, I brought you something this morning."

"Oh?" Saul raised his head slowly, as though unable to believe so many women would be so thoughtful.

Well, Clara thought smugly, *that's because you haven't been in a place with people as wonderful as this. By the time we're though, you'll never want to leave Buttonwood.*

"Apple fritters." Opal set the plate in front of him.

"I see." Saul looked from the plate, to Opal, to Clara, and back to the plate. "That sounds wonderful, Miss Speck. I wonder if you would humor my curiosity?"

"What?" Opal spoke aloud the question knocking about Clara's mind.

"After I asked you to help me tend a man who'd shown your father disrespect, why would you bring me apple fritters?"

"Because you asked me to help." Opal's answer clearly didn't satisfy Saul any more than it did Clara, and she must have realized it because she went on. "I liked what you said about me having a good head in a crisis. You didn't see me as a Speck or a Grogan—just saw that I was willing and able to lend a hand."

"Then I'm honored to take your apple fritters." Saul gave her a wide grin. "It's not every woman who appreciates getting roped into holding a man's dirty boot while he tries to kick her."

"It's not every man who appreciates a capable woman," Clara called out. *Saul and Opal really are well suited.* She smiled about it long after her friend left.

"You're looking pleased with yourself." Saul's observation gave her a guilty start.

"I'm glad to be getting things done." Clara swiftly turned the conversation back on him. "That's quite a stockpile of sweets you have there."

"Yes." He gave the assortment an assessing look. "Though I'm beginning to become suspicious."

Oh no! They shouldn't have all come this morning.

Clara could have kicked herself. *Three unmarried women bearing desserts to the new bachelor in town? Of course he's becoming suspicious!*

"Of what?" She pasted a smile on her face.

"Miss Field, I'm going to ask you a question." His tone became somber. "And I need you to answer it honestly."

"Of course," Clara squeaked past the lump in her throat. *Saul is a smart man. Has he figured out that I'm trying to marry him off?* "Ask away."

"This many baked goods makes a man wonder." Saul leaned forward, fighting to maintain his serious expression as Clara's eyes went wide and round. "Does Buttonwood harbor a secret?"

"A secret?" she repeated the word innocently.

Too innocently. *What if I asked what secrets you hold, Clara? Would you tell me?* He pushed the thoughts away when the silence stretched too long, like brittle taffy. "A hidden orchard perhaps?" He straightened up, creating more distance between them. "Some undisclosed location where the women of this town grow apples to satisfy their demand?"

"What do you—" Confusion gave way to merriment as she caught on to his joke. Laughter spilled from her lips, lighter and sweeter than any of the confections gracing his shelf.

He wanted a second serving. "Is there a reason no dish seems complete without this particular fruit?" Saul gestured to the row of offerings on the shelf. "Apple cobbler, apple pie, apple fritters—that's more than a coincidence."

"You've eaten many meals here with no apples," she protested. But no giggles peppered her words. Clara, for all her denials, hid something. Even more intriguing, she wasn't good at it.

Saul decided to dig a little deeper. "Then is it some sort of holiday I'm unaware of? A day wherein we celebrate apples?"

"That's ridiculous." The words came out in a small huff, causing a saucy tendril to dance at her forehead for a moment.

"Is it?" *More ridiculous than wanting to wind that springy curl around my finger and give it a tug?*

The bell over the shop door shattered the silence, not the first time a customer provided an unwelcome interruption. Saul's humor came flooding back when he saw who'd arrived.

Amanda Dunstall minced up the center of the store, carefully balancing a large, covered plate as she made her way toward them. "Good morning!"

"Lovely to see you, Amanda!" Clara's obvious relief over the change in conversation made him all the more determined to get back to it.

"What do you have there, Miss Dunstall?" He made a great show of peering at the dish then sending a quizzical look toward Clara.

"Crumb cake." Her cheery answer almost disappointed him.

"If I didn't love crumb cake so much," he admitted, "I'd be saddened to hear it wasn't apple."

"Everything in town can't be made with

apples." Clara's triumphant tone matched her grin. "It isn't as though we have a secret orchard."

"Of course not." Miss Dunstall sent Clara a concerned look. "The only trees around here are cottonwood and black walnut."

"We know," he broke in. "It was just a joke about the apples. We were having a conversation about them when you came in."

"Oh yes!" She brightened. "Well, no worries, Dr. Reed. It's apple crumb cake."

"You don't say?" His smile proved a direct counterpoint to the defeat written in Clara's expression, but he held his peace until Miss Dunstall left. Then he let loose. "'*Apple* crumb cake,' she said. I wonder what the odds are of four women each baking a dish and all of them having to do with apples?"

"I'd be more likely to wonder how often a man finds himself in a town where the people are so thoughtful." She served him a pointed glare. "Why don't you enjoy your food, thank the ladies for their kindness, and finish filling out your orders?"

"That would be a fine idea," he agreed, "if I liked apples."

"Of course you like apples!" She tapped her foot in impatience.

"What makes you think so?" Saul sensed they were getting to the meat of the matter.

"Everyone likes apples!"

"I don't." He plunked the crumb cake on the shelf beside the other dishes. "Which seems an awful waste."

"There's no reason to joke about something like that." Clara's glower wouldn't scare a chipmunk from an acorn. She looked too cute, but Saul could see she meant business. "Those women worked hard to make those for you, and you'll need to tell them how much you enjoyed their efforts."

"No one's disputing that. I'll enjoy watching you and your aunt eat them."

"Oh, I admit it!" She held up both hands, palms outward. "I told the girls it was a shame you'd missed out on your ice cream and that you liked apples."

"Did you?" Chuckles broke free at her earnest expression. "Well, even if you made a wrong assumption, it's good to know your friends trust your judgment."

"I didn't assume anything." Her brow furrowed in puzzlement. "Your father told me when I asked him what you liked to eat."

"Dad told you I like apples?" Saul stopped laughing. Either Clara misheard, wasn't telling the truth, or Dad had forgotten.

"Yes, I'm sure of it." She squinted at him. "You're certain you don't?"

"Absolutely." A muscle in Saul's jaw jumped. "I haven't eaten an apple I didn't have to since I was seven."

"What changed?" Clara knew she had no right to ask, no reason to expect an answer. But the question tugged at her heart so insistently, she had to try.

"What makes you think something changed?" Saul's voice went low and gruff, a warning she delved too deep.

"You said you haven't eaten an apple you didn't have to since you were seven," Clara spoke softly. "That means you ate apples before because you wanted to. Something changed."

"My sister." He thrust his hands in his pockets, eyes staring past Clara.

She got the sense he stared past the shelves, past time itself, as the memory unwound around him.

CHAPTER 18

My sister. Nellie loved apples." Saul's eyes grew bright then dimmed. "She started to feel sick, but no one listened. I didn't listen." His jaw clenched for a long moment. "Until she wouldn't eat the apple bread at dinner. Then I knew Nellie was sick."

"It wasn't your fault," Clara whispered. The reminder of her presence seemed to jerk him back to reality. "I'm sorry."

He pulled his hands from his pockets, blinking hard. "There's nothing you can do about it. Nothing I could do." Saul drew a ragged breath. "I can't believe Dad forgot. Apples."

"Is Nellie the reason you became a doctor?" It fit so perfectly and made Clara wonder, too, about Saul's need to help an orphan like Midge.

"I'm finished talking about it." The words came out clipped as he turned away, moving from behind the counter and toward the door.

"Wait." She reeled from the abruptness of how he'd pulled away. "I didn't—"

"Clara." The sound of her name on his lips halted her apology. "The stage is here."

"The stage?" She struggled to make the transition, not wanting the connection to be broken.

"Midge." His stride grew longer. "Come meet Midge!"

"Dr. Reed!" Midge couldn't break free of the stagecoach fast enough. She ran, flinging her arms around his middle in a great hug. "I'm so glad to see you!"

"I'm glad to see you, too." He wrapped his arms around her, tight and safe, before straightening up. Dr. Reed smiled, just like she remembered, and Midge knew she'd be all right in this dusty little town.

She hung back while he talked with Mrs. Henderson, drinking in the space. Her gaze flicked from where the stage master unloaded her luggage to a small wooden building that looked like a restaurant. Midge's grumbling stomach made her hurry her observation of the stables, the smithy, and a fine house that looked as though a giant plucked it from a grand city and plopped it on the prairie.

Just in front of her was the general store, its windows bright in the midday sun, dust already invading the clean-swept boards of the porch. But what really caught her eye was the lady who stood out front, watching. Midge cocked her head to the side and looked straight back.

The woman looked older and taller than she

was—about the same age as Nancy. Midge felt a horrible pang at the thought then tried to ignore it by concentrating instead on the other girl's steady scrutiny. With her golden hair all up in a bun and a light-blue dress and soft apron over it, she looked normal enough. But it was her smile—nice but not trying too hard, like some folk when they heard Midge was an orphan—that made her stick out in a good way.

Well, that and the way she'd snuck happy glances at Dr. Reed before she saw Midge keeping track. Yeah, the lady seemed the sort she'd like. The town—though *town* seemed almost too long a word for a place so small—was short on buildings but big on room to run. Midge could slip away and stretch her legs and thoughts when she needed to in a place like Buttonwood. She liked that, too.

"Midge"—Dr. Reed gestured for her to come over—"Mrs. Henderson will go back to Fort Laramie with the stage, if that's all right with you. My father hired two ladies to help with the house and the store, so Mrs. Henderson can get back to Baltimore unless you want her to stay."

"That's all right," she assured her traveling companion. After spending every waking moment with Mrs. Henderson for days on end, hardly ever escaping her watchful eye and critical comments, Midge was ready to part ways. "I'm here safe and sound. Thank you, Mrs. Henderson."

"I do miss the city," the older woman confessed. "And it seems God's provision that the stage master found a letter slipped down between the cracks like that and needs to go back to Laramie right away. Bless you, Dr. Reed. Mind you behave, Midge."

"Yes, ma'am." With that settled, Midge turned her attention back to the woman with the yellow hair, who'd drawn closer.

"I'm Miss Field, one of the women Dr. Reed mentioned who helps with the store and the house." She stooped a little so she stood eye to eye with Midge. "You can call me Clara."

"You probably already know I'm Midge." She'd see how Clara responded before making any decisions. Midge might not have any family left, but she wouldn't play the poor little orphan girl for anybody. Not even Dr. Reed.

"Yes"—Clara's smile widened—"Dr. Reed told us how smart you are. We've readied a room if you'd like to see it."

Midge shot a glance at Dr. Reed, making sure he nodded before she agreed. "All right."

"My aunt is at the house." Clara walked toward the fancy building Midge noticed earlier. "Her name is Mrs. Edgerly, but she'll want you to call her Doreen."

"You must be Midge!" An older lady with dark-brown hair shot through with silver met them at the door. "Come in!"

"They'll take you upstairs," Dr. Reed told her. "I'll see to your luggage while you look around." With that, he was gone.

Midge tried not to gawk too much as she went up the stairs and passed several rooms before everyone came to a stop. Clara and Mrs. Edgerly didn't go inside, but she figured this must be hers, so she edged around the doorframe.

"Oooh, it's beautiful." She just stood against the wall, taking the room in little sips to make it last longer. Wispy buttercup curtains danced in a breeze from the open window, beckoning her close to a small table complete with two chairs, a fine linen tablecloth, and a tea set.

"For me?"

"All yours," the older lady promised.

Midge extended a hand toward the teapot, waiting for their agreement before she picked it up. The porcelain felt cool and smooth beneath her fingertips as she traced strands of buttercups and greenery. She set it down gently, careful not to let it clink against the teacups or saucers as she moved toward the bed.

"It's so tall." The top of the mattress reached as high as her hip, the dark wood of the headboard stretching higher. Someone had carved flowers on the center post, and she traced the grooves before brushing against the softness of the quilt. "Green and yellow are two of my favorite colors."

"Dr. Reed told us so," Clara said from the doorway.

"I—I'd better go see if he needs help with my things." Midge pushed past them. She hurried down the stairwell, rushed through the door, and didn't pause for breath until she stood in front of the general store.

It was a good thing nobody caught her, or even tried, because Midge didn't have any good reason for running off like that. How could she explain that when she looked at that room, decorated so perfect just for her, a corner of her mind had started whispering thoughts she'd considered long dead. Thoughts about growing up in a normal house, with a family who knew her favorite colors and cared enough to choose them. Thoughts about what it'd be like to have a real home.

And Midge had seen enough to know where hopes like that led.

Disappointment. Clara watched the hated emotion unfold on Aunt Doreen's face, sweeping away the startled expression of a moment before when Midge raced past. *Not again. Aunt Doreen's had too much disappointment recently.*

"Midge didn't like it."

"She's overwhelmed." Laying a hand on her aunt's arm, Clara tilted her head. "Let me bring her back." She waited for the older woman's nod then hastened down the steps. Following Midge didn't take much, as the girl stood on the porch in front of the general store.

Clara made sure the sound of her voice reached the girl before she did. "Dr. Reed probably carried your things in through the kitchen entrance."

"Why?" Midge's shoulders hunched up, crowding the brim of her bonnet into a calico barrier.

"It's closer."

"No." The girl spun around, eyes wary. "Why are you being so nice?

"Why wouldn't I be?" Clara didn't come closer. Midge's posture and question were walls to protect the girl. But from what?

"That's not the way the world works." She pressed her fingers to the locket at her throat. "Folks are only nice when they have a reason. What's yours?"

"What do you think it is?" Clara read pride in Midge's gaze and thought she knew the answer, but she wanted to hear it.

"I don't need anyone to look down on me." Her hand dropped to her side.

"Good." Clara moved past Midge to sit on a bench outside the store. She waited for the girl to turn and join her. "I don't."

"You and your aunt didn't make those curtains and set up my room so nice out of pity for the orphan?"

"Why waste time on something as useless as pity?" She adjusted her skirts to leave more room on the bench for Midge and patted the area beside her. "I feel compassion for you, not pity. Never mistake the two."

"What's the difference?" She edged closer but didn't sit.

"Pity almost implies a person is looking down on another, which doesn't help either one of them. In fact, it's a bit insulting for the person being pitied, don't you think?" Clara fixed her gaze on Midge as she explained. "Compassion, on the other hand, means that maybe we aren't the same—no two people are—but I can try to understand how you feel and respect how difficult things are."

"That is a big difference." Perching on the far edge of the bench, Midge mulled it over. "All right then. What did you decide?"

"About what?"

"When you were trying to understand how I feel," she clarified. "I'm wondering whether you came close or not, if your way will work any better than Mrs. Henderson feeling sorry for me."

"I thought that after everything you've lost, it'd be important for you to feel like we wanted you here. That knowing we were excited to meet you and tried to make you comfortable would go a long way toward easing any feelings that you didn't belong." Clara shrugged, using the movement to make sure Midge's gaze followed her. "I know it was important to me when I lost my family and came to live with Aunt Doreen."

"You're an orphan, too?" She scooted closer. "Your aunt took you in and fixed up a room for you like you did for me?"

"Yes." Shutting her eyes for a moment helped push back the pain from remembering the day she'd left home. "My mother and father left me behind to go on a business trip." Clara left out how she'd begged to go, too. How Daddy had laughed and said his little girl would be in the way and he'd see her later. "They both died in a carriage accident."

"I'm sorry." Midge slid her hand in Clara's and squeezed.

"Ah, but you're not sorry for me?" She squeezed back. "You wish it hadn't happened, understand that it hurt, but don't pity me or think you're better than me because I had a hard time?"

"No." A shy smile tugged at the corners of Midge's mouth.

"Then I appreciate your compassion, just as I appreciated the time Aunt Doreen spent to make me feel welcome in her home." Clara looked Midge up and down. "I was only a little younger than you at the time." No matter that she'd looked older than Midge did now. The girl before her was a late bloomer, but when she blossomed, she'd be a sight to see. Clara stifled a pang at the thought she wouldn't be around to see it.

"So that's why you're nice—not because of pity but because you *do* understand." The girl sucked in a breath. "I love my room, and I'm sorry I was rude."

"Thank you for the apology, but it was Aunt Doreen whose feelings were hurt." Clara stood up. "It'd make her feel better if you told her how much you like everything."

"I will."

"Dr. Reed mentioned you lived with your sister." Clara delicately felt around the topic, only now realizing how little she knew about this young woman. "I don't know much else, but he's asked us to help with your schooling and such while you're here."

"Anything he wants, I'll do my best." She sounded so serious that Clara was torn between smiling and crying. Midge obviously wanted to please the man who'd saved her.

"Then here's your first lesson. The next time

you're upset, don't scamper off." Clara opened the door and followed her charge inside. "You never know what you're missing when you run away from a conversation."

CHAPTER 19

Saul rounded the corner as the girl bounded up the stairs. Your aunt said you'd gone to talk with Midge."

"Yes." Clara seemed a little lost in her own thoughts, making him wonder where they led her.

"I could use some insight, if you wouldn't mind sharing." He grasped her elbow through the soft cotton of her dress and steered her toward the parlor. "What I know about girls wouldn't pack a tooth."

"You were close with your sister." Her murmur wasn't a question, precisely, but it hung in the air like a challenge.

"Midge, I'm sure you'll agree, can't be compared to anyone else." He sidestepped the trap, adamantly refusing to be drawn into the conversation he'd so narrowly avoided earlier. *I won't talk about Nellie.*

Clara's voice rescued him from the memories. "I received the impression she's lived a hard life."

"What did she say?" Saul paced behind the settee to mask his expression. He'd been careful not to give any details of Midge's background but hadn't cautioned the girl to do the same. Mrs. Henderson should have warned Midge not to tell others about Nancy's circumstances, lest she be judged for a situation beyond her control.

"Nothing specific. Nor did I ask." She paused as though hoping he'd volunteer information. When he didn't speak, Clara twisted in her seat to peer up at him. "I trust you would fill in any missing information we'd need to be able to help her."

He wouldn't have Midge tarred with the same brush as her sister, and that meant keeping her past firmly in Baltimore. "If she said nothing, how did you gather she's had a difficult time?"

"Her general wariness and mistrust say enough, though her comment that people are never nice unless they have good reason made me ache for the life she must have led." Clara's gaze held censure for his secrecy and sorrow for Midge's suspicions. "For one so young to believe people only do things to benefit themselves. . ."

"I know." Saul moved to take the seat opposite her. "Most don't learn that lesson until much later in life."

"It's not a valid view, no matter one's age," she corrected. "In Midge, it's merely more jarring to see such a jaded perspective since she's so young."

"Clara"—Saul passed his hand over his face— "I'll grant the idea is disheartening, but that doesn't make it invalid. It's true—the majority of people won't lift a finger unless they reap a reward for their efforts."

"We'll have to disagree on that." She sat so still and straight a casual observer could be forgiven for thinking her spine had frozen stiff. "Not all people in the world think solely of themselves."

"Of course not—often they act on behalf of the people they love." His initial agreement made her relax before his final words hit her with the force of a physical blow.

"And caring for those one loves is selfish?" Clara's voice came out taut and brittle, like a piece of leather stretched too thin and baked in the sun.

"You mistake my words. Caring for others is the antithesis of selfishness, but when you look at the decisions people make every day, my point stands. What they do is chosen, almost without exception, to benefit themselves or those close to them."

"Then you see even an act of love as a sad truth of humanity." She refused to see herself that way. "I suppose, then, it's not the actions themselves but the lens through which one views them. Perhaps yours need changing."

"Perhaps yours need cleaning. A rosy tinge can only last so long, Clara." He clasped his hands together as though preparing to deliver a lecture. "Midge knows reality, and you won't reach her with platitudes."

"Since you've come to Buttonwood, have you not seen people look beyond themselves to help others?" Her voice gathered strength as she proved him wrong. "To welcome you and Midge, for instance, or thank you for something you've done on behalf of a neighbor? These are hardly platitudes, Dr. Reed. These are people living good lives and spreading kindness as best they can."

"The people here have big hearts, but I'm in no rush to place them on a pedestal." His words came out as unyielding as his argument. "The Specks and Grogans mill around each other waiting for an opening, tempers grow short when the days stretch long, and no one cultivates patience along with that grain. They help each other, knowing when the time comes their neighbors will return the favor. It's a system just like any other."

"I disagree. They work together to accomplish what they can't achieve alone. Admitting they need help and appreciating the skills others have to offer are virtues to be applauded." Clara stood up, measuring the length of the room with her strides. "Why do you have to narrow it down to materialistic loss and gain statements without taking into account the gracious spirit of the town?"

"Why does it disconcert you that people ultimately do what's best for themselves, and that Midge and I acknowledge it?"

"Because no one deserves to be seen as grasping or opportunistic for taking care of themselves or the ones they love." Clara came to a halt, fingers digging into the brocaded back of the settee. "Not when it takes everything they have just to try."

"I didn't mean you." His voice moved closer, though Clara kept her gaze fixed to the velvet beneath her fingertips. "It takes courage and conviction to come out here and try to provide for your aunt. Selfishness doesn't come into the equation."

Even if I'm trying to marry you off to one of the local girls so I can earn this house? Guilt clumped in the back of her throat, behind her eyes, gathering in tears as she realized what she'd done. *To take care of Aunt Doreen, I'm nudging you into one of the most important decisions you'll ever make—and you don't even know it.*

"Clara," his warm breath fanned against the nape of her neck as he spoke, "I'm wrong."

"No." She raised her head and pulled away, putting as much distance between them as she dared. "You're right, Dr. Reed. If you look closely enough, every decision has its roots in what a person wants. Scratch the surface, and you'll find a reason behind any action."

"Reason is one of the gifts God gave mankind," Saul agreed. "There's no shame behind using logic so long as it's combined with conscience."

"And compassion." Clara forced herself to meet his gaze. "That's what I spoke with Midge about—the difference between pity and compassion. We discussed the mistake of looking down on people less fortunate and the value of trying to understand their feelings."

"She doesn't want to be pitied." His jaw clenched, a protective gesture that shot straight to Clara's heart.

"No one does. Just as no one wants to think

that behind every action lies self-centered thought." She took a deep breath. "But both are realities to be faced. Dr. Reed, Midge will face pity so long as she is an orphan under the care of a bachelor. Your motives for taking her in will be questioned by those whose own intentions are less than altruistic."

"A moment ago you protested this idea and said that people deserved better." He moved to stand at the mantel. "Why the change?"

"Because you don't plan to stay in Buttonwood, Dr. Reed." Clara paused to let that sink in. "Because these are the suspicions you will face in a big city. But most of all"—she closed her eyes before admitting the last—"because perhaps I have a few motives of my own."

"Such as?" His palm pressed flat on the mantel, Saul waited for Clara to open her eyes.

When she did, he saw the tumult of her thoughts. Vulnerability yielded before resolve, conviction warred with regret, and the velvety softness of hope held firm against the harsh edges of doubt. "I want you to stay."

His breath left him in a great *whoosh* at the determination in her words. *She wants me to stay. Here. With her?* An unexpected elation washed over him at the thought. Waiting for her to continue, the silence grew until he could no longer stand the delay. "Why?"

"For what your father has done in helping

Aunt Doreen and me, I owe him whatever I can do to bring him joy." She took a step forward, her expression as she spoke of his father wanting him to stay—not her own wishes—painfully earnest. "He wants you near him, longs to share the rest of his life with family, needs to see you happy. You can make that happen."

"My work lies in Baltimore." He took his arm off the mantel and straightened up. "There are many in need clustered around the city, overlooked by the medical community."

"Has the medical community made provision for Buttonwood?" She glanced around as though searching for spare doctors. "For any of the outposts on the Oregon Trail or frontier towns in the wilderness? The town's residents need care, and in spring many others will pass through. You'll find need wherever you look for it, Dr. Reed."

"It came to me in Baltimore." He struggled to keep his tone even. "Midge's sister is just one example of thousands of poor living piled atop one another, unable to afford help and told they're not important enough to warrant assistance. The people coming west make the choice to try for a new life. They had the ability to pick up and move on. Others don't possess the means for such a change."

"With all the tales of epidemics plaguing travelers, many are dissuaded from trying. Help along the way means more successes, more hope, less crowding in cities." Clara didn't so much as blink at his protests, instead countering with points so clear, he found himself considering the possibilities.

"I have a responsibility to Midge," he stated. "She's lost everything she knows, and I'll not break my promise to return to the city where she's spent the whole of her life until now."

"Have you asked Midge what's most important to her—staying in Baltimore or staying close to you?" She tilted her head. "I should be surprised if her answer would be Baltimore."

"Midge needn't choose. She's had too much wrenched from her. I won't take anything else. I'll establish my practice in Baltimore as planned." He moved past the settee, heading toward the door in an obvious signal the conversation had ended.

"If that is your choice, you will lose Midge to the city." The quiet certainty in her voice stopped him when desperation or histrionics wouldn't have. She sat down again while she waited for his answer.

"Improbable." Saul turned, lifting a single brow to show his dismissal of the idea. "She'll be well cared for."

"But not by you." Each word hammered into him. "When you return to Baltimore, keeping her in your home would lead to unsavory rumors and reflect poorly on her moral character and your professional ethics."

"We've already established she'll go to school." Saul rested on the arm of an overstuffed chair. "It's been seen to."

"Precisely." Clara laid one hand atop the other in her lap, all angles and finality as she continued.

"Midge's lack of family and education will cast her to the fringes there, and while you may live mere blocks away, you'll not be part of her daily life. The isolation inflicted by her status as an orphaned young woman of a family with no status at an elite institution will stifle her spirit and strength."

"I will find a way." The words fell flat even to his own ears. Clara would know far better than he the expectations and petty distinctions drawn among schoolgirls.

"Staying in Buttonwood *is* a way." Her gaze implored him to see things as she did. "The only way to keep Midge close without the unforgiving speculation of high society and to maintain a connection with your father."

"How can that be?" *How dare you tell me to stay when you aren't going to?* "When you and your aunt join another wagon train come spring, Midge's presence with two unmarried men would still be cause for conjecture."

"Not to the same extent as it would be in the city," she conceded, "but that is true. That brings me to the solution I hope you'll consider despite it going against your plans."

"What?" Saul knew he invited disaster, but his curiosity wouldn't let him walk away.

"I'm asking you to look beyond your own reasons—beyond personal gain—to see how what I'm about to propose would be the best course of action for everyone involved."

"Stop hedging." He shifted closer, noting that she fidgeted but didn't pull away. "What solution?"

"Dr. Reed." She drew a deep breath and met his gaze squarely. "Consider how a wife would solve several of your problems."

"A wife!" He sprang from the chair. "Every sane man knows that the more women added to an equation, the more complex it becomes." Saul shot her a pointed glance. "You prove it."

"For now I'll ignore how that statement rankles." Clara remained seated, every inch rigid with icy disdain. "Should you remain in Buttonwood as a married man, Midge's presence wouldn't raise so much as an eyebrow. She'll stay secure and accepted, and you'll fulfill your father's dearest wish. You'll have patients aplenty to tend and epidemics to halt in their tracks. Far from complicating matters, marriage offers an expedient resolution."

"Marriage is more than a contract of convenience. I needn't look beyond that of my own parents for a perfect example of why such arrangements fail." Saul shook his head. "Hasty weddings create problems only funerals can resolve."

"I know." Sorrow crept into her voice, pulling him from the memories of his tension-filled childhood home.

"Do you refer to your uncle?" Saul moved to stand beside her.

"Aunt Doreen married him to be able to support me, and not a day went by I didn't wish she'd found another way." When Clara looked at him, sadness leached away the color in her cheeks. "But that needn't be the case here. Several girls in

Buttonwood would make fine wives for you and kind mothers to Midge, if you opened yourself to the possibility."

"Girls in Buttonwood?" The enormity of what she'd said crashed over him all at once, making it impossible to speak aloud all the realizations clashing in his head.

She'd brought her friends over to ready Midge's room, insisted he come to lunch to show his appreciation, and seemed upset by the addition of the other men. Her approval when he asked Miss Speck to join him at the table wasn't due to relief over her friend's avoidance of embarrassment. The apple desserts trickling in all morning after she'd told them it was his favorite treat. . .

"You've been trying to match me with your friends." In his exertion not to shout, the words came out in a deceptively soft tone.

"I've made efforts to give you the opportunity to know them." Her admission only fanned the flames of his anger. "By now I'd hoped you'd have narrowed your interest to one or two."

"You're to be congratulated, Miss Field." He clasped his hands behind his back and turned to face her. "The effectiveness of your plot will astonish you, I'm sure."

"Oh?" Her entire visage lit up with such hope and joy that Saul almost regretted his next words.

"Yes. I've come to know the young ladies in a variety of situations—aside from church and the threshings—thanks to you. I have seen enough of the women to determine how I feel and have narrowed down my interest"—he paused and waited until she leaned closer—"to none of them. You will cease your matchmaking efforts immediately."

CHAPTER 20

She's trying to marry off my Dr. Reed! Midge could scarcely believe what she was hearing through the cast-iron grate in the floor of her room. She'd come upstairs to apologize to Mrs. Edgerly, but the older woman had gone off to clean something, she supposed.

That left Midge alone in the cheery yellow and green room, where she'd edged up to the bed and fluffed herself down upon it to see if it felt as soft as it looked. It did. But more importantly, from where she lay she could hear Clara and Dr. Reed talking in the parlor.

She's trying to marry him off, all right. Incredible as the thought seemed, more unbelievable still came the following realization. *And she's botching it. How can anyone* not *find a wife for a man as kind and smart and handsome as Dr. Reed?* That boggled her brain, but she decided to be thankful. *If Dr. Reed married, where would that leave me?*

A few moments later, Midge sucked in a sharp

breath as Clara explained exactly where that would leave her. Or, rather, where she'd wind up if Dr. Reed didn't marry. A boarding school? Dr. Reed hadn't mentioned sending her away to a fancy all girls' school, but there was his voice, agreeing with the plan.

Even after Clara's warnings about those places. There the other girls would pity her, or laugh at her, or look down on her, or be cruel because she wasn't born into a rich family that was still alive. She'd have to trade Dr. Reed for all those snooty little princesses? *Nuh-uh, I'm not getting stuck at a boarding school.*

The other choice sounded much better. Since Baltimore didn't seem safe anymore, especially if she'd be trapped at some fancy school, she wasn't so keen on going back. If getting Dr. Reed hitched meant she could stay with him and not pretend to become a prissy nose-tilter, that's the choice she'd make.

Not that she'd let Dr. Reed marry just anybody. When Midge met everyone in town, she'd be keeping both eyes open for the right woman. Then, with a few nudges and some sneaky scheming, it shouldn't be too hard to make things go the way they ought.

Dr. Reed's voice interrupted her schemes when he forbade Clara to keep trying to marry him off. *Well, he doesn't have to be so stubborn about it.* Disgruntled, Midge swung her feet over the side of the bed and sat up. *What would it hurt him to think it over?* If Dr. Reed wanted to be difficult, she'd have to be especially clever about finding him a bride.

She didn't have time to dawdle, either. Midge waited until she heard the front door close. She scurried down the stairs to find Clara still in the parlor, sitting on a plush sofa, looking sad. Sad wouldn't get them very far, but something else flashed across her new friend's face when she glimpsed Midge—determination. Ah, now that was an emotion Midge could understand. . .and, better yet, use.

"I couldn't find your aunt."

"Dr. Reed said she went to the Dunstalls' café for a moment." Clara gave a tight smile, the kind held in place by tense edges and an unwillingness to reveal one's upset. "Did you see that he'd brought your things up?"

"Yes." Midge waited a moment before settling on the sofa beside Clara. "Clara? Sometimes it's not so bad to have reasons to do things. So long as they're good ones." She snuck a quick glance and saw some of the tightness leave her friend's smile.

"I'm glad you see the difference."

"Yeah, so I was thinking I could help you marry off Dr. Reed, because I listened and you have good reasons." Midge sat real straight on the sofa, finding it harder than it looked. "Your voices came up through the grate in my room."

"I see." Clara looked shocked and horrified. "You heard everything?"

"About Baltimore and boarding schools and people Dr. Reed can help here in Buttonwood and making his pa happy?" Midge nodded. "I heard all of that. I don't want to go to one of those schools, and

I think Dr. Reed takes care of enough people. He needs a good wife to take care of him."

"You're right, Midge." Clara sighed. "He didn't take my advice very well."

"And now his guard's up." Midge scooted a little closer. "That's why we'll have to work together and catch him by surprise. . . ."

                       ~∞~

Time slipped by in drips and drabs, days Clara whiled away teaching Midge to read and write or finishing the inventory for the store. With no moment left unfilled, more than a week passed before Clara refocused on ending Dr. Reed's bachelorhood.

"Summer's almost gone." Midge turned mournful eyes from the window, where she'd been staring outside. "And Dr. Reed's father will come back in a couple of weeks."

"Yes." Clara checked the spelling words scrawled across the slate before passing it back to her pupil. "You've been in Buttonwood for a couple of weeks now. Are you certain staying is what you want?" She didn't want to press, but Clara had to know. If Midge's deepest desire was to return to Baltimore, Clara couldn't go through with the scheme to marry Dr. Reed off. Too many lives would be changed, and Mr. Reed would understand her decision. Neither of them had known about Midge when they struck the bargain. Worse, he'd left too soon after they found out for them to discuss the ramifications of it.

"It depends on Dr. Reed." The younger girl set

the slate down on the tabletop with a sharp click. "I want to stay with him, but I want him to be happy, too. It's hard."

"Yes." Clara put an arm around Midge's shoulders for a moment. "My hope is you could both be happy here, and that would please Dr. Reed's father, as well."

Midge took a deep breath, almost as though swallowing her doubts. "The way I figure it, the man has to propose, so we can't rope Dr. Reed into anything he doesn't choose, anyway. All we can do is guide him in the right direction."

"True. Enough time has passed since our first. . . erm. . .conversation," Clara glossed over the disagreement and pressed on, "that I doubt he'll suspect we still harbor any hopes."

"Take him by surprise, like I said. So I'll ask him to come gather walnuts with us this afternoon." Midge tapped the edge of her slate with anxious fingers. "You've already asked the others?"

"Yes. Opal, Willa, Sally, and Amanda will all be there, along with us and Aunt Doreen." Clara smiled. "It will be the perfect opportunity, if we can leave him with the right women."

"Amanda's nice but too young." Midge's fingers stopped tapping. "And Matthew Burn has already spoken for Sally. That leaves Willa and Opal."

"It shouldn't be hard to split into groups. If you go with Amanda, I'll maneuver to be with Aunt Doreen and Sally." Clara kept her voice to a whisper so her aunt wouldn't overhear their scheme. "So Dr. Reed will be with Opal and Willa, which is fine since he's trying to get the Specks and Grogans to stop fighting."

"He can't resist trying to fix things." A somber nod accompanied this wisdom. "It could work."

"As long as we're subtle." *Caution* wasn't exactly Midge's watchword, but Clara needed to give one last reminder. "If he suspects a plot, that's the end of it."

"Right. I'll go get him for lunch then." Pushing away from the table, Midge pursed her lips. "We're all ready?"

"As ready as we can be." Thin assurance, Clara knew, but the best she could honestly offer. Since her ill-fated conversation with Dr. Reed about the possibility of marriage to a Buttonwood bride, he'd walked a fine line between pointedly avoiding the ladies and remaining sociable.

Please, Lord, Clara prayed as Midge left, *let this work. I followed You to Buttonwood. I followed Your guidance to stay here. Josiah's offer can't be anything but the next step on the path You laid before me. Help Saul see that this is right. His marriage will make Josiah happy, give Midge the family she deserves, enable me to support Aunt Doreen, and allow us all to stay close together. Jesus, I don't want to leave my friends.*

She raised her head when she heard the door open, signaling Midge's return. In a few moments, they all sat around the lunch table. Clara looked at the faces surrounding her, from Aunt Doreen's gentle smile to Midge's puckish charm and Saul's chiseled features. *It feels right to have friends so close, a home to call our own.*

"Did you have a busy morning at the shop?" She knew full well only a trickle of customers wandered in—most of the townsfolk were too busy with harvesting to spare any time.

"Not a soul in the place but me." Saul cut into a thick slice of ham. "If it weren't for taking inventory, I'd have nothing to do."

"Good." Midge seized the opportunity without a second thought. "Then you can come with us this afternoon. It'll be fun! Clara's going to take us to collect walnuts."

"That's a wonderful idea!" Aunt Doreen unwittingly played her part to perfection. "You're tall enough to shake higher branches that we could only hope to reach."

"I'd be glad to help." He swiped another biscuit from the basket set before him. "Why the sudden interest in walnuts?"

"The time is right." Clara passed him some of Opal's honey. "Besides, walnuts make delicious additions to coffee cake and breads."

"What better reason could there be?" His grin showed enthusiasm at the prospect of Clara's promised baking, but the question stung.

Midge slid a swift glance her way before giving a careless shrug. "You never know what you'll find when you're out and about."

Never know what I'll find. The words thrummed in Saul's mind as he surveyed the bevy of females lurking among the trees. He spotted no other men in the vicinity, a surefire sign he'd been duped. The corners of his mouth tightened, and he slowed his pace, letting Midge and Miss Edgerly pass him.

"Where's the parson?" he gritted out when Clara drew abreast of him. The guilt stamped across her features did nothing to restore his good humor.

"Perhaps he doesn't have a taste for walnuts." Her blithe reply was at odds with her stiff posture.

"Clara," he growled her name as his hand curled over her elbow. Ignoring the heat searing his fingertips, he pulled them both to a stop. "Give me one good reason why I shouldn't turn around and go back to the store."

"Is it so awful?" Her wide eyes pled with him to deny it. When he held his silence, a wistful sigh escaped her lips. "You'll stay because you won't disappoint Midge."

"Dr. Reed!" Almost as if on cue, Midge's voice came piping back to them. "These branches are so full all you'll have to do is tap them!"

"If I weren't so angry at that underhanded tactic"—he started moving toward Midge as he spoke, never relaxing his grip on Clara's arm—"I'd almost admire your aptitude for diabolical scheming."

"There's nothing diabolical about gathering walnuts," she hissed. Clara tried to disengage her arm, but Saul wouldn't allow it.

"Allow me to make one thing clear—under no circumstances will you or Midge leave my sight this afternoon. I'll not be maneuvered into a sham courtship."

"Then don't let it be a sham." Despite her fixed smile, the words uttered from the side of her mouth were underscored in steel as she pulled her arm free. "Oh, Sally! Midge and I have been wanting to ask about the pattern of your green dress. Why don't we gather the fallen walnuts over there while Dr. Reed shakes these branches?"

"Then these will need to be collected." Saul wasn't about to let her disregard his orders.

"Oh, that's not a problem. We'll remain in your sight while the others stay here." Her smile could have sweetened lemons. "Opal? Willa? Amanda? You won't mind helping Dr. Reed over here, will you?"

"Of course not!" The other women drew close, boxing him near the wrinkled bark of a nearby trunk.

With a triumphant glance over her shoulder, Clara took Midge, Doreen, and Sally far away, leaving him behind. With the three eligible women of Buttonwood.

Saul climbed the tree at record speed, wrapping his fingers around the thinnest parts of the branches and shaking with all his might. Walnuts rained down upon the earth, striking grass and dirt with thuds not nearly loud enough to appease his frustration. A few of the green pods knocked the girls about their heads and shoulders, giving a brief flash of satisfaction before remorse had him calling out apologies.

"That's to be expected!" came the cheerful replies as all three women stooped to gather the harvest.

"It's the reason Ma lets me come do the collecting,

instead of asking too many questions." Willa Grogan stiffened as soon as she said the words, avoiding the gazes of the other girls as she stooped. She didn't say much else as everyone worked.

When he moved on to the next tree, Saul bellowed for Midge to come join them. From his vantage point, shadowed in the yellow-green of the autumn walnut leaves still clinging to the branches, he could see her laughing with Clara.

Why isn't she here with the other unmarried women? The realization that Clara didn't see herself as one of his prospects rankled. *Out of all the women in town, she's the only one I'd want to spend time with alone. And just look how well she gets on with Midge. . . .*

Since he'd last seen them, they'd flung decorum to the winds and abandoned their bonnets—obviously certain they'd ventured far enough to be shielded from any disapproval. Both of them hunched in the cool shade, squirreling out the soft green husks of ripe walnuts and adding them to bulging sacks. The trees veiled Clara's smooth white skin from the sun's rays, and Midge's freckles soaked up every drop whether she wore a hat or not. The two wore matching smiles as they worked together.

And pretended not to hear his calls.

Understanding rushed him with enough force to knock the breath from his lungs. This afternoon's interlude with the ladies wasn't just another stage of Clara's matchmaking attempts. No, this latest machination, executed with the precision of practiced surgery, had blinded him to a crucial truth.

Midge is in on it.

CHAPTER 21

He's yelling pretty loud now." Midge tilted her head toward the direction of Saul's shouts. "I think he wants us to know that he knows we can hear him."

"Nobody likes to be ignored." Clara deposited a handful of husks into her sack. "After the way he disregarded my advice, he needs a good reminder."

"Since he's with Opal and Willa now, we've done what we can." Midge shuffled toward another heap. "At least for today."

"We'll see how things unfold, but we fulfilled the basic goal." Clara picked up their bonnets and followed. A cool breeze lifted the ribbons, sending them dancing in the air. It felt good to stand in the quiet shade for a moment. "You said just the right things at the perfect times."

"Good." A smile flashed across Midge's sun-kissed face before worry lit her gaze. "He'll know I helped."

"Hopefully that will help make him see how important it is and get him to change his mind."

"Him marrying is important to me." Midge set down her sack. "But I haven't figured out why it's so important to you. Why are you trying to marry off Dr. Reed, anyway?"

Clara thought for a moment and chose her words carefully. "Do you remember how I told you that Aunt Doreen and I got kicked off our wagon train just a little ways from Buttonwood?"

"By that no-good Hickory McGee." The fierceness of the girl's glower warmed Clara's heart. "You could've been hurt or gotten lost or something terrible, and he didn't care."

"Well, he made a decision. . .that much is certain. My point is Dr. Reed's father took Aunt Doreen and me in. Oh, he said he wanted some help, and he was glad to have us making his meals, but he didn't have to ask us to stay. We owe it to him to do anything we can to make him happy."

"And Dr. Reed marrying someone here and staying nearby would make his father happy?"

"Yes." Clara leaned against the rough, wrinkly bark of a nearby trunk. "So that's one reason."

"I remember the part about the boarding school." Midge kicked a small stone, sending it tumbling across the grass. "Clara? Do you think having a wife and staying in Buttonwood will make Dr. Reed happy?" Eyes made big with worry stared up at her.

"If she's the right wife, yes. Dr. Reed wants to help people, and he could do a lot of good right here. He wants to make sure you're happy, and staying here would keep you close, too. So there's all of that and getting to see his father every day." Clara nodded. "I'd say a good home in a nice town with plenty of friends and family should make anyone happy."

"You're right." Midge eyed her speculatively. "So you do want Dr. Reed to be happy."

"Of course." Clara frowned at the idea she'd want anything else. "He's a good man."

"So you like him, even if he doesn't listen to you and he's probably very mad at us both right now?" The sidelong glances Midge kept sending her while she tossed more walnuts into her bag began to make Clara uncomfortable.

"Yeeeees."

"That's interesting." Her friend didn't say anything more.

"Why is it interesting?" Clara knew she'd regret asking but couldn't stand the way curiosity niggled at the back of her mind while Midge calmly continued with the chore at hand.

"Well, did you ever stop to think that maybe you could fix all of your problems if you just went ahead and married Dr. Reed?" Midge abandoned all pretense now, clutching her bag of nuts and staring intently at Clara to gauge her reaction.

"No! I mean, no." Heat swept up Clara's neck and to her cheeks. "The thought never crossed my mind."

"Huh." With no more than that grunt, Midge dismissed the topic.

Clara stayed rooted to the spot. *Me? Marry Saul?* The idea made no sense, not when she worked to get the house for Aunt Doreen. *But Midge doesn't know about the house.* Shame streaked through her at the reminder of her mercenary motive. True, making Josiah—and now Midge—happy was part of it, but caring for Aunt Doreen and gaining her independence were primary.

Marry Saul—the thought had no business buzzing around her head.

"Why not?" Midge's voice drew her back.

"Why not, what?" Clara shook her head as though to reorganize the muddle of her thinking.

"Why didn't you ever think about being Dr. Reed's wife?"

"Because marriage isn't the solution to a woman's problems." Uriah's grim features as he cut a switch from the tree in the yard flitted across her memory. "Never forget that, Midge. Don't marry because you think it will make life easier."

"But that's why you want Dr. Reed to marry." Midge gaped at her. "Why is it different for you?"

"When a man marries, he gains a wife at his side, a helper in his home, and a mother for his children." Clara struggled to explain. "He keeps his profession, his property, his name, everything but his bachelorhood. Can you understand that?" She waited for Midge's nod. "A man still makes his own way in the world, his own decisions, and his wife is expected to follow him. She leaves her home to join his. That's the difference."

"Then they make a life together," Midge pointed out.

"In a sense. Think about it this way—a woman gives up her name and leaves her family and home. Everything she owns and who she is now belongs to her husband. Her clothes and jewelry aren't hers anymore, but his. Her husband makes the decisions for the rest of their lives, and for the most part she has to live with that."

"And if she marries the right man, they'll agree most of the time." Midge's face took on an obstinate look. "Or she makes him listen."

"But if she marries the wrong man because she needs money, or her family needs the connection with the other family, that woman is bound to her husband for the rest of her life. And in the eyes of the law and society, he rules her."

"I don't like that." Midge's face scrunched into a frown. "There's a big difference for men and women in marriage."

"You have to be sure you marry for love and respect when the time comes, Midge, so you can avoid all those other problems." Clara forced a smile. "And remember that Dr. Reed will make a wonderful husband, so Opal or Willa will be lucky to have him."

"Dr. Reed is a good'un." A wide smile broke across Midge's face. "And since you've gotten to know him better, now maybe you can think about him being a wonderful husband for you."

Time to bring in reinforcements. Saul made a quick getaway, using Clara's disappearing act to his advantage for the first time all afternoon. While the women laid their harvest on flat areas in the stone outcropping beside the meadow, Saul went to fetch a few extra hammers. Husking the walnuts would take a lot of work. Enough work that he might be able to persuade a few other men to lend a hand.

Mouth curled in a smile, Saul headed straight for the blacksmith's shop, where Matthew and his brother seemed eager to help. It didn't take long before Nathan Fosset and Elroy Speck swelled the ranks, and the whole group of them trooped off to meet the girls at the meadow.

Clara's eyes widened when she caught sight of him, and even at a distance Saul knew they'd darkened with simmering anger. When he drew close enough, the stormy jade of her gaze proved him right. Her lips thinned in a grimace of a smile, which raised his spirits more than the merry greetings of the women surrounding her.

"Things seemed uneven this afternoon," he drew out the words, "so while I picked up the hammers, I rounded up a few more men to level things out."

"Shared burdens make the load lighter." Amanda Dunstall's singsong comment couldn't have been better timed.

"Exactly." Saul watched Clara's hands clench into fists. "Here you go." He passed her a hammer, relishing the way her fingers curled around it as though longing to throttle something—or someone.

She turned away, straightened her leather work gloves, and began pounding away at the hapless walnuts before her in what should have been an obvious attempt to vent her ire.

At least her motive shone through to Saul as she hefted the mallet and struck the hulls again and again. It didn't take too much guesswork to imagine she likened his head to those obdurate casings.

Well, it'd take more wiles than she and Midge can summon and combine to weaken my resolve. Jaw set, Saul went to work. Dull thuds of hammers against nuts—punctuated by the sharper clang of metal against rock after an occasional miss—filled the afternoon. Inky brown stained the rocks, everyone's gloves, the hammers' heads, and the sacks filled with walnuts still encased in thick shells, and everyone continued to work.

Even Midge's glee at the demolition eventually wore off, but others in the group still found reason to smile. Saul made a point of staying between his ward and Mrs. Edgerly, keeping far away from any of Clara's friends. The other men practiced no such restraint.

According to established pattern, Matthew Burn sought out Sally Fosset's company. Elroy Speck maneuvered to work alongside Amanda Dunstall while Nathan Fosset paired up with Willa Grogan. That left Matthew's younger brother, Brett, to cozy up to Opal Speck.

Instead, Brett edged his way in next to Clara, who initially brushed off his occasional comments. The youngest Burn blacksmith didn't seem deterred but kept on cracking casings with deft blows of his hammer and sliding smiles her way whenever he could.

Saul made a point of moving to the side. "Come over here, Midge, and give Brett some more room."

Clara's disgruntled glance earned her a smug grin. *You have no room to complain,* his expression told her. Though she gave an exasperated huff, he knew she acknowledged the truth in it when she looked away.

As the day wore on, young Brett's attentions toward Clara became less amusing. His arm would brush hers, his gloved hand rasped across her wrist when reaching for another walnut. The boy's bulk crowded Clara, letting him get too close. The longer Saul watched this progression, the more it chafed.

Still, Clara did nothing. No frowns chased away the insolent suitor. No widening of her stance forced him to retreat. Clara didn't encourage him, but she didn't discourage him, either. In short, she carried on as though she didn't notice Brett's advances.

Everyone else ostensibly detected his interest. When the young blacksmith wrapped his fingers around Clara's under the pretext of showing her how to better grip the hammer, Saul shouldered his way between them. "That's it. We're done." He cast a pointed look at their bags. "Everyone else goes home to full families and should get a larger share."

"No one will argue with you about that, Doc." Elroy hefted a sack as though judging its weight. "Amanda here gets the same as everyone else since she and her ma will use them in the diner."

"We certainly will." Amanda flushed with pleasure.

"I'm building some shelves for the medical supplies I ordered for the store." Saul handed half-filled bags to Mrs. Edgerly and Midge, lifting a large one to carry.

"It seems a shame to leave now." Clara made one last effort to salvage the afternoon, and Midge opened her mouth as though to support her.

"We came early," Saul reminded her. "And Midge needs to keep up on her lessons."

"All this has left me a bit tired," Mrs. Edgerly admitted. That did the trick like nothing else would have.

"Are you all right?" Clara moved with lightning speed, slipping her arm beneath her aunt's elbow to offer support.

"Let me take that, Mrs. Edgerly." Saul took the bag back.

"I'll be fine so long as you start to call me Doreen." She gave a tight smile. "With Midge and Clara calling me by my Christian name, you're the lone hold out. I never cared much for Edgerly, anyway."

"Doreen, it is." Saul let that last enigmatic comment slide, not pressing her as to whether she meant the sound of the name or the husband who'd given it to her.

Clara said a flurry of good-byes and sidestepped a crestfallen Brett Burn, and they all headed home. Midge and Doreen kept up a constant stream of chatter, but it couldn't mask the tension underlying the walk.

When Clara made as though to go to the

kitchen, Saul snagged the door to keep her outside with him. "We need to have a conversation, you and I."

"After today, we've both made our aims quite clear, Dr. Reed." She lifted her chin. "There's nothing more to say."

"I disagree." He crossed his arms and leaned against the doorjamb, blocking her entry. "You specifically disregarded my instructions today."

"Midge and I stayed in sight," she countered. "With you up in the trees, you could see for miles on end."

"Those aren't the instructions I meant, though you didn't keep to the spirit of those orders, either."

"Dr. Reed, you may not have noticed, but I'm not one who does well with orders." She folded her hands together primly. "Not without good reason, and not without proper authority."

"I forbade you to meddle in my affairs and told you to stop matchmaking." A muscle worked in his jaw. "As this pertains to my future directly, my reasons are none of your concern and my authority is absolute."

"Had I shown up with a parson in tow and a loaded shotgun in hand, I might concede your point." Her nostrils flared slightly. "As it is, arranging situations where you spend time in the company of others can't be deemed a hardship."

"In the company of women." Saul uncrossed his arms. "Unmarried women." He leaned forward. "With no other men around."

"The arrangement presented itself as ideal for

you to further your acquaintance with the ladies,"
Clara acknowledged.

"I tire of this game." Saul stepped away from
the door, leaving her avenue of escape clear. "So I'll
get to the point. What if I told you this afternoon
gave me second thoughts?"

CHAPTER 22

An icy shiver tingled down Clara's spine, flooding her senses and making her mouth go dry. Where was the warm rush of elation, the heady flush of success she expected to feel?

Missing. Clara's brows lowered as she realized the reason for her odd reaction. "Dr. Reed, I'm in no mood for jokes. I prefer your irritation, which at least is in keeping with the serious nature of what is at stake."

"What makes you think I'm not serious?" The surprise in his voice left no doubt as to his sincerity, but the mysterious tilt to his grin left her unsettled.

She'd tread softly to start. "Who caught your interest?"

"Due to your *foresight*," he lingered over the word, obviously refraining from using a less flattering description, "I've spent considerable time getting to know the women of Buttonwood. While I'm not about to propose, I've decided to consider the option."

Relief surged through her nerves. *Thank You, Lord!* "You don't know how happy I am to hear you say so." She inched closer and looked up at him. "Which girl?"

"That's what I wanted to discuss. Your knowledge of the women in town ranges farther than my own, and I'd like your input. Will you walk with me?" He offered her his arm.

"Certainly." She laid her fingers on his strong forearm without hesitation, the bolt of heat an indication that her victory was sinking in. "I'll help in any way I can."

"Nothing could please me more than to hear you say that." His sidelong glance sent her stomach aflutter.

"Oh?" Reborn suspicion put a damper on her enthusiasm.

"When choosing a wife, a man needs to have all the information possible at hand. It makes sense to start at the basics. Miss Reed, what qualities did you look for in the prospective brides?"

"Wouldn't it make more sense to discuss the aspects of the women you're currently considering?" Clara itched to know who stood the best chance. *Opal, most likely.*

"No. *You* may have started the process weeks ago, but *I'll* begin anew." He leveled a look of admonition. "Preferably with your cooperation to ensure nothing is overlooked."

"Very well." Clara quelled her resentment over the implication she might have overlooked something. Obviously, Saul needed to feel he'd taken control, so she'd do her best to be gracious. After all, he'd come around to her way of thinking. "After discerning essential eligibility—"

"Ah, ah, Miss Reed. We'll apply scientific principle from the offset. How did you determine eligibility?"

"You know the fundamental criteria as well as anyone." She didn't bother to hide her annoyance but decided to humor him regardless of it. "The women cannot bear direct relation to you or already be married, but must be of suitable age for matrimony without having an understanding or engagement with another man. Additionally, her reputation must be in good standing to reflect well on her husband-to-be."

"Very thorough," he praised. "I agree with every requirement listed and am now prepared to move on to personal qualities and wifely attributes."

"How gratifying to hear I didn't overlook anything thus far." Clara straightened her shoulders. "Any wife of yours must be a godly woman with integrity and intelligence. Caring for her family and loved ones is of utmost importance, and she'd not be one to shirk her responsibilities. Essentially, the woman you marry will be a good mother to your children, a helpmeet in your home, and assist with your patients."

"Excellent." Saul gave a firm nod. "I assume that includes all the skills to run a household. Your advice holds merit."

"Any of the women would make a good wife to you and a loving guide for Midge," Clara urged.

"Your father would be so pleased to hear you're considering staying in Buttonwood!" *And so will Aunt Doreen, if all goes as planned!*

"Wait." He jerked them both to a stop. "I said I'm considering a wife. Did you hear me say anything about staying in town? This is precisely the type of assumption that can derail the best-laid arrangements."

"But. . .why wouldn't you stay?" Clara dug in her heels as he started to walk again, making him remain at her side. "If you marry one of the women here and can have Midge stay with you while you keep close to your father, why would you leave?"

"Marriage will allow me to have Midge stay in my household regardless of its location." His calm observation cut through her hopes like a dagger. "Remain focused on the issue at hand."

"You'd ask your wife to leave behind her home and family—everything—to follow you to Baltimore?" Her heart sank at the thought. Not only would she not earn the house and Josiah not know the happiness of keeping his son close, but also one of her friend's joy would be mingled with wrenching sorrow.

"I will not discuss that now." Saul strode ahead, and Clara moved with him, too lost in thought to protest. "Let's review the women who met the criteria we've both agreed upon."

"The initial candidates included Sally Fosset, Amanda Dunstall, Vanessa Dunstall, Opal Speck, and Willa Grogan." Clara ticked off the names, concentrating on the current issue. Once Saul chose a wife, she'd work with the woman to get him to stay in Buttonwood. For now, she'd take his interest as a step in the right direction. A sizeable step."

"The Dunstalls?" His brow furrowed. "How do they fulfill your standards?"

"To be truthful, I always felt Amanda seemed a bit young for you." The admission didn't cost her much, as the tone of his voice made it clear he held a similar view. "Yet I couldn't exclude her from the gatherings. Elroy Speck will be a much better match for her, should things progress in that direction."

"Agreed. And her mother, the Widow Dunstall?"

"While Amanda's mother, Vanessa, is still young enough to make a good wife since she married early, the obstacle there has more to do with her continued mourning of her husband." Clara's voice softened. "He was her true love, and even after fourteen months, she's not ready to move on."

"I wouldn't want to compete with a previous relationship or show disrespect to the memory of her first husband." Saul patted Clara's hand as though to assure her he agreed with that assessment. "So that leaves Misses Fosset, Speck, and Grogan on your list."

"Yes. Sally met all the requirements, but in the past weeks it's become clear to me that Matthew Burn cares deeply for her." She slanted a glance at Saul to make sure he wasn't disturbed by the comment. If Sally were the woman he'd settled on, there'd be trouble ahead. "What do you think?"

"I expect their wedding to come before

my father returns from Baltimore." Saul's easy acceptance of the fact belied her qualms. "They'll make a good couple."

"Indeed." Her stomach flopped a little as Clara realized they'd finally come down to it—the two women Saul was seriously considering as his wife. "That leaves Opal and Willa."

His nod, unaccompanied by any statement, was frustratingly noncommittal.

"Both women are God-fearing, strong, loving, and kind. Either would make a fine wife and mother," she pressed. When he still didn't respond, she pushed harder. "So what do you have to say about Buttonwood's prospects?"

"I'd have to say, based on our specifications"—Saul's gaze bored into hers as he finally answered—"you overlooked someone."

Saul watched as Clara's brow furrowed at his comment. To her credit, she didn't immediately dismiss his statement. Instead, she caught her lower lip between her teeth in dismay at the very thought she'd failed him in such a manner.

He hid his amusement as she tilted her head to the side as if running through the names of every woman in town, considering and discarding potential applicants for the position until her shoulders slumped in defeat.

"I can't think of anyone else. If Amanda's too young, everyone else already married or spoken for. . ." She looked up, so adorably disgruntled he couldn't hide his smile for another minute. "Oh, you're pulling my leg!" Outrage darkened her features. "After all your talk of scientific process, you make a jest just when we get down to the nitty-gritty of things."

"This is no joke." Saul reached down, clasping both her hands in his as his chuckles faded. "Can't you think of at least one other single woman in Buttonwood, Clara?" He drew out her name, relishing the sound of its soft syllables.

"Me?" The word came out in a squeak, her brows raised so high they disappeared beneath the brim of her bonnet.

"You're single, not related to me, and of the proper age." He stroked his thumb across the back of her hand with each point he made. "We get along well when you're not trying to foist me on any other woman in town."

Her eyes had softened to the color of spring moss as he spoke, but at that last comment Clara yanked her hands away. "How dare you," she hissed.

"How dare I what?" He reached for her, only to have her back away, eyes snapping. "Clara, you have to admit you belong on my list of possibilities." Saul attempted an engaging smile.

"No. Don't turn my words against me." She backed farther away as he tried to shorten the distance. "Be as annoyed as you like at my interference, but don't pull me into it to toy with my thoughts. To pretend you would be interested in me—to want to marry me—mocks a lifetime commitment. This is beneath you."

"Is that what you think?" Saul came to a halt, lowering his hands to his sides. Anger flared to life, lending heat to his words. "That I'd toy with you? When have I ever been less than honest?"

"Never." Fury formed tears of frustration in her eyes as she glowered at him. "You've been clear about your intention to leave from the start. I should have known something was afoot the moment you told me you'd had second thoughts."

"Because you're so unyielding, you assume the same of others." He stood his ground. "You take my words and twist them."

"No, you led me into this conversation, step by step, guiding me to form a list of qualities you could turn on me." Her words came out thick, heavy. "It's despicable you'd resort to such a tactic. You tried to humiliate me by drawing me into this ruse, but you've only shamed yourself."

"You honestly believe that." The realization struck a nerve deep inside. "I meant what I said, Clara. If you stop and think about it, we're well matched to each other. Any man would be proud to take you as his wife"

"It's a ploy to make me stop trying to meddle." Her breath rasped out in bursts. "Well, I'll tell you this much, Saul Reed. . .it won't work. You need a wife, and I intend to see that you get one—if not for your own good, then for everyone else's." With that, she whirled away and hurried back in the direction they'd come.

"Good!" He called after her. "Just remember the list is longer, now, Clara Field! And if I marry one of those women, it may very well be you!"

"No, it won't!" Clara didn't even stop to yell the words back, but from where Midge stood behind a cottonwood tree, she saw Dr. Reed's face when he heard them.

He wore the look of a man issued a challenge.

Midge didn't need any more prompting to go fan the flames. As soon as Clara vanished behind the door to the house, Midge sprang into action. She reached Dr. Reed's side fast enough to see his eyes still shooting sparks. Good. If he was going to convince Clara to be part of their new family, he'd have a fight ahead of him.

"I'm real sorry that didn't work out, Dr. Reed." She put on a mournful face and peeked up at him.

"Humph." The grunt was his only response.

Not good. He'd need more fire than that if he was going to win—and Midge had already decided Dr. Reed needed to win. She thought for a minute and tried again. "That's all right. I'm sure you can get Opal or Willa." She waited a beat. "Probably."

"What?" He looked at her like she'd insulted him, which, come to think of it, had sort of been the point.

"Well, sometimes folks have to settle."

"I choose Clara," he told her, "but I wouldn't say having either Miss Speck or Miss Grogan for a wife would be settling."

"Oh, I didn't mean *you'd* be settling." Midge flashed him a bright smile as he went reddish purple. "Just that since Clara turned you down, you're already passed-over goods."

"She did not turn me down." The words came out all stiff. "I haven't asked her to marry me."

"But she said she won't marry you," Midge pointed out. She shrugged to grind the rejection in a little deeper. "That's the same thing."

"No, it is not the same thing." He peered down at her, eyebrows scrunched together in one long line. "It's not the same unless I ask her."

"But she'd say no."

"She says she'd say no. That's a different matter entirely," Dr. Reed corrected. "If I asked her, she'd say yes."

Midge fought to keep from smiling. Now she had him right where she wanted. She gave a teensy snort to make sure he knew she didn't believe it. "But you're not ever going to ask."

"Scamp!" He burst out laughing so loud, she jumped.

"What?" She stared up at him, wondering if she'd overdone that last bit.

"You pushed too far, Midge." Dr. Reed smiled at her, all that determination she'd worked to provoke gone in a second. "You're trying to goad me into proposing to Clara."

"It almost worked," she grumped. "Tell me the truth—it was the snort that did me in, wasn't it?"

"That. . .and you were starting to look smug." He tapped his index finger on her nose. "So you like the idea of my marrying Clara, eh?"

"Yep."

"Clara in particular, or anyone? I know you

helped with her matchmaking this afternoon."

"You're not mad?" She held her breath while she waited for his answer.

"I was," he finally said. "But I could use a little turncoat to help convince Clara to marry me. What do you say?"

CHAPTER 23

*S*aul Reed doesn't know what he unleashed. Clara's desire to thwart the doctor grew with each passing hour. Today the whole town would turn out for a picnic and taffy-pulling to mark the end of ensiling. She still wasn't clear on what all the process of ensiling entailed. It involved cutting down stalks of corn before they dried and fermenting them into silage for cattle, but the precise method didn't interest her.

The celebration, on the other hand, presented a day full of sweet opportunities to pair Saul with Opal or Willa. Taffy-pulling, conveniently enough, required two sets of hands, and Clara couldn't think of a better way to stick Saul far away from her. The mere memory of how he'd played on her sincere attempts to find him a good match made her blood boil.

If he thinks his ploy yesterday will distract me from marrying him off to one of the other girls, he'll soon regret his gambit. Her eyes narrowed as she recalled how he'd held her hands when he declared his intent to court her. *My opponent may be devious, but my cause is righteous.*

With that last reassurance, she set out to find Midge. Right or not, Clara would take all the help she could dredge up to win the war. She found her young ally still in her room, tugging the green and yellow honeycomb quilt up and smoothing it over her bed.

"Good morning, Midge." She waited outside the doorway until Midge gestured for her to come inside. "Are you looking forward to the taffy-pull?"

"Who doesn't like taffy?"

"My Uncle Uriah didn't like taffy." Clara fingered one of the small teacups sitting on Midge's tabletop. "I always thought perhaps if he ate more sugar it would improve his sour disposition."

"Maybe." Midge giggled. "Everyone in town will be there, won't they? Especially the girls?"

"Exactly. Can I count on you to help me make sure Dr. Reed is paired with one of the girls to pull taffy?"

"Absolutely." Midge's eyes sparkled. "I'll ask him to be my partner, and then I'll call you over for some reason and say I can't do it."

"Then we'll arrange a last-second switch so he can't finagle his way out of it." Clara hugged Midge. "Brilliant!"

"Clara, did you fix up this quilt?" She walked back to the bed and traced one of the hexagonal pieces of fabric. "It's been repaired real nice, and I wondered who took the time."

"I found it in a trunk above the store, but all of us girls worked together to make it ready for you. Opal, Willa, Amanda, and Sally all came over, and we spent a morning stitching it back together." As she drew closer, Clara saw Midge rub at her nose.

"Thanks. I like it. All of you are so nice to me, I know Dr. Reed won't regret his wedding." Her friend's voice came out hesitant and concerned. "You don't feel guilty sneaking around though? Like you're fooling someone you care about and it's wrong?"

"Not over something so simple as a partner for pulling taffy," Clara reassured her. "Especially when it's for his own good. Sometimes, when people won't listen, you have to nudge them in the right directions."

"All right then." Her smile back and brighter than ever, Midge headed for the door. "I'm willing to nudge. And if that means eating lots of taffy, so be it!"

"I'm not sure I see the connection." As they made their way down the stairs, Clara gave up trying to link eating taffy with getting Saul safely married and settled in Buttonwood.

"A girl can only hope." Midge skipped over the last step. "Maybe if I give up my partner, I'll somehow end up tasting everybody else's batches?"

"If there's a way to wrangle it, I'm sure you'll manage." With that, Clara went to join Aunt Doreen in the kitchen. She gathered the dishes they'd contribute to the picnic and passed a few for Midge to carry before they left.

As they neared the church, she saw Saul with the other men. He'd come early to help set up the makeshift tables and scattered cookfires, which suited Clara straight down to her bones. The less she had to speak with him directly, the better. As it was, getting through the day without the whole town suspecting she wanted to tar and feather the man would be a difficult feat.

"Good morning, Clara!" Opal bustled up to join them. "I hear the men will be patching the roof on the church while we start the taffy boiling."

"An excellent use of time." *And another reason to stay far away from Saul. I never imagined tar would be so readily available. . . .*

Clara made a note to ask Opal to take Saul some water later on. Any pretext to throw the two of them together was an opportunity not to be overlooked.

The morning whirled by as they boiled huge pots full of sugar, vinegar, water, and butter until spoonfuls of the mixture formed hard lumps when tossed into cold water. To these batches, they'd add vanilla or honey flavoring as they poured them into cooling pans. For the molasses taffy made with sorghum, the flavor was already set.

While the pans cooled, everyone flocked together for an informal lunch. The men came over after finishing repairs to the church, jockeying for position as they heaped their plates full of everything within reach.

"Midge, why don't you show Dr. Reed that seat over there." Clara indicated the bench where Opal sat.

"Will you be there to help?" Midge cast a quick glance around. "In case he tries to leave?"

"Yes." She suppressed a surge of irritation that she had to watch over every move Saul made. It wasn't Midge's fault the man's behavior was erratic. "I'll join you in a minute."

"All right then." Midge headed off to fetch Saul, leaving Clara alone for a moment to ready herself for the trial to come.

"Miss Field?" Brett Burn appeared at her elbow, holding out a mug. "Would you like some cool cider? It looked awful hot over those taffy fires."

"Oh. . ." Clara was about to refuse when the fine hairs on the back of her neck prickled. A swift turn, and she saw Saul staring at her, brows beetling as he took in the blacksmith's presence. "Thank you." She accepted swiftly. "My friends and I will be eating over there, if you'd like to join us."

"I'd like that." His eager smile sent a pang of guilt through her. Obviously, young Mr. Burn read more into the invitation than she meant.

"Excuse me." Clara drifted toward Opal, resolving to be more careful in how she handled her suitor. She welcomed him as a barrier between her and Saul, but as nothing more.

"Seems as though you've picked up a stray friend." Saul's comment sounded innocent enough, but his gaze spoke volumes as she walked up to join him, Opal, and Midge.

"Mr. Burn's offered me no insult." If she stressed his name slightly for Saul's benefit, no one would blame her. "Here he comes now."

"Miss Speck, Dr. Reed." The young blacksmith sank down on the grass beside the bench, balancing a full plate on his knees. "Miss. . ."

"Midge. Everyone calls me Midge."

Clara shot her friend a censorious glance. Obviously she'd need to have a chat with Midge about certain proprieties. At thirteen, the girl wore her hair up, her skirts long, and needed to be addressed by her surname as any other respectable lady.

"Miss Northand," Saul corrected. "This is Mr. Burn."

By all rights, Clara should have applauded Saul's swift handling of the situation. Instead, she noticed the sharpness of his tone, as though he deliberately sought to make the other man feel distanced from the rest of the group.

"Brett," she added, "runs the blacksmith shop along with his father and older brother." A zing of satisfaction at the peeved expression on Saul's face faded when she saw the delight written across Brett's features.

Oh no. What have I gotten myself into now?

A mess. No matter how he tried, Saul couldn't see the goopy pan of sticky candy smeared with butter as anything but one huge mess.

"I don't see the appeal," he told Midge.

"You're a doctor." She rolled her eyes at him. "Of all people, you know that to get the job done sometimes you have to get your hands dirty."

KELLY EILEEN HAKE

"Not that—I meant I don't see how this is considered romantic." Saul frowned at the glop before him. "Spending the afternoon yanking on tacky candy won't win Clara's heart."

"It's not about the candy. . .though eating it at the end doesn't hurt," Midge whispered. "Think of it this way—if you don't ask her, she'll spend the whole time with that blacksmith she brought over at lunch."

That galvanized him. "She won't say yes. We'll have to think up another way."

"Just leave it to me." Midge waited for a few moments, until the taffy-pulling contest was about to begin. "Clara!" she shouted loud enough that everyone heard her. "Clara!"

"Yes?" Sure enough, Clara came running—with Brett hard on her heels. "Are you all right, Midge?"

"I think I ate too much at lunch." Saul watched in fascination as Midge's eyes drooped and she laid a hand over her stomach. "I'll be fine, but I don't want to leave Dr. Reed without a partner. Will you take care of it?"

"Of course." Her quick capitulation made sense—Clara had always been one to think of others before herself. "I'll make sure Dr. Reed has a partner."

"Thank you." Midge put on a brave smile. "I think I'll go sit in the shade for a little while and watch."

"Would you get her some water?" Clara asked her oversize suitor, nipping about her heels like a big puppy. Of course it worked, and Brett went loping off toward the water bucket.

"I would have seen to it," Saul told her now that he didn't have to leave her alone with the blacksmith.

"Yes." She gave him the first genuine smile he'd seen from her since yesterday morning. "You're good to Midge—to all your patients. I haven't forgotten that."

"Especially the ones I like." He raised a brow.

She immediately retreated to polite conversation. "But how often does a big-city doctor get to have all the fun of a taffy-pull?"

"Rarely," he acknowledged. Saul shot Midge a big smile to let her know everything was working perfectly. "So what now?"

"First. . ." Clara craned her neck as though searching for someone. "Opal!" She gestured for her friend to come over.

Saul listened in stony silence as Clara explained the situation, relaxing only when Opal gave an apologetic shrug. "I already have a partner." With that, she left them alone again.

"Working with you would be an honor." Saul stepped closer.

"Hmmm." Clara's lips tightened to a thin line. "Willa!" She waved her arms wildly until she caught Miss Grogan's attention.

"Yes?" Willa waited during Clara's quick clarification of the problem then ventured a quick glance at Saul. Apparently, that one glance told her everything she needed to know, because she beat a hasty retreat.

"Now will you be my partner?" His patience wore thin, but since Clara had no more maidens to call over, he could keep things pleasant.

Brett returned, complete with menacing frown. "She's already agreed to be my partner."

"That's true." Clara looked from him to Brett and back again.

"Take your places. The contest is about to begin!" the parson called out to everyone. "Remember that the pair with the best consistency and most pleasing design will win, so be as thorough as possible!"

"We belong over there." Brett's hand curled around Clara's elbow, making Saul step forward.

"But she promised Midge she'd see to it I had a partner," Saul pulled out his trump card.

"What's wrong?" As if on cue, Midge appeared at his side. She kept one hand pressed to her stomach.

"I couldn't find a partner for Dr. Reed, and I already told Mr. Burn I'd work with him this afternoon." Distress raised Clara's voice. "Someone will have to do without."

"Oh, but Dr. Reed was so looking forward to his first taffy-pull!" At Midge's statement, Saul put on his best hangdog expression. But it was too late.

Clara's eyes narrowed as she looked at the pair of them. Without her eyes drooping, her shoulders hunching, or her hand over her stomach, Midge looked the picture of health. Saul knew it, and Clara wouldn't miss the truth.

"Oh, how silly of me!" When Clara spoke again, the words came out loudly. She reached for

Midge's hand and drew the girl close. "The answer is obvious. I'll look after you this afternoon, since Mr. Burn and Dr. Reed are both so anxious to pull taffy." She seared Saul with a malevolent glare as she tugged Midge away. "They can partner up with each other!"

CHAPTER 24

Clara sat pressed up against the end of the pew the next morning, Aunt Doreen a comforting presence on her other side. She'd not said more than a handful of words to Saul or Midge since the taffy-pull and wasn't about to relent now.

The unmitigated gall of the man! She twisted her gloves in her lap as she thought of how he'd not only continued this ludicrous pretense of courting her but also hoodwinked Midge into helping him. *It's bad enough to make sport of my emotions, but to cavalierly raise the hopes of a young orphan longing for a family?* One of the buttons popped off her gloves and pinged to the floor below.

When Saul bent to retrieve it, she eyed him wrathfully and refused to accept the fastener. *I won't take anything you offer, Dr. Reed. Not when I know your manners for the facade they truly are.*

It wasn't until the congregation began to sing that Clara shook free from her ruminations. Bowing her head, she listened for a moment to identify the hymn so she could join in. Within the first line, she recognized it and raised her voice.

> "Safely through another week
> God has brought us on our way;
> Let us now a blessing seek,
> On th' approaching Sabbath day;"

The verse rang true. How else could she have struggled through such a trying time, if not for God's grace? More importantly, she would need His blessing if she were to continue to press on in the face of such opposition. At the reminder she didn't face the challenge alone, Clara's voice grew stronger.

> "While we pray for pardoning grace,
> Through the dear Redeemer's Name,
> Show Thy reconciled face,
> Shine away our sin and shame;"

She silently asked forgiveness for her frustration and impatience as well as how she'd tried to creep around to accomplish her goals. Clara snuck a glance at Saul's profile as he sang in a husky baritone, suddenly regretting her short temper. Trying to manipulate him was wrong, no matter how much it rankled to admit it, and she owed him an apology for the way she'd handled things.

The parson launched into the next hymn, the familiar melody washing over Clara in a mingle of regret and hope.

"Guide me, O Thou gracious Savior,
Pilgrim through this barren land.
I am weak, but Thou art mighty;
Hold me with Thy powerful hand."

The song continued, and she sang along by rote, but the words of that last stanza occupied her thoughts. *Lord, I am a pilgrim in this land—a traveler. You brought me to Buttonwood, too weak to provide for Aunt Doreen despite my determination. That we made it even this far is a mark of Your might and power, not my own. Why, then, have I tried to strong-arm Saul into bending to my will?*

Saul turned his face toward hers. Their gazes caught and held. The intensity of his scrutiny made her chest go tight with shame. By all rights, Saul should be furious with her plot to marry him off. That maneuver yesterday, leaving him with Brett Burn as his taffy-pulling partner after she failed to match him with Opal or Willa, should have him smoldering.

Instead of censure or anger, his brown eyes held apology. Clara tilted her head in a small show of acceptance. Her own actions had forced him to resort to using Midge as a buffer between him and the other women of the town.

Clara sank back onto the pew as the sermon began, grateful for the support. Drained of her fiery resolve, she realized for the first time in a long while just how tired she felt.

"Now we reap the harvest of all the work we've done and lay in stores for the hard winter to come."

The parson straightened his spectacles while he spoke. "As summer draws to a close and autumn changes the land around us, it is tempting to mourn the bright days passing away. In the third chapter of Philippians, we're reminded that we're to keep our focus on Christ."

Tears pricked the back of her eyes as Clara listened and realized the awful truth. *I've focused on getting the house, not following Your way.* Regret clawed at her. *How can I make it right, Lord?*

"Just a moment. . ." The parson ran his finger down the thin parchment of the pages in his Bible until he came to the proper place. "'But this one thing I do, forgetting those things which are behind, and reaching forth unto those things which are before, I press toward the mark for the prize of the high calling of God. . . .'"

This is the end of my machinations to make Saul wed a Buttonwood girl, she decided. *When Josiah returns, I can tell him in all honesty that I gave it a valiant effort but failed.* Peace settled over her at the thought. *I'll follow His word and forget what's behind, reaching for what God has in store. The future has never been in my hands.*

Saul's grip tightened around the small button he'd retrieved from the floor. It never failed to amaze him that words written dozens of centuries ago spoke so clearly to his heart.

"'I press toward the mark. . . .'" The parson's reading resonated with such depth, Saul wondered whether he intended today's message to affect his parishioners so personally.

The significance of the passage wasn't lost on Clara, either. Her earlier nod after the uplifting hymns had given him hope that she softened toward him, and the contentment on her face now bolstered his anticipation. Together, they'd put the mistakes of the past weeks behind them.

And Saul would see to it that everything went smoothly from there on out. New tactics were called for. No more antagonistic plotting or chesslike opposition would be employed. Instead, he'd make her understand he hadn't spoken lightly about courting her.

He squared his jaw. Today marked a new beginning. Oh, Clara would need a lot of convincing, but by the time he finished, he'd have her eating out of his hand. As the parson moved on, Saul refocused his attention to make sure he didn't miss anything.

"Today we'll close with one last hymn." With that, the preacher led them in a rousing chorus of one of Saul's favorite praise songs.

He rose to his feet and lifted his voice along with the others, relishing the purpose behind the words.

"Forward! be our watchword,
Steps and voices joined;
Seek the things before us,
Not a look behind. . ."

When they left the church to walk home, Saul kept his gaze fixed firmly ahead, to where Clara spoke with Midge.

"You're not angry with me anymore?" Hope shone through Midge's guarded tone.

"No." Clara reached out and grasped the girl's hand. "And we're not going to try to make Dr. Reed marry anyone. We're finished pushing him when it's his choice to make." She peeked over his shoulder as though to be sure he was listening.

"Good." He flashed her a wide grin as she and Midge hurried out of earshot and began whispering.

"Is that what's been afoot?" Doreen's murmur took him by surprise. "I wondered why everyone's been so quiet lately."

"Your niece is of the opinion I should marry a Buttonwood girl and settle down near my father." Saul looked down at the older woman, whose hand rested on his arm. "Despite my explanations that I had different plans, she's insisted on throwing me in the company of her friends."

"I suspected as much," she admitted. "I'd held out some hope it might work. Your father longs to have you stay."

"My practice is based in Baltimore." He didn't offer further explanation, instead choosing to change the subject. "Though Clara's efforts have piqued my interest in marriage."

"Oh?" Doreen's bonnet brim nearly caught him in the eye as she turned. "Is that why she won't be matchmaking any longer? I find that easy to believe—it's unlike Clara to abandon any undertaking unless she's already succeeded."

"Determined women such as your niece are rare."

"Yet you find yourself in a house with two of them." Doreen raised a single eyebrow. "It's uncanny how alike Clara and Midge are when it comes to pure strength of will."

"Perhaps that's why they get on so well." Saul thought about that for a moment. "For all that, the two of them are very different. Perhaps if Midge hadn't grown up in such difficult circumstances. . ."

"I won't pry," the older woman assured him. "You mean their perspectives differ even if their personalities run parallel."

"Exactly." He searched for words to describe it. "Midge is all sharp angles hewn by hardship. Clara's strength seems. . .softer somehow. But that's not the right word."

"The edges of her past are worn smooth from weathering," Doreen supplied. "In time, love will level out Midge's rough spots, too. But the sheer force or character it took to withstand their losses will always be the foundation of their worlds. Everything becomes shaped by how they perceive it."

"All this time, you've kept such wisdom to yourself." Saul stared at the woman whose quiet presence he'd taken for granted. "I should have asked sooner."

"You wouldn't have heard it." She sat down on the bench before the general store and gestured for him to join her. "It took you this long to realize you should be wooing my niece."

"How do I go about it?" Saul rubbed at the tension in the back of his neck. "When I tried to tell her, she decided my declaration was a ploy to stop her from matchmaking anymore."

"She's never seen her own value." Grief and remorse flashed across Doreen's usually calm face. "My husband saw to that."

"Why?" Saul's jaw clenched. "What did your husband do?"

"Uriah made it clear from the start that he saw women as inferior to men in every way and expected both of us to cater to his every whim." Doreen's eyes lit with fury, her words coming out faster. "Clara, in particular, he deemed useless. 'A penniless orphan brat,' he called her."

"If it weren't for the Lord's mercy softening my heart, I'd consider the man fortunate to have died." The words came out low and harsh, from his very gut. "Had I ever met this Uriah, he would have rued the day."

"The worst of it is I married him so I could take care of her. My inheritance wouldn't support both of us, so I needed a husband." Doreen drew a shaky breath. "If you want Clara, you'll have an uphill battle convincing her. She'll never marry for less than genuine love and respect."

CHAPTER 25

"How's that?" Midge peered over Clara's shoulder and waited for the verdict on her penmanship.

"Beautiful." Clara set down the slate. "We'll move on to pen and ink soon. In fact, I'll bring some back from the store this afternoon."

"Thank you." She scooped up the slate and took it from the table. "I'm glad you and Dr. Reed are getting along so well."

"Now that I'm not pestering him about getting married, things go much more smoothly." Clara stood up. "Today I'll be emptying and rinsing all those bottles of useless tonics. That way we'll have vials for powdered medicines when the new supplies arrive."

"Dr. Reed says you're real smart to have thought of that." Midge slid out of Clara's way and followed close. "He likes having you around to come up with ideas and help organize things."

"He's kind to say so." Red color climbed up Clara's neck and spread across her cheeks in a telltale sign of pleasure.

"One of the things I like about Dr. Reed is that he doesn't say anything he doesn't mean." Midge clasped the slate to her chest. "Like he told me back in Baltimore he wouldn't make me go to church if I didn't want to, and he meant it. I go while we're here because it would make him sad if I didn't, and I don't want to disappoint him, but he would keep his word if I tried to stay home."

"Yes, he would." Clara paused, one hand on the doorknob. "Why wouldn't you want to go to church, Midge?"

"Sometimes I forget that you've only known me for a little while." She rubbed her finger over the rough splinter on the right side of her slate. "You know, you and Dr. Reed and Aunt Doreen are all so wrapped up in church and prayer and everything, sometimes you forget other people don't think the same way."

"Midge, does it bother you when we pray?"

"No. I like the way we all hold hands around the table." She released the slate when Clara tugged it from her hands. "And the songs in church are real nice, too. They remind me of ones my sister used to sing to me."

"Nancy." Reaching for her hand, Clara led Midge to the parlor and sat down on the settee. "I remember you said she prayed a lot."

"Yeah, but she still lost her baby and died." Midge kicked the settee's leg with the heel of her boot since she couldn't say what she wanted to— that Rodney beat down the door and choked her when she tried to get in his way. That the man in the dirty suit shoved Nancy on the ground and took away the child growing inside her, making her bleed until she died. That Midge hadn't been able to stop it, and all her sister's cries didn't help, either. "Like I told Dr. Reed, it may sound good, but praying doesn't work."

"I've never heard anybody talk about it like that before." Clara's voice jerked Midge back. "Is that what you think? That prayer has a job to do, and if nothing happens, it's useless?"

"Well. . ." *Yes.* But the wonder in her friend's expression stopped Midge from saying so too fast. "It makes sense."

"I can see why you'd think so. Let me try to explain it another way, and you tell me if you understand what I mean. Okay?" Clara waited for her to nod then went ahead. "Do you remember when you wanted more taffy on Saturday evening and you asked for another piece?"

"You said no because it would spoil my supper," Midge recalled. A thought struck her. "Do we have any taffy left?"

"I'll look in a minute." Clara didn't seem very excited by the idea. "When you think about that conversation, do you look back and say that talking to me is a waste of time?"

"No, talking to you isn't a waste of time." Midge could hardly get the words out fast enough. "Even if you never give me another piece of taffy again, I'd still talk to you."

"I'm glad to hear it." A smile stretched across

Clara's face. "You know, a lot of times I'll ask God for things and I don't get the answer I want."

"Oh." Midge looked down at the toes of her boots. "You mean you prayed."

"I prayed for God to see Aunt Doreen and me safe to Oregon before winter," she pointed out. "But if that happened, I wouldn't have stayed in Buttonwood and met you."

"What you're saying is that even if you pray and you don't get what you ask for, it's not a waste of time." Midge heaved a sigh. "But it's not the same as talking to a person, Clara."

"No, because you're talking to God. Time spent praying is never wasted, Midge, even if you don't like the answer."

"Then I still don't see what good it does."

"Will you try something for me?"

"Depends on what it is." Midge snuck a glance at Clara out of the corner of her eye.

"You know how when you talk with people you say 'please' *and* 'thank you?'"

"Yes. That's just being polite."

"Have you ever been polite to God?" Clara raised both eyebrows when she asked. "Or have all your prayers been 'please' without any 'thank you?'"

"When I could talk to Him, I concentrated on the important stuff." Midge's nose tingled, so she kicked the sofa leg again. "If God has the whole world, why waste time on a 'thank you' from me when He could've saved my sister?"

"I don't have all the answers." Clara reached over to fold her in a hug, but Midge hopped up off the sofa.

"Well, neither do I." She headed for the door but stopped long enough to say one last thing. "And neither does prayer."

"Where's Midge going in such a hurry?" Saul kept one hand behind his back as he walked into the house.

"She needs time to think a few things over." Clara absently ran a fingertip over the thick velvet of the settee. "My talk about prayer upset her."

"And you, from the looks of it." He strode into the parlor and pulled the gift from behind his back with a flourish. "Perhaps these will cheer you up?"

"Oh, Dr. Reed, how lovely!" Clara took the bouquet of purple flowers he'd gathered and raised them to her nose. "Aunt Doreen will be so pleased to see them on the table."

"I picked them for you, Clara." Saul settled next to her. "To show how much I appreciate the time you've spent making our stay in Buttonwood a time to cherish."

"You'll have me thinking I should apologize more often"—she fingered a petal of one of the delicate blossoms—"if this is how you make amends after our battle over trying to get you married off."

"These humble flowers are meant as more than amends." He reached to take one of her hands in his. "I hope you're ready to hear me when I tell you there's only one woman in Buttonwood I'd consider courting."

Her lips parted in a small O of surprise, the

flowers tumbling to her lap. "You. . .I. . ." She took a breath and started again. "The evening after the walnut gathering, when you said you'd put me on the list. . . ?" her voice trailed off in a question.

"As true then as it is now." His pulse kicked up a notch at the shy hope flitting across her face.

"Midge was right. Just this morning she told me you don't say anything unless you mean it." She gave his hand a tentative squeeze. "I'm ashamed I even suspected otherwise."

"We'll put it behind us and move forward." Her mention of Midge made him remember his charge's hasty departure a moment before. "What else did your conversation include this morning?"

"She mentioned your promise not to force her to go to church, and she revealed her disbelief in prayer." Clara's gaze sought his. "Saul, curiosity ranks among my vices, but I've refrained from asking about Midge's past. I hoped you or she would come to tell me in your own time, but it seems she connects her sister's death with God not answering prayer."

"That's true." He tightened his grip yet didn't reveal more. "What else did she tell you?"

"Nothing particular." Tears shimmered in her eyes. "That girl's heart is still raw with grief for her sister, and the thought she has neither faith nor family to sustain her makes me ache."

"We stand as her family, and our faith will bolster hers." Saul prayed it would be so. "The loss of life is never easy to understand or accept."

"She mentioned a baby." Clara sat bolt upright,

her hand sliding from his grasp. "Did she watch her sister die in childbirth, along with the infant? Such a tragedy would test anyone's character, and she's so young."

"Clara, I intend to ask you to become my wife." He held a finger to her lips when she would speak. "Don't answer now. I tell you this so you know what I say is in hopes you'll join me and Midge to make our little family complete. To do that, there are things you need to know."

"I'm listening." Her expression gave no hint to her thoughts, forcing Saul to continue.

"When I told you I took Midge in after I arrived too late to save her sister, I spoke the truth. This is all most people need to know, all they can know if Midge is to have the kind of life she deserves." He rose to his feet, measuring his words with steps. "What you've earned the right to hear is the part of the tale I omitted to protect her reputation."

"Whatever her past, she needs us now." Clara's selfless response proved, as nothing else could, that he'd made the right decision in telling her. In choosing her.

"Midge found me after her sister's bully sent her out on the street for the first time." He chose his words carefully, pausing to make sure Clara understood his meaning. "To sell herself." Saul hated having to say the words, but she had to understand the full horror of it.

"No." She went white. "Midge didn't—"

"She found me." He cut off the words, wishing he could cut away the ugliness. "Filthy, skin and bones, dress too small, Midge looked to be no more than ten. I stopped and offered to find her respectable work. That's when I saw the bruises around her neck. From what I gather, Midge's older sister took up with a bruiser named Rodney, who forced Nancy into prostitution. When Nancy found herself in a delicate condition, Rodney hauled in a quack to terminate the...problem."

"The baby?" Clara's whisper scarcely floated to his ears.

"Yes. Nancy resisted but couldn't stop them." Saul began pacing again, the words coming low and furious. "When Midge tried to intervene, Rodney all but choked the life out of her before sending her out to take her sister's place. By the time I got there, Nancy had passed away."

"Oh, Saul."

The strangled sob drew him right back to Clara. Tears streamed down her face as he lowered himself onto the settee and wrapped his arms around her. He held her for long moments, until her cries softened and her breaths returned to normal once again.

"I'm sorry I had to tell you." He kept one arm around her waist while he handed her his handkerchief.

"I needed to know." She dabbed the linen beneath her eyes. "Thank you for telling me. Thank you for saving Midge and bringing her here."

"Thank you for understanding." He reached out to cup her cheek in his hand. "I'm blessed to have found you. Once we return to Baltimore, the three of us will be able to move forward."

Clara slowly lowered his handkerchief, her hand covering his and bringing it away from her face as her brows knit together. "Baltimore?"

"Hello?" A feminine voice preceded a knock at the door. "Dr. Reed? Do you have anything for a toothache?"

CHAPTER 26

B altimore!" Opal's gasp of indignation went a long way toward soothing Clara's exasperation.

"Yes! After all this time, how can he not understand that I won't drag Aunt Doreen back East? That we traveled all this way to prove we can make something of ourselves, start fresh, and he wants us to forget all about that?" The words came out in a huff. "He didn't even consider it. . . just informed me we'd be going."

"He did bring flowers." Opal's eyelids, made heavy from the laudanum she'd taken to dull her toothache, drifted shut. She snuggled deeper into Midge's quilt, making herself comfortable on the settee as she spoke with Clara. "How romantic. It must be nice to have a man be romantic like that."

"That part was nice," Clara admitted. *And Opal doesn't have an inkling how wonderful Saul truly is because I can't tell her about Midge. Not many men in this world would disrupt their own lives to care for an orphan.* "It makes no sense how he can seem so thoughtful and kind one moment, and be a tyrant the next."

"Mmmmhmmm." The drowsy agreement signaled Opal's descent into sleep. Hopefully, the ache would be gone by the time she awoke again. If not, Saul would have to pull the bothersome tooth.

Clara tucked Midge's quilt tighter around Opal, remembering how proud and pleased the girl had been to share it. Belying everyone's expectations, Midge's favorite item in her yellow and green sanctuary wasn't the dainty porcelain tea set, but the quilt she so carefully tugged into place each morning and curled under each night.

A swift glance out the window didn't show any sign of the girl, who must still be on the far side of the meadow, cracking walnuts on the flat rocks. Aunt Doreen had just left to tell Saul it was time for the noon meal, so Midge should turn up at any minute.

An acrid tinge of smoke tickled Clara's nose. The Dunstalls' trash burning had lasted longer than usual this week, leaving a sulfuric trace still strong in the air. As Clara made her way to the kitchen to check on lunch, the odor of burned food grew stronger until she opened the kitchen door.

She stood rooted to the spot in horror at what she saw. Greedy flames engulfed the worktable. When the shelf above it collapsed in a shower of sparks and cinders, Clara slammed the door shut and raced to the parlor, where Opal slept on.

"Wake up!" Grasping her friend's shoulder, Clara gave a violent shake. She pulled Opal to a sitting position, only to have her friend sag back onto the settee. "Opal, the house is on fire!" It was no use. The laudanum kept her friend locked in sleep.

There wasn't time to get help. Tendrils of smoke curled around the doorway. With so much wood in the house, the flames would reach the parlor before Clara returned with anyone strong enough to carry Opal out.

"Lord, help me!" Desperate, she jammed her shoulder into Opal's stomach, trying to lift her friend. Her knees buckled before she got Opal off the settee, sending them both crashing to the floor.

Gasping for breath, Clara wriggled out from beneath Opal's weight, kicking off the quilt, which had tangled about her legs. At the flash of an idea, she seized the blanket, tugging, shoving, pushing, and pulling to get it beneath Opal as a makeshift travois.

By now, everything had turned a murky, grayish haze. Clara grasped the edges of the blanket, sliding it—and Opal—across the floor in a frantic bid for safety. Coughs wracked her as she fought for every inch. Flames danced around the edges of her vision, crowding out the darkness as she stumbled.

"Clara!" Strong arms wrapped around her waist and hauled her toward air so clear it hurt her chest. "Clara, honey, breathe." Saul carried her far from the house, bracing her shoulders.

"Opal," she managed to croak before the coughs overtook her again. "Still. . .inside." Clara struggled to see beyond Saul's face. Fire engulfed both stories of the house now.

"I have her." A familiar voice came from beside her, but Clara couldn't place it.

"Opal," she murmured, trying to turn her head to see that her friend had made it out. She couldn't twist far enough, so she reached out, grasping hold of some fabric nearby. Clara yanked it as close as she could, throat dry and aching so she couldn't speak.

Beneath the soot and smoke, her fingers rubbed enough grime away for Clara to see the green and yellow of Midge's quilt. It was enough to let her know they'd saved Opal. What could be more important?

"Clara, look at me," Saul ordered as he set her down a goodly distance from the house, propping her back against a large stone. "Breathe deep for me."

She looked up at him through eyes made bleary with tears, obediently drawing a deep breath of untainted air as Adam laid Opal beside her. Coughs wracked Clara's frame as she did as he urged, expelling some of the smoke from her lungs. Her shoulders drooped, head lolling to the side in exhaustion.

"Water." He spared only the one word for Adam as he crooked a finger beneath Clara's chin and tilted her face upward once more. "Look up, sweetheart." Saul ran his hands over her sleeves and skirts, checking for telltale scorch marks or any tenderness to indicate injury. He found nothing.

Thank You, Lord.

"Opal," she rasped after the spasms subsided once more.

"I'll check on her." Saul shifted, looking for the first time at the other woman pulled from the fire.

Still under the effects of the laudanum, Opal Speck lay curled on one side, partly bolstered by the quilt twined around her. Though her breath came in slight wheezes, no coughing or gasping plagued her. Obviously, she hadn't breathed in as much smoke.

"Here, Doc." Adam set down a bucket of cool water and crouched beside him. He slid an uncertain glance toward Clara, who still coughed. "She all right?"

"I pray so. She seems to have taken in more smoke and ash than Miss Speck." Saul dipped his handkerchief in the water, wrung it out, and moved toward Clara. "Don't move."

He used the cloth to wipe soot away from her eyes, already cleansed by the tears, to lessen the stinging. Only after she'd sipped from the tin cup he'd given her did he turn back to Opal and repeat the process.

"How come she's out like that?" Adam stayed close to Opal but didn't touch her. "Did she hit her head? She was on the floor when we got there."

"She came to me for help with a toothache." Saul closed his eyes at the memory of his frustration over her interruption. "I gave her some laudanum to dull the pain, so she'll sleep for a while yet. You say you found her on the floor?"

"Yep, all twisted in that quilt." Understanding flashed across his friend's features. "Miss Field was trying to drag Opal out of there."

"Couldn't." The word came out in a husky scratch as Clara's eyes filled with tears again. She reached out to put a hand on Adam's sleeve. "Thank you."

"Don't talk anymore, Clara." Saul refilled the cup and passed it to her. "Just deep breaths, then small sips of water. That's better. Easy does it."

"Why isn't Opal coughing?" Adam looked from Clara to her friend and back, his brow furrowed.

"She was on the floor, below the smoke. Clara was standing, trying to pull them to safety, so she breathed it all in." Saul swallowed at the thought of it.

Behind them, everyone in town or near enough to see trouble formed a bucket brigade. Midge stood in line with the others, her return with the shelled walnuts at the moment he and Doreen discovered the fire a blessing in and of itself.

Otherwise, he'd be tearing the place apart searching for her, just in case the collapsing second story had trapped Midge. Bucket after bucket of water hissed as they clashed with the flames, slowly vanquishing the destructive force.

Saul knew Dad's house was ruined, but it didn't matter. As long as Clara's lungs weren't scorched and she suffered no permanent damage, he'd praise the Lord for this day's work. They'd lost no lives, and the fire hadn't spread to the dry prairie grasses to devastate the town and surrounding farms. Overall, a crisis had been averted.

Why, then, Saul wondered as he braced Clara through another paroxysm of coughing, *does it feel as though everything has changed?*

Ruined. Even if her throat weren't raw and aching, Clara wouldn't have been able to speak as she surveyed the smoldering remains of Josiah's once-fine home. *Everything is ruined.*

Jagged talons of guilt slashed at her, cutting off the air Saul kept insisting she breathe. She gasped at the sharp pain in her chest, tears stinging her eyes though she'd thought them all spent. Thick coughs bent her double, blotting out the thoughts of her failure for a blessed moment.

Saul shifted beside her, warm and solid, one arm bracing her back so she could inhale more easily. How was he to know regret tainted every breath, scraping her throat and bruising her heart?

She closed her eyes against the sight of charred bricks heaped in smoking ashes. *Why, Lord?* Against thoughts of what Midge had suffered before Saul found her. *Why?*

Memories long held at bay rushed forward, sliding like storm clouds one atop the other until their rumbling deafened her to everything else.

"Not now, Clara. Mommy and I will be home in a few weeks. You'd be in the way on this trip. . . ." The last words her father spoke to her before he and her mother died in the carriage accident.

"Useless," Uriah's voice hissed. *"Penniless orphan brat. There's no place in my house for a willful woman."*

The verses he'd made her memorize, write over and over, recite nightly as a reminder she'd be nothing but a burden her entire life.

"*It is better to dwell in the wilderness, than with a contentious and an angry woman.*' '*A foolish woman is clamorous: she is simple, and knoweth nothing.*'"

His favorite proverbs from the Word resounded in the passageways of her mind, striking at her every decision. Anger over his unfair judgments filled her with a desire to prove herself. Settling in Oregon seemed the perfect opportunity to stand on her own, provide for Doreen, and be a burden to no man.

Or was it pure foolishness that drove her to bring them to the middle of the wilderness? After a lifetime of rejecting Uriah's prejudice, her own actions had come to epitomize the worst of it.

Clara slumped into the crook of Saul's arm, sobs merging with coughs she couldn't control until black spots danced in her vision. And still the tears came.

I failed us all.

CHAPTER 27

Midge stared at what was left of the house. Only the brick husk of the first floor remained in place, the wooden second story having collapsed in the blaze. Smoke still hung heavy in the air, steaming bits of broken house still sending tendrils upward.

Tears streamed down her face from the stinging smoke and the new layer of loss. Her fingers closed around the locket she'd not taken from her neck since the day Nancy died, squeezing tight as though to hold on to the only thing she had left.

Things. Midge straightened. *Memories count, too.* Blinking, she turned away and looked toward where Dr. Reed tended Clara. She stumbled a little as she headed toward them, until a soft hand smudged with soot reached out to clasp hers.

Aunt Doreen didn't say anything, didn't try to smile or pretend everything was all right. She just held Midge's hand in a firm grip as they made their way over to Clara and Dr. Reed. That made her feel better than any slick smiles or shiny promises could have.

Midge dropped to her knees beside Clara, still keeping hold of Doreen's hand. She released her clutch on the locket to reach out and comb her fingers through her friend's hair. There wasn't much to say, nothing good to tell, so she settled for the obvious. "We're here now."

"Good." Clara's voice sounded far away and gravelly from all the smoke and coughing. Her eyelids sank low, but she still moved to draw Midge close to her side.

All of her worries merged with the smoke she'd breathed to clog Midge's throat as she snuggled close. Aunt Doreen settled on her other side, between her and Opal, who hadn't woken up yet from the laudanum. At least, that's what Dr. Reed was saying.

"She'll be fine." He had his arm around Clara's waist and looked down at her while he spoke. "Clara will need to take it easy since she breathed in so much smoke. It doesn't seem as though she scorched her lungs, but we can't be too careful."

They all sat for a moment, huddled together. Them, against this terrible thing that had almost taken Clara away. The thought brought fresh tears to sting Midge's eyes, and she swiped at them with the back of her hand.

Not Clara. She scowled and looked overhead. *Or Dr. Reed or Aunt Doreen, either.* No matter how hard she rubbed her eyes, the tears kept coming, so she just let them. *You've already got Mama and Nancy and Nancy's baby up there in heaven.*

No answer came. No voice sounded from the

heavens or whispered in the wind as the rest of the town doused the rubble of the house one last time. The silence rushed in her ears until it became an unbearable taunt.

Midge held on tighter to Clara and Doreen and finally asked the question that had plagued her since Nancy died. *How am I supposed to believe in You, and all Your love and goodness, if You keep trying to steal everything I love?*

"Saul?!" Josiah bellowed as he burst into the shop, the acrid stench of smoke and ashes spurring him forward in the darkness. "Doreen?" Receiving no immediate answer, he pounded up the stairs.

The icy hand of fear clamped around his heart, making it hard to breath, hard to move. He moved anyway, not stopping until he ran into his son at the top of the steps. Josiah wrapped Saul in his arms and held tight for a moment to assure himself his son was safe and sound before he let go. "Where are Doreen and Clara?"

"In the dugout with Midge." Saul led him into the crowded room. Everything had been shoved against one wall, making room for a mattress and washstand near the stairwell. "I insisted the girls sleep here, but. . ." A gesture at the cramped space finished the statement for him.

"No one was hurt? They're all fine?" Josiah's pulse kicked up a notch when Saul hesitated.

"Clara inhaled a lot of smoke, and I can't get her to rest as she should." A frown furrowed his brow. "Her coughing has lessened in the two days since it happened, though I'd be more satisfied if she'd stop sifting through the remains of the house, trying to salvage things. She needs to recover fully."

"And Doreen?"

"She was with me in the store when the fire started." Saul's assurance drained some of the tension from Josiah's shoulders. "Midge came back from the field to find the house aflame, so neither one suffered any injury."

"What trapped Clara inside?" *I thought the place safe, but if something collapsed and endangered her, I'll never forgive myself.*

"Opal Speck." Saul's expression softened. "I'd given her laudanum for a toothache, and she'd dozed off in the parlor. Clara wouldn't leave her behind."

"She's a good woman."

"A stubborn woman." He turned away so Josiah couldn't see his eyes. "She tried to drag Opal out on a quilt. When Adam and I burst in, she'd all but collapsed mere feet from the door. Praise God we were able to save them."

Rage and gratitude warred in his son's voice, and Josiah knew the emotions centered around a woman. *But which one?*

"You carried Opal out of the house?" He kept his tone casual to hide the importance of the question.

"I reached Clara first. Adam managed Opal."

"She seems to have made quite an impression since I left." Josiah kept the observation neutral.

"You could say that." A wry smile tilted the

corners of Saul's mouth. "Clara understands I intend to marry her."

For the first time since he'd seen the skeletal brick outline of his house, smelled the ashes of charred wood and tang of overheated metal, Josiah grinned. *Clara. My boy inherited my good sense after all.*

"Fine." He dragged off his hat and leaned against the wall. "Fire doesn't matter then. No harm done."

"No harm?" Saul gave a short bark of laughter. "The house burned down. The women lost their clothes and belongings."

"We'll rebuild from the bricks and replace everything lost." Josiah squinted at the glower on his son's face. "That's one of the advantages of owning a general store."

"It's more than that." Saul paced three steps, executed a tight turn in the narrow space, and kept going. "Since the fire, Clara's changed. It's not just that her throat hurts so she doesn't talk a lot." He gave a helpless shrug. "I don't know how to fix what's wrong."

"Well, it makes sense she takes the loss of the house personally." Josiah moved over and sank onto the mattress on the floor, stretching out his feet. "The only thing she wanted was a way to provide for Doreen and give her a good life. It was underhanded of me to use that against her, but how else could I have gotten her to agree to our little bargain?"

"What bargain?" Steel edged Saul's words.

Now I've gone and stepped in it. Josiah didn't

move a muscle, too busy trying to figure out how to squirm out of the mess he'd made without twisting any more of the truth.

"What bargain," he parroted his son. "Good question."

"Dad, what did you do?" Saul loomed closer.

"Sit down, son." Josiah waited as Saul silently debated whether or not to give ground, finally settling next to him. "The easy answer here would be to remind you of the deal I made with Doreen and Clara when they first showed up in Buttonwood. In exchange for room and board, they'd cook the meals and keep house."

"Keep house," Saul muttered. "I know she feels responsible because you left them to take care of the house while you were gone, but it goes deeper. Tell me the rest."

"It's going to stick in your craw, but every man learns that when it comes to women, he has to swallow his pride."

"Go on." Saul stared straight ahead like a man bracing for a firing squad.

"In the letter I wrote asking you to come, do you remember me mentioning that you might find a wife while you were here?" Josiah knew that wasn't enough warning for what he'd done, but he'd bring up whatever points he had in his favor.

"You hadn't even met Clara when you wrote that." Saul pinned him with an impatient glower.

"You might not have been set on finding a wife, and Clara skittered away like a gun-shy mare at the very idea, but I'm not fool enough to miss an opportunity like that when it walks right into my store."

"Skittered away at the idea? She could have at least met me before ruling out the possibility."

"You're a fine one to speak." Josiah bit back a grin at the disgruntled note in his son's tone. *Maybe this talk won't go too badly.* "Did you come willing to consider the girls you met during your stay?" The silence between them was answer enough to suit him. "So I decided you needed some guidance, a nudge in the right direction."

Saul snorted. "You expect me to think that's all of it?"

"Yep." Josiah stretched, trying to end the conversation right there. "That's all." He threw in a yawn for good measure. "What say we turn in?"

"Not so fast, Dad." Saul didn't budge. "You put Clara up to all that matchmaking, didn't you? I have my own father to thank for her incessant attempts to throw me together with every unmarried woman in Buttonwood the entire time you were gone?"

"If you knew what she was up to, why pry it out of me?" Josiah yanked off a boot. "The whole thing worked in the end. I counted on you to pick Clara, you know."

"That I believe." Saul shook his head. "You're crafty, Dad, setting it all up that way. And since it's Clara you chose, I'll forgive you." He got up, walking to the kerosene lamp as though about to put it out.

"Good. Now maybe we can get some shut-eye and put this whole thing about the house behind us. With you marrying, Clara, she doesn't need it anymore."

Saul froze, hand still reaching for the lamp. "The house?"

"It was the only way to get her to play match-maker, son. As much as I hate to admit it, I was devious enough to offer her the house if she could get you married off and settled down."

"Why?" His arm fell to his side.

"All that girl wants is to be able to provide for Doreen. After Hickory kicked them off the wagon train, it looked like they couldn't ever make it." Josiah stood up. "I offered her a home if she could give me my family."

"And if she doesn't marry me?" Saul swung around to face him. "What then? You knew I wouldn't wed any of the other women here. Now she and Doreen can't even stay to keep house for you. Clara isn't marrying me because she wants to, Dad." His voice went hoarse. "She has no other choice."

CHAPTER 28

"Good morning." Clara's subdued greeting the next day tightened the vise around Saul's chest.

Sleep evaded him the night before, and now words played the same trick. He rubbed some of the grit from his eyes. "Why are you doing laundry? You should be resting."

"I feel much better today." She kept at it. "After all, there isn't much laundry left since everything burned."

"Take it easy," he ordered. "My father came home last night."

"Home?" Her lips trembled, and she stopped stirring the laundry she heated in a large pot. "I'll go explain."

"You have nothing to explain." His hand shot out and caught her by the wrist, drawing her away from the laundry. Saul's jaw set. "At least, not to my father."

"He trusted me to look after his house." The green of her gaze darkened. "I failed."

"In more ways than one." The harsh statement came out before he could stop it. "What about marrying me off to a Buttonwood girl? Dad's more disappointed about that than the house."

Clara tried to tug her hand away. "I promised him I'd try, and I did. But after the walnut gathering, and the message that Sunday, I couldn't keep forcing you into those situations. Your father will understand that it didn't work. As for the house. . ." She lifted her chin. "I'll pay him back in time. Somehow. Turn loose of me, Saul. I need to go to him. He deserves an explanation."

"*I* deserve the explanation, Clara." Saul stepped closer, refusing to let the feel of her soft wrist beneath his fingers or the rosy blush of the morning sun on her hair sway him. "Why didn't you tell me about the bargain?"

She paled. "That was private. It wasn't my place to break a confidence, although you knew I was angling to see you wed. What more did you need to evade my efforts?"

"The truth," he all but growled it. "I needed to know that the time you spent with me meant nothing more than gathering information. That the way you made me and Midge feel welcome all had to do with your ambition to get this house. I needed to know your *real* motive behind it all."

"Why?" This time she snatched her hand from his grasp. "Why did you need to know that if I saw you happily married, your father delighted to have family nearby, I could make a home for Aunt Doreen and myself?" Her eyes shone bright and fierce. "Would you have married one of the other girls out of charity for us? What would it have changed?"

"I would have known that you were using me from the moment I came to town." He spoke low, shadowing her steps as she backed up. "I would have known better than to start looking for you in a crowd, to wait for your hair to escape your bonnet and gleam in the sun. I would have known it was a waste of time to watch how your eyes change color according to how you feel, and that for all your big heart and kindness, you calculated every step of the way."

"No, Saul," she whispered the plea.

"Most of all, I would have known why you never put yourself on that list of brides-to-be. You never wanted to marry me. You still don't." He reached toward her face but curled his fingers back before he touched her. If he touched her, he'd be lost. "Isn't it ironic how you wanted to marry me off and I swore to avoid it, but now I'm going to be the one taking you to the altar?"

"How could you still want to marry me?" Wonder filled her face. "In spite of the bargain I made with your father?"

"Because you didn't trick me into choosing you, Clara." He took a deep breath. "I did that on my own."

"It's not too late to fix that mistake." Anger flared to life in her gaze as she crossed her arms over her chest. "Neither of us is bound by any promise."

"But you will marry me."

325

"No." She uttered the syllable as though it were an immovable mountain.

"Don't be foolish, Clara."

"I won't be." Her lips pressed in a thin line. "Only a foolish woman would marry a man who didn't want her. Who said he'd been tricked into it."

"It's my decision." He closed the distance between them so his boots brushed against her skirts.

"Marriage vows take two people, Saul Reed." She unfolded her arms to plant her hands on her hips. "So it's my decision. And I say no." Her voice caught. "I won't marry a man who'll resent me for it."

She thinks I don't really want her anymore, that I'm just going through the motions out of a misplaced sense of obligation.

"The only thing I'd resent"—he wound one arm around her waist as he spoke—"is your refusing to be my wife. We'll have a good life, Clara."

"Then why all of this?" She pressed against his chest in a bid for freedom.

"We're not leaving anything out this time." Saul kept one arm at her waist and reached up to trap her palm against the beat of his heart. "No more secrets."

She stared at their joined hands, "Are you sure?"

The heat of their contact seared him. "Never doubt it." He leaned to press a kiss on her brow before freeing her hand so he could tilt her chin up. Their gazes held. "And I'll spend the rest of our lives convincing you that you made the right choice."

He lowered his head to hers, his mouth pressing

against the softness of her lips for a long, heady moment. *Marrying me may not be her first choice, but I'll make sure she never regrets it.*

"I never suspected you could be so persuasive." She touched the tips of her fingers to her lips and gave him a shy smile.

"From now on, Clara, there will only be one bargain. You'll become my bride, and together we'll give Midge the family she deserves. It'll be a new start for us when we return to Baltimore."

"Baltimore?" Her echo made the memory of their conversation the day of the fire resurface. Just before Opal came, hadn't she said the exact same thing—with that same look of mulish stubbornness?

"Where I'm establishing my practice," he reminded. "The city that's the only home Midge has every really known."

"Oh, Saul." She pulled away from him, tears sparkling in her eyes. "After everything we've been through, how could you think I would go to Baltimore? I can't go back East."

"It's the only way." He caught one of her hands in his. "Be sensible, Clara. In Baltimore, I can provide for you and Doreen. The loss of the house here doesn't matter—Dad can live above the store. You won't have to wait for a new wagon train or endure the hardships of the trail ever again, and Midge will finally have the family she deserves. It's the perfect solution to every problem."

"You're wrong." She pulled away for what seemed like the last time. "Marriage is never the solution for a woman."

With her head bowed, Clara almost ran straight into Josiah.

"Chin up," he warned. "Or I might think you're unhappy to see me."

"Never," she promised. The now-familiar guilt speared her. "I'm so sorry about the house, Mr. Reed." Her throat ached with memories of helplessness. "By the time I found the kitchen aflame, I couldn't stop it."

"It's not your fault." Saul came behind her and tried to put his hands on her shoulders, but she stepped aside.

"All that matters is all of you came out fine." Josiah craned his neck. "Where's that aunt of yours?"

"Inside, cleaning up after breakfast." Clara saw his hesitation. "Go on ahead. She'll be happy to see you."

"Will she?" His murmur almost slid past her, but Clara heard it as Josiah Reed went down the steps of the dugout.

Saul blocked her when she would have followed. "Our conversation isn't over."

"I will not marry you for convenience. I will not go back East." She looked up at him, searching for an answer—any answer—for the question she had to ask. "What more is there to say?"

"Morning, Dr. Reed!" Midge came bouncing out of the dugout. "Your pa brought me a peppermint from the store."

"He's looked forward to meeting you." Saul's smile strained around the edges. "Is he talking with Doreen now?"

"Mmmmhmmm." Midge answered around the minty candy. "Aunt Doreen said I should see if I could help you with anything."

Clara cast a last look at Saul. His stony expression smashed her last fragments of hope. *He doesn't have any other reason. Saul doesn't want to marry me because he loves me—it's just the easiest way to make things work out for him and Midge.* Hot tears pricked behind her eyelids, but she blinked them back, forcing a smile for her young friend.

"I have a surprise over here." Clara reached out and grasped Midge's hand, tugging her toward the pot where she'd been laundering the quilt. "Opal stopped by this morning with something for you."

"What is it?" Midge's jaw dropped as she peered into the steaming pot. Her voice came out in a whisper. "My quilt?"

"That's right." Clara used the wooden paddle to pull the bed covering out of the hot water and deposit it in a cooling rinse. "She'd already washed it once, but I could still smell the smoke. I thought I'd give it another wash before you used it tonight."

They swirled it in the rinse water, watching as yellow and green melded in a whirl of color. It took both their efforts to pull the heavy quilt from the pot and try to coax the excess water out.

A shadow fell over the fabric, lending a bluish hue to the greens as large hands reached to help them. Saul didn't say a word as he wrung the fabric in the middle so she and Midge needn't do a delicate balancing act to keep it from dragging in the dirt. He didn't look at Clara even as he spoke.

"I can see why this is special to you, Midge, since it's the only thing that made it out of the fire."

"No, it's not." The young girl's hand crept up to the locket she always wore about her neck, only to hastily catch up her corner of the quilt when it sagged toward the earth. "I mean, that's not what makes it special."

"She loved this quilt before the fire," Clara agreed. "As an act of kindness, she fetched it for Opal that day. One good deed deserves another, and that's why she still has it today."

"Well, fair's fair." Midge carefully tugged her end over the rigged clothesline and pinned it in place. "Opal helped fix it for me, so she deserved to use it."

"Is it the color?" Saul's voice came out low and serious. "The green reminds you of Nancy?"

"Partly. Nancy's favorite was green and mine's yellow, so it's like both of us together." Midge pursed her lips as she looked up at him. "Do you want to know what's really so special about this quilt, Dr. Reed?"

For the first time that day, Saul said the right thing. "Of course I do. If it's important to you, it's important to me."

"All right." Midge traced her fingertips along the wet fabric, outlining the honeycomb pattern as she spoke. "It's more than the colors and more than it coming out of the fire. When I came here and saw it waiting for me, I thought it was real pretty and nice, but it didn't matter all that much."

"What changed?" Clara had to know. She'd

been wondering about the significance for a long while.

"That first night, I laid down and thought about what you said. You remember coming after me that day?" At Clara's nod, Midge kept on. "No one had ever been excited to meet me or done anything nice like fixing up a room for me. I liked that. And when I woke up, I looked at the pattern because I hadn't seen the same one before. That's when I saw that it'd been repaired. Someone put a lot of time into making it beautiful again."

"I can see why you'd appreciate that." Saul clapped a hand on her shoulders. "That'd make it special to anyone."

"No." A frown creased Midge's features as she stared up at her hero. "A lot of people would have thought it was junk and thrown it away or wanted something new. They'd say it was a waste of effort for something old and worn."

"Such a shame," Clara sighed, "when people can't recognize the value of what lies right in front of them." She stared at Saul as she spoke, willing him to hear the meaning beneath the words. *Look at me, Saul. Ask me to marry you because you love me. Ask me to make a home with you here, in Buttonwood, where we've already shared so much. See what's right in front of you.*

"Exactly." Midge walked around Saul to loop an arm around Clara's waist. "You saw that quilt and knew it had been through a lot. Maybe somebody loved it to pieces, and somebody else gave it a good thrashing, and it wasn't much to look at when you found it. But you saw that it could be made whole and beautiful again, and it was worth saving." She reached out and curled her other hand around Saul's forearm. "Just like I was when Dr. Reed found me."

Oh, Lord. . . Clara gave up trying to stop the tears. There were only so many times per morning a woman could be expected to hold them back under such circumstances. *Is this the same girl who came to Buttonwood defiantly asking whether I pitied her? She's not accepted Your love yet, but I see Your hand at work. Thank You, Jesus.*

CHAPTER 29

*N*either of us is bound by any promise..." What he'd give to have extracted Clara's pledge of her hand in marriage before everything had gone wrong.

Fragments of his conversations with Clara and Midge rang through Saul's mind the rest of the day, giving him no peace.

"That's not what makes it special." Midge's frown chastened him as she revealed the depth of her loving heart.

"Such a shame when people can't recognize the value of what lies right in front of them." Clara's gaze was full of meaning, but the words did not follow due course. It made no sense.

He was good at recognizing what stood in front of him. He'd found Midge. He'd asked Clara to marry him. Fisting his hands at his temples, Saul leaned on the counter for a moment while Dad went up to the room overhead. *What more can Clara want?*

"Whiskey." Larry Grogan's voice broke through the muddle of his thoughts. "Where's your whiskey,

Doc?" The man's bloodshot eyes scanned the shelves. His wrinkled clothes and the stubble on his cheeks, bisected by the still-angry pink of his scar, spoke of days of neglect.

"We only sell medicinal whiskey here, for cleaning wounds and such." Saul straightened. He purposefully omitted mentioning whiskey's other use for muting pain. Larry was long past suffering from his injuries. "You know that, Larry."

"I know." He slapped some crumpled money on the counter. "Two bottles, and make it snappy."

"Who's hurt?" Saul reached for his medical bag even as he asked the question. If Larry looked this bad, even after his ribs and face had healed, the sick family member must be far worse off.

I've been too preoccupied with Clara and the fire to have paid attention. He tamped down the surge of remorse. A doctor didn't have time for such things in a crisis.

"What?" Larry's astonishment would have been more at home on a cartoon caricature. "Nobody I know of. Why?"

"I see." Saul put back his bag and placed both palms flat on the counter. He took in his customer's disheveled state with new eyes. "Then it's best you leave, Larry."

"Soon as I get m' whiskey." The fool gave the counter an imperious thump. "Better make it three bottles."

"We only sell whiskey for medical use," Saul rephrased his earlier statement, speaking slowly to clarify his meaning.

"Yeah, that Gilbert and Parsons stuff." Larry grimaced. "Don't matter much though. After a few belts you can't taste the difference anymore. Bring it out, Doc."

"No." It would have been amusing to watch Larry try to figure out what he meant, but today Saul was in no mood for it.

"No?" The man sounded incredulous.

"No."

"You can't do that!" Outrage beetled Larry's brows. "You can't turn down a paying customer!"

"What are we turning down?" Dad came down the steps just in time to spare Larry from being escorted to the door by Saul's hand on the scruff of his collar.

"Josiah! Come tell your boy how men handle things in Buttonwood." Larry puffed up like one of the roosters his family used to terrorize Sadie the cow.

Saul, for one, would rather deal with the animals.

"Keep your hat on, Larry." Dad approached slowly. "My son's got five years and a medical degree on you. Buttonwood's the same as anyplace else in that you show respect."

Trust Dad to put that little weasel in his place with a few words when I was ready to toss him on his ear.

"He won't sell me any whiskey." The petulance in their customer's voice grated on Saul's nerves. Sober, Larry acted like a spoiled brat. Drunk, he could be dangerous. Saul shouldered his way between his father and Larry.

"We only sell the hygienic stuff." Dad's repetition

of Saul's warning didn't sit too well with Larry.

"I know, and I want to buy three bottles." He jabbed his money with a grubby finger. "So what's the holdup?"

"There's no reason under the sun why you'd need three bottles. . .unless you Grogans have finally had it out with the Specks?" The look Dad shot him meant that was a question.

"No." Saul crossed his arms over his chest. "It seems Larry's developed a taste for the stuff."

"This isn't a saloon, Grogan." Dad's growl made Larry back up against the counter. "We've worked hard to keep that sort of thing out of Buttonwood, and you won't get it from my store. Saul's right—you can take your money and leave."

"One day, you Reeds'll be sorry you crossed me." Larry scooped the money into his pocket. "Same as those Specks." He kept muttering as he stalked out the door.

"What a piece of work." Dad shook his head. "The Grogans and the Specks are fairly good bunches as long as you don't mix them, but that Larry seems to have gotten all the rotten in his batch. What happened to his face?"

"I stitched him up after a threshing accident where he just about got himself killed. As for the others, Adam and his sister are fine folk," Saul agreed. "And I'd say the same for Elroy and Opal Speck. Larry, on the other hand, attracts trouble like a trash heap attracts maggots."

"Let's not think about that." A grin spread across Dad's face. "I've got some good news to tell you."

At least one of us is having a nice day. Saul lounged against the counter. "What's your news?"

"You're getting married?" Clara repeated dumbly, staring at her aunt as though she'd gone mad. Which, come to think of it, was as good an explanation as any.

"Josiah asked me this morning." Aunt Doreen's eyes shone with suspicious moisture in the dim light of the small dugout. "I said yes."

"How could you?" Clara sank onto the bed, her knees unable to keep her upright. Sitting didn't ease the cramped feeling of walls and the earth itself crowding down around her.

"How could I not?" The woman who'd raised her looked astonished by the question. "After all that's happened..."

"After all that's happened," somehow she managed to choke the words past the lump in her throat, "you're giving up?"

"What am I giving up by choosing to marry Josiah?" Doreen's weight made the mattress dip slightly. "Think of all that I'm gaining."

"Just as you thought of what you'd gain when you married Uriah?" The words shot out of Clara's mouth before she could bite them back. Before she could decide if she wanted to.

"The two have nothing in common."

The vehemence in Aunt Doreen's tone spurred the roiling frenzy in Clara's heart. "Even their names are similar," she snapped. "Both men seek your hand only after you've withstood devastating change, preying upon you in a difficult time."

"How dare you say such things about Josiah!" Aunt Doreen rose from the bed, gray eyes darkening to the color of thunderclouds. "He's offered nothing but kindness, and you equate him with your *uncle*?" A long pause filled the room before sorrow softened her gaze. "Can you honestly not see the difference?"

"I see a difference," Clara admitted. "Else I would have pressed onward until we caught up to Hickory or found Oregon on our own rather than accept his help."

"Josiah knew it, too. Without even knowing us, he went out of his way to make us feel needed, although the trade was never a fair one."

Her point didn't ease Clara's mind at all. "Why is that? Why take in two women he just met, know them for only a few weeks, and suddenly return with a proposal?" She set her jaw. "It doesn't sit well, Aunt Doreen. You don't have to accept his offer."

"It's my choice, Clara."

"I don't accept it." Clara reached out, holding her aunt's shoulders. "You needn't marry Josiah to see us through. You'll never need to make such a sacrifice again." Tears couldn't seep through her determination this time. Nothing would.

"Oh, Clara." Her aunt reached out to stroke her face. "Is that what you think? That I'm marrying Josiah because we didn't make it to Oregon?"

"And I didn't stop the fire." Shame made her voice as hollow and dark as the depressing place where they now lived. She hung her head. "I failed us both."

"No, Clara." Doreen pulled her close and wrapped her in a tight embrace. "I told Josiah I'd marry him because I want to."

"Don't pretend for me. We'll find another way." She babbled now, trying to withdraw but unable to because she'd backed against the bed. "Marriage isn't the solution. That's what I told Saul when he asked me to marry him and said it would fix everything. We'd go to Baltimore because that's where Midge wants to live, and the house burning down wouldn't matter."

"I'm not marrying him to solve anything. We could stay in this dugout through spring and go on to Oregon, Clara." Doreen finally eased back to look her in the eye. "I'm engaged because I want to be. The way Josiah looks at me makes me feel beautiful and cherished."

"Hurrying into anything would be a mistake. Can you have a long engagement, get to know each other better?" *Give me more time to grow accustomed to the idea?*

Silence spooled between them as Doreen eased down beside her once more. When she spoke again, it was almost a whisper. "He says he loves me."

Clara saw her aunt touch the third finger of her left hand briefly and belatedly noticed the sparkle upon it. "You deserve to be loved. Did he give you that as an engagement ring?"

"Yes." Doreen's face flushed with pleasure as she splayed her fingers to better display the finery.

"Isn't it lovely?"

Clara looked at the rose gold ring set with small diamonds and seed pearls. It looked like something she would have chosen for her aunt, had anyone sought her opinion. "There's no question Josiah has good taste. He chose you."

"Won't you be happy for me?" The vulnerability in her aunt's gaze proved Clara's undoing.

This is about her, not me. Aunt Doreen's given up so much for me through the years; so long as she's not tying herself to another man for the wrong reason, it's time for me to let go of my own plans. She took a deep breath and found a small smile. "I'll try."

Midge backed away from the dugout slowly so she wouldn't make any noise. The roof raised in a hill-like mound, with the stovepipe poking through it. The last thing she needed was for Clara to know she'd heard everything.

Aunt Doreen is marrying Dr. Reed's father, which means she'll stay in Buttonwood. Midge walked briskly, stomping out her thoughts and her energy as she went along. *That'd be fine if Clara married Dr. Reed and we stayed, too.*

She paused to aim a savage kick at an un-suspecting rock. *But Clara won't marry Dr. Reed because marriage isn't for fixing problems and she doesn't want to go to Baltimore. Well, neither do I. Why can't we stay with Aunt Doreen and Opal and everybody here? And why can't Dr. Reed just come out and say he wants to marry Clara for Clara?*

An exasperated huff sent some wisps of hair around her face dancing. She shoved them behind her ears and kept walking. *And what was that about me wanting to live in Baltimore? Nobody asked me. I'd have told them even if we have to stay in the dugout where dirt sprinkles into our food in the morning and on our noses at night I'd stay. It's worth it for the open space and the big sky and not running into Rodney on the street.*

When she reached the river, she made an about-face and marched back the way she'd come. *Clara wants to marry Dr. Reed, but only if he wants to marry her. Dr. Reed wants to marry Clara, but somehow bungled it up so she thinks he proposed to fix everything and she said no. And now that Dr. Reed's father is back, we'll go back to Baltimore on the next stage.*

Midge flopped to the ground, plucked a blade of dry grass from the stalks surrounding her, and placed it between her lips. A puff of air made it hum. A good blow and it whistled. She pulled it to her lap and stared at it for a second.

Maybe. . .just maybe Clara and Dr. Reed were like this blade of grass. When they met, things started humming, but it wasn't enough to get things off the ground. They needed something to knock them into shape and make it work.

The longer Midge sat, the more the prairie grasses poked through her skirts and jabbed her legs, prickling until she had to get up. It was like the land itself was shoving her away, ordering her to get going. *But where?*

Suddenly, she knew what she had to do. It shouldn't take much, but if she handled things right....

Midge whistled as she headed for the general store.

CHAPTER 30

"Why aren't you marrying my son?" Josiah's abrupt version of "good morning" took Clara aback the next day when she went to get a few eggs from the general store.

"Excuse me?" She could hear herself spluttering but couldn't manage to exert more dignity than that.

"You heard me." He rapped his knuckles on the counter. "The first night I came back, scared half to eternity that everyone had died in a fire, Saul told me you two were getting married. Then, yesterday, the bottom fell out. So while he's out taking a look at the Specks' sick cow, I'm asking for an explanation."

Clara raised an eyebrow at his high-handed speech. "That's between your son and me."

"The way I look at it, since I'm marrying Doreen, that makes you family." The smile spreading across Josiah's face at the thought of marrying her aunt went a long way toward softening Clara's reaction. "So I'm asking, as family, what went wrong?"

Clara took a moment to study this man who'd

swooped into their lives, given them a home, and recognized her aunt for the treasure she was. Josiah didn't so much as bat an eye when his grand house burned to cinders, but as a concerned family member, he'd brook no obstacle. *He's a good man, Lord. Thank You for that.*

"Saul only wants to marry me because he thinks I'm in a bad situation, out here alone with just my aunt." Pain streaked through her chest as she spoke the painful words. "Your son just can't resist trying to fix things, but I won't marry a man who doesn't love me."

"Who'd have thought my son would've inherited all my good taste without a lick of sense to go with it?" Josiah's snort shook Clara from her melancholy. "He hasn't told you he loves you then?"

"No." She sniffed back the surge of emotion his thoughtless words caused. "He told me the truth— marriage is the perfect solution."

"That's Saul's way of saying he loves you." Josiah shook his head. "Though he's foolish not to realize you wouldn't see it that way."

"I'm afraid you're mistaken." Clara abandoned the eggs and began inching back toward the door, hoping to leave before the tears caught up with her.

"Don't run off now." He tugged a handkerchief from the display and waggled it at her. "Listen to me for a minute so we can clear this up."

Clara kept moving. "I need to go." A few more steps. . .

"What do you know about Saul's sister?" The words stopped her cold.

The image of Saul's expression on the one day

he'd mentioned Nellie flashed through her mind. The raw grief, the sorrow mixed with helpless rage she recognized all too well, had struck a chord she still couldn't deny.

Clara walked back to Josiah and took the hankie. "That she loved apples, and he only realized she was really sick when she wouldn't eat apple bread." Her tone softened. "You told me he liked apples, but that was wrong. You got him mixed up with his sister."

"No, I told a falsehood." Creases around Josiah's eyes grew more pronounced as he winced at the memory. "I knew if you had the other gals bake apple desserts but you made something different, yourself, he'd notice yours."

"A side scheme all along?" Funny how she couldn't even work up much indignation over it. Not when she was so close to finding out the reason behind Saul's drive to be a doctor. "What happened to Nellie, and why does Saul blame himself?"

"She was his twin, you know." Josiah's eyes clouded over as he looked past her to years long gone by. "Saul wanted to go to the park. Nellie said she felt sick, but he told her not to be a baby. So she went. The next day she was worse and wouldn't eat anything. By the time the doctor came, it was too late. She died that night."

"No," Clara breathed. "It's not Saul's fault."

"He's always believed he should have listened to her and asked for a doctor earlier, that she would still be alive if he'd cared enough to fix the problem." Josiah mopped his face with a bandanna before turning a gimlet eye on Clara. "When anyone he cares about—anyone he *loves*—has a problem, there is nothing Saul won't do to fix it."

Understanding dawned. "You mean—"

The jangle of the bell above the door interrupted her as Doreen rushed into the shop, waving a piece of paper. "Josiah! Clara!" She ran up against the counter, breathing hard. "Midge has run away!"

Saul returned from the Doane farm after setting their youngest boy's broken arm. When he entered the store, he found Clara, Doreen, and his father gathered around one of the counters. Obviously agitated, everyone spoke at once.

"What's the problem?" Saul strode up to see a slightly blotchy letter lying there, so he plucked it up and began to read.

> *Dear Everyone,*
>
> *I'm sorry for all my bad habits. Eaves-dropping is hard to stop. I heard Clara and Aunt Doreen talking through the stovepipe in the dugout. I know that Aunt Doreen is going to marry Dr. Reed's father and stay here. Dr. Reed thinks I want to go back to Baltimore. Clara won't marry him just to fix problems.*
>
> *I'm going to go away awhile. Dr. Reed, you can marry Clara and she won't think it's for me. You both stay in Buttonwood with Aunt Doreen and your father.*
>
> *Love,*
> *Midge*

"Where would she go?" Saul stared at the loopy writing scrawled across the note, heart clenching. "Why would she leave?"

"We'll find her." Clara put her hand on his forearm, her warmth seeping though his sleeve and easing some of the tightness in his chest. "As for why she left, she says it right here. She didn't want us to get married just because of her."

"But we weren't!" Saul's grip tightened, crushing the paper.

"We weren't?" Hope and wariness flickered in her gaze. "Was it so Aunt Doreen and I would have a home?"

"No." He shook his head as though to clear it. *Had everyone gone mad?* "I chose you because you're the only woman I'd want for my wife, Clara Field." Saul returned her gaze, willing her to accept his meaning. Accept him.

"You're the only man I'd want for my husband." A shy smile blossomed across her lips before horror flashed across her face. "Midge wouldn't try to go to Baltimore?"

"Surely not," Doreen protested. "It's too far. She has no money and no direction. Midge has more sense."

"But isn't that what her letter says?" Clara tugged it from his fist, scanning it with anxious eyes. "Yes, she's going away so we can stay in Buttonwood, because she wants to go back to Baltimore."

"She can't have gone far. We'll find her and bring her home," Saul promised. He reached out to tuck a tendril of Clara's soft blond hair behind her ear. "She'll learn to love it here."

"You mean. . . ?" The woman he'd make his bride didn't finish the question, but the sparkle in her eyes said it all.

"I know you won't leave your aunt, and I've done a lot of thinking. Adam Grogan is right about Buttonwood needing a doctor. I can do just as much good right here as I could in Baltimore." Saul reached out to draw her close. "Midge will just have to learn to live with that."

"Good!" His precocious ward's voice rang down the steps moments before she appeared, a triumphant smile across her face. "I like it here, too!"

"Then why the letter?" Clara brandished the missive. "You frightened us all!"

"I'm sorry about that." Midge bit her lip. "I really do want to stay in Buttonwood with Aunt Doreen and Opal and everyone, but that wasn't the big reason. It seemed like the two of you might get married just for me, and I wanted to be sure that you were in love."

"Clara knows I love her." Saul slid an arm around her waist. "Don't you, sweetheart?"

"You never said so." Her blush tattled of doubts, but the way her hand rested on his forearm told him he had the power to dispel them.

"Forgive me, Clara." He put his other arm around her to draw her close, relishing her warmth. "Let me tell you now that I love you and intend to marry you as soon as you'll say the word."

"I'm sorry it took me so long to trust you and trust that God had brought someone so wonderful to me." Her smile shone bright and tender, promising years of joy. Her light touch as she reached up to tuck an errant lock of hair behind his ear sent shivers through him. "I love you, too, Saul."

"It's about time!" Midge's exclamation made everyone laugh.

"Yes, it is." Doreen slid a glance at his father. "We could have a double wedding, if you like."

"Yes." Saul couldn't stop grinning at the feel of Clara in his arms at last. "I don't want to wait any longer than necessary to make good on this bride bargain."

ABOUT THE AUTHOR

KELLY EILEEN HAKE is a reader favorite of Barbour Publishing's Heartsong Presents book club, where she released several of her first books. A credentialed secondary English teacher in California with an MA in Writing Popular Fiction, she is known for her own style of witty, heartwarming historical romance.

JOIN US ONLINE!

Christian Fiction for Women

Christian Fiction for Women is your online home for the latest in Christian fiction.

Check us out online for:

- Giveaways
- Recipes
- Info about Upcoming Releases
- Book Trailers
- News and More!

Find Christian Fiction for Women at Your Favorite Social Media Si

 Search "Christian Fiction for Women"

 @fictionforwomen